OUTWITTING TROLLS

WILLIAM G. TAPPLY

THORNDIKE
C H I V E R S

This Large Print edition is published by Thorndike Press, Waterville, Maine, USA and by AudioGO Ltd, Bath, England.
Thorndike Press, a part of Gale, Cengage Learning.

The text of this Large Print edition is unabridged.
Other aspects of the book may vary from the original edition.
Set in 16 pt. Plantin.

LIBRARY OF CONGRESS CATALOGING-IN-PUBLICATION DATA

Tapply, William G.
   Outwitting trolls / by William G. Tapply.
     p. cm. — (Thorndike Press large print mystery)
   "A Brady Coyne novel."
   ISBN-13: 978-1-4104-3195-0
   ISBN-10: 1-4104-3195-9
   1. Coyne, Brady (Fictitious character)—Fiction. 2. Lawyers—Massachusetts—Boston—Fiction. 3. Murder—Investigation—Fiction. 4. Boston (Mass.)—Fiction. 5. Large type books. I. Title.
PS3570.A568O99 2011
813'.54—dc22   2010044109

BRITISH LIBRARY CATALOGUING-IN-PUBLICATION DATA AVAILABLE
Published in 2011 in the U.S. by arrangement with St. Martin's Press, LLC.
Published in 2011 in the U.K. by arrangement with St Martin's Press.

U.K. Hardcover: 978 1 445 83608 9 (Chivers Large Print)
U.K. Softcover: 978 1 445 83609 6 (Camden Large Print)

Printed and bound in Great Britain by
the MPG Books Group.
1 2 3 4 5 6 7 14 13 12 11 10

To . . .
My Readers
My Students
My Friends
My Editors, especially Keith Kahla
My Agents, Jed Mattes and Fred Morris
My Parents and Sister, Tap,
Muriel, and Martha
My Adored Children, Mike,
Melissa, Sarah,
Blake, and Ben
My Beloved Wife, Vicki

Thank you for everything.

To be sure, most lawyers today recognize that their most important work is done in the office, not in the courtroom; the elaborate masked ritual of the courtroom holds attraction only for the neophyte and the layman.

— DAVID RIESMAN,
Individualism Reconsidered

"I am coming to eat you," said the troll, his voice rumbling so deep that it shook the whole bridge.

"Eat me?" asked Little Billy Goat Gruff, shaking from head to toe. "I am too little. . . . You should wait for my middle brother to come. He is much bigger than me."

— "THREE BILLY GOATS GRUFF,"
RETOLD BY S. E. SCHLOSSER

ONE

I spotted Ken Nichols about the same time he spotted me. He was sitting at the end of the hotel bar, and when I started toward him, he grinned and raised what looked like a martini glass.

I took the stool beside him. He held out his hand, and I shook it.

"Glad you could make it, Brady," Ken said. "Jesus, it's good to see you. What's it been?"

"Ten years," I said. "At least."

He was wearing a pearl-colored button-down shirt under a pale blue linen jacket, with faded blue jeans and battered boat shoes. He had a good tan, as if he played golf year-round. His black hair was now speckled with gray and cut shorter than I remembered.

Ken had big ears and a meandering nose and a mouth that was a little too wide for his face. He grinned easily, he loved animals, and when he spoke, I could still detect the Blue Ridge Mountains of his childhood in his voice. Ken Nichols was an easy guy to like.

He was a veterinarian, and back when we were neighbors in Wellesley, Ken was the one who gave my dogs their rabies and distemper shots, and I was the lawyer who handled the legal work for his business. We used to play in the same foursome on Sunday mornings, and we invited each other's families over for backyard cookouts on summer weekends.

Then Ken got divorced, dissolved his veterinary practice, and moved to Baltimore, and shortly after that, I got divorced, too.

We'd been out of touch ever since, but Ken and I used to be pretty good friends, and when he called me earlier in the week, saying he was coming up to Massachusetts to attend this veterinarian convention in the big hotel in Natick and would love to meet me for a drink if I could sneak away, just for old times' sake, I agreed instantly. Friends, old or new, were always worth sneaking away for.

"You're looking good," I said to him.

"I work out," he said. "You get to a certain age, you've got to take care of the machine, you know what I mean?"

"Yeah," I said. "I do know. Change the oil, replace the filters, rotate the tires. I keep thinking I should do something about my brake pads, but . . ."

He smiled. "Same old Brady." He showed me his empty martini glass. "So what'll you have? The usual? Jack, rocks?"

I smiled and nodded. "You remembered."

"Some things never change."

The bartender, a Hispanic guy in his twenties with a pencil-thin mustache, must have been listening, because he came over and said, "Gentlemen?"

"Another for me," Ken said, "and a Jack Daniel's on the rocks for my friend."

After the bartender turned away, Ken said, "So how's your golf game these days?"

"I quit golf a few years ago," I said. "It came down to golf or fishing, and I picked fishing."

"Tough choice, if you love both."

"I figured out I didn't love them both the same," I said, "so it was easy. Quitting golf was a helluva lot easier than quitting cigarettes. You're still playing, I bet."

He nodded. "I joined a country club just outside of Baltimore, and —" He stopped when a cell phone began buzzing and dancing around on the bartop beside his elbow. Ken picked it up and looked at it, flipped it open, and said, "Clem? That you, man?" He listened for a minute, frowned down at his wristwatch, then lifted his head and gazed around the room. "Yeah, okay," he said. "I see you. Wait there."

He snapped the phone shut, stuck it in his jacket pocket, and looked at me. "I'm sorry," he said. "I've got to do something. It'll take just a minute."

I waved my hand. "Don't worry about it."

The area where I was sitting consisted of a short bartop with a dozen stools plus five or six small tables, all crowded into one corner of an open area off the hotel lobby. Beside the bar was a small raised platform with a piano and a drum set. I guessed a jazz quartet might be performing later on this Friday evening. People — mostly veterinarians, I assumed — were milling around and lounging on sofas and soft chairs, some of them with laptops propped open on coffee tables, some of them looking up at a wide-screen TV mounted on the wall that was showing a Red Sox game.

As I watched, Ken weaved through the crowd to the other side of the room and went up to a man who was leaning against the wall with his arms folded over his chest. This man had a neatly trimmed dark beard streaked with gray and a high shiny forehead. He was wearing a dark suit with a maroon necktie. He looked to be in his late forties, early fifies, about the same age as Ken. He kept his arms folded as Ken approached him.

Ken said something to the man and held out his hand. The man grinned quickly, and they shook. Ken said something, and the other guy frowned and gave his head a quick shake. Ken shrugged and said something else, and the man looked up and turned his head toward the bar. His eyes found me across the room, and he lifted his chin and smiled at me as if he knew me.

I nodded to him. Maybe I was supposed to recognize him, but I didn't.

The man turned back to Ken, reached out, put his hand on Ken's arm, pushed his face close to Ken's, and began talking.

After a minute or two, Ken nodded and stepped away from the bearded guy, who smiled, made a pistol out of his hand, and pointed his index finger at Ken's face. Ken nodded, and the other guy turned and walked out of the room.

Ken stood there for a minute watching the man go. Then he started back to where I was sitting.

When I swiveled around to face the bar, I saw that my drink was sitting there on a coaster for me. Ken's new martini had appeared as well.

Ken eased himself onto the stool beside me. He picked up his martini, downed half of it, and said, "Ahh. I needed that."

I turned to him. "Everything okay?"

He shrugged. "Sure."

"That guy you were just talking with . . ."

He waved the back of his hand at me. "No big deal."

"Sorry," I said. "None of my business."

He grinned. "You don't want another case, do you?"

"Massachusetts or Maryland?"

He laughed. "You name it, pal. I got cases here, there, and the Arctic fucking Circle."

"I never passed the Arctic Circle bar," I said. "Otherwise . . ."

"Yeah," he said. "Too bad."

"I assume you've got somebody handling your business," I said. "Someone you can trust."

"Oh, sure." He nodded. "Some things, it takes more than a lawyer to fix, though."

I looked at him. "Are you in some kind of trouble, Ken?"

"Who? That guy?" He smiled. "Nah. Not really. He's an old friend." He flapped his hand. "It's just life, you know?"

"Because if you are . . ."

14

He smiled. "I know. Thanks. Good to know. But really, that's not why I wanted to get together. This was just about, you know, hey, it's been, what, ten years — eleven, actually — I got divorced eleven years ago. We were pretty good friends, you and me. Things were simpler back then. We had some good times, though, didn't we?"

"Yes, good times," I said. "Different times."

"They sure were," he said. "Hell, we were both married, for one thing. You haven't remarried, have you?"

"Me?" I shook my head. "No. I've had a couple of pretty serious relationships, but I always managed to screw them up, and they never got quite that far. I still have an open mind on the subject. You?"

He grinned. "I'm having way too much fun." He drained his martini glass. "Another?"

"You go ahead," I said. "I'm good."

Ken downed two more martinis while I nursed my single shot of Jack Daniel's, and we talked about the good old days when we both were younger, living in the suburbs, raising our kids, mowing our lawns, and playing golf on the weekends. When Ken talked, his eyes bored into mine as if he needed desperately to be understood. He peppered me with a lot of questions — what were my sons up to, how was my law practice going, what was Gloria, my ex-wife, doing, where was I living — and when I tried to answer them, his eyes would shift and he'd be looking past my shoulder, scanning the roomful of people as if he were expecting somebody, not really listening to me.

Ken's cell phone, lying on the bartop in front of him, buzzed two or three other times while we were sitting there, and each time he picked it up, frowned at the screen, gave me a quick, apologetic smile, and did not answer it.

We'd been there for a little more than an hour when he looked at his watch, drained his glass, took out his wallet, and put some bills on the bar. "Well," he said, "I gotta go."

I reached for my wallet, but he put his hand on my arm. "I got it," he said. "Worth it, seeing you again, getting caught up a little."

"Worth it for me, too," I said, "but we barely scratched the surface."

"Well, we'll do it again, and next time you can buy the drinks."

"Good," I said. "Means there will be a next time."

"Wish we could make an evening out of

16

it," he said, "but I'm on a damn committee, and we've got a meeting in ten minutes. Thanks a million for trekking over here. Let's not let another ten years go by, okay?" He held out his hand.

I shook it. "I agree," I said. "We should keep in touch."

"So if I had a legal problem some-time . . . ?"

I nodded. "Sure. Of course."

"That's great." He slapped my shoulder. "Say hi to Gloria for me next time you see her," he said.

"And you give my best to Sharon."

"I will," he said.

"Ken, really," I said, "if you just want to talk, you know, legal problems or whatever, don't hesitate to give me a call. Anytime."

He nodded. "I might do that."

"I mean it," I said.

"I do, too," he said. "I'll call you."

TWO

To anyone who didn't know better, the four of us probably looked like some nice well-adjusted American family from the Boston suburbs, out for an authentic North End Italian dinner on this Saturday evening in April. There was the man, a tall guy, and sitting across from him his wife, still blond and pretty, an attractive couple, both of them fit and trim, somewhere in their forties. The college-aged son, although a little rebellious with his ponytail and scruffy beard and sunburn, was nevertheless clearly enjoying this get-together with his family, as was the pretty girl, small and quick, with flashing dark eyes and straight black hair, the boy's younger sister apparently, judging by the casual way they appeared to be ignoring each other.

We were sharing a platter of antipasto and a bottle of Chianti. Gloria, my ex-wife, was telling Gwen, our son Billy's friend from

San Francisco (not his sister, not even close), about her new photography exhibit in a Newbury Street gallery, while Billy was telling me about the good trout fishing he'd had on a little spring creek in east-central Idaho, where he was living and working these days.

Nobody had yet addressed what Billy — Gloria still called him William — had said when he told me he was coming home for a few days. He said, "I'm bringing a friend. Her name is Gwen, and we have something to tell you. Both of you. You and Mom."

"A friend, huh?" I asked.

"Actually, yeah," Billy said.

"A girlfriend, you mean."

"A friend," he said.

"Well," I said, "you got something to say, why wait? Not that it won't be great to see you again, meet your friend Gwen. That will be excellent. But if you've got something to tell me, why not just spit it out?"

"We want to do it in person," Billy said, "and we want you and Mom to both be there and hear it at the same time from both of us."

Billy's use of the first-person plural wasn't like him. He'd always been a first-person singular type of guy. I was curious about what the two kids had to tell us. A few obvious scenarios played themselves out in my imagination.

So here we were, eating olives and hot peppers and artichoke hearts, prosciutto and salami and mozzarella balls, dipping our bread in saucers of olive oil and oregano, and sipping a musky Chianti at Mosca's Trattoria on Hanover Street, and whatever it was that Billy and Gwen had to tell us sat at the table with us like a shy elephant, impossible to ignore but pretending to be invisible.

I hadn't seen my number-one son for nearly two years — since two summers earlier when I had ten glorious days of fly-fishing in Montana and Idaho and managed to spend a couple of those days in his drift boat, splitting time with him at the oars. Billy was a Rocky Mountain fishing guide in the summer and a ski instructor in the winter, and I envied him. When I was his age I was plowing through college and law school, hell-bent on starting my career and getting married and having a family and saving up for retirement.

Billy was hell-bent on having all the fun while he was young that I'd mostly postponed until I was middle-aged.

It had been even longer since I'd spent any time with Gloria, even though my former wife still lived in our old family house in Wellesley, a suburb of Boston, which was where I lived. We did talk on the phone now and then, mainly when one of our two sons — Joey, the younger, was a prelaw sophomore at Stanford — had some kind of issue, usually involving money, that required parental consultation.

Billy had started to tell me about his five-day float trip down the Middle Fork of the Salmon River through the Frank Church–River of No Return Wilderness when my cell phone vibrated against my leg. It felt like an angry bumblebee had gotten trapped in my pants pocket.

I fished out the phone and looked at it. UNKNOWN CALLER, the screen read. I didn't recognize the number. It had a 617 area code. Somebody local.

"Go ahead and answer it," said Billy.

I shoved the phone back into my pocket. "I'm having dinner with my family," I said. "It's Saturday night. Whatever it is, it can wait."

"Maybe it's important," he said. "One of your clients. If they're calling on a Saturday night, it's probably some kind of emergency, don't you think?"

I shrugged.

"Well," he said, "who could it be?"

21

"I don't know."

"Why don't you see if they left a message?"

I nodded and took out the phone. MESSAGE WAITING, it read.

I accessed my voice mail. A woman's voice said, "Brady? Where are you? I need you. This is Sharon Nichols. I'm . . . it's Ken. My husband. Ex-husband. He's . . . I'm at his hotel room. There's so much blood. Please. I don't know what to do. I'm kind of frantic. I definitely need a lawyer. Please call me." She recited a number, the same one that appeared on my phone's screen.

It took me a minute to process what Sharon Nichols had said. Twenty-four hours earlier Ken Nichols and I had been drinking at a hotel bar, reminiscing about the days when we were golfing partners.

Now his ex-wife was calling from a hotel — the same one, I assumed — talking about Ken and blood and asking for a lawyer.

I snapped my phone shut and stood up. Billy, Gwen, and Gloria all looked at me. "I'm sorry," I said. "This actually *is* an emergency. I'll be back in a minute."

Gloria arched her eyebrows, and I could read her expression. *What the hell do you think you're doing?* it asked. *What's more important than dinner with your family?*

"I've got to answer it," I said to her. "I'm going outside and make the call." After being divorced from Gloria all those years, I still felt obligated to explain myself to her.

I went out to the sidewalk. The dampness on the pavement from a soft April rain shower reflected the yellow streetlights and the red and green neon restaurant signs. I stood under the canvas awning and pecked out the number that Sharon Nichols had left.

She answered on the first ring. "Brady? Is that you?"

"It's me," I said. "What's going on?"

"It's Ken," she said. "He's — I think he's dead. He must be dead. There's blood everywhere."

"You said you were in his hotel room?"

"Yes. It's —"

"The Beverly Suites in Natick?"

"Yes. How did you —"

"I had drinks with Ken there last night. Did you call the police?"

"No," she said. "I called you."

"Hang up and call the police. Dial 911. Do it right now. Okay?"

She hesitated. "But somebody killed him. Murdered him, I mean. Don't you see?"

"You want my advice," I said, "you want me to help you, you want to consult with a lawyer, then do what I tell you, and that is, call the police. Do it now. You do want me to help you, right?"

"Yes," she said. "Will you be my lawyer?"

"Sure. I'm your lawyer, and I'm telling you to call the damn police. Okay?"

"Okay," she said.

"Get out of that room," I said. "Right now. Lawyer's orders. Don't touch anything. Step out into the corridor and stand outside the door to his room and call the police. Then wait there for them."

"It's kind of late for that."

"For what?"

"For don't touch anything."

"Whatever," I said. "Just get the hell out of the room."

"Will you help me?"

"I am helping you. I'm giving you good advice. I'm telling you to vacate that room and call the police, and I'll be there as soon as I can. What's the room number?"

"Um, 322."

"I'm on my way."

"Okay," she said. "Thank you."

After I disconnected from Sharon Nichols, I stood there on the Hanover Street sidewalk watching the rain drip off the awning. I was remembering when we brought Bucky, our sick old beagle, to Dr. Nichols's veterinary hospital for the last time. Billy and Joey were just kids. Bucky had been part of our family for as long as either of them could remember.

A few months earlier, Ken had told me that Bucky's tumor was inoperable and it was just a matter of time. We'd nursed the old dog until he continually whined from his pain and could no longer get his legs under his hind end. He lost his interest in food — eating had always been Bucky's favorite activity — and I had to carry him outside and up and down the stairs.

When I told the boys that we were going to have to put Bucky down, and I explained how Dr. Nichols would do it with an injection, and how it wouldn't hurt, how Bucky would just go to sleep, they both said they wanted to be there. Gloria and I had a quiet argument about it. She thought they were too young to witness the death of a loved one, even if it was a dog. I thought it would be a good experience for them.

In the end, Gloria conceded. She admitted that she was probably projecting, that *she* certainly didn't want to be there, so on a Saturday morning in October, Billy, Joey, and I took Bucky to the vet's office. Ken and Sharon were both there, wearing white coats. I lifted Bucky onto the stainless-steel table. The two boys and I patted him and talked to him, and then Sharon held him and Ken slid the needle into his foreleg, and Bucky exhaled once and it was all over.

When I looked up at Ken and Sharon, both of them had tears in their eyes. I always liked that about them.

They had two kids, a girl, Ellen, who babysat for our boys a few times, and a son named Wayne, who was about Billy's age. Our kids all knew each other, though I didn't remember that they were friends.

Ken and Sharon got divorced a year or two before Gloria and I did. They sold their veterinary practice, including the animal hospital and the kennels, and I took care of the business end of it.

Ken relocated in Maryland. Sharon bought a townhouse in Acton and brought up her kids there.

All of that happened ten or eleven years ago, and except for a few of the typical lingering tax issues related to the sale of their business, I hadn't had any further professional or personal dealings with Sharon or Ken Nichols before my reunion with Ken the previous evening.

Now Ken had apparently been murdered in a hotel room on Route 9 in Natick, and Sharon had found his body, and I was the one she called.

I went back into the restaurant and stood beside our table. "I've got to go," I told Gloria, Billy, and Gwen. "I'm really sorry."

Gloria opened her mouth, then shook her head, picked up her wineglass, and took a sip.

"You gotta do what you gotta do," said Billy. "We'll catch up later."

"You want to tell us what it is you've got to tell us?" I asked.

"It'll wait," he said. "Give us an excuse to do this again."

"And we will," I said. "Definitely." To Gwen I said, "It was great to meet you. Next time I won't crap out on you, I promise."

She gave me a terrific smile.

"Next time, okay?" I asked Gloria.

She nodded but did not smile.

I clapped Billy on the shoulder, turned, and left the restaurant. I'd walked to the restaurant in the North End from my townhouse on Mt. Vernon Street on Beacon Hill. It took about twenty minutes, which was as fast as a taxi could negotiate the one-way city streets even in the sparse Saturday evening traffic, so I walked home. When I got there, I let Henry out back to pee, gave him a bully stick, and told him I'd be back.

27

Then I walked down to the end of Charles Street, fetched my car from the parking garage, and pointed it at the Beverly Suites Hotel on Route 9 in Natick, where Sharon Nichols was waiting for me with the murdered body of her ex-husband, my old friend.

THREE

The Beverly Suites Hotel was one of the countless big-box commercial establishments that lined both sides of the Framingham and Natick stretch of Route 9. Before last night, I'd never been inside this one, nor had I felt deprived. Now it was twice in twenty-four hours.

I stopped under the portico by the front entrance, got out of my car, and gave my keys to an attendant. He gave me a plastic receipt with a number on it. I slipped it into my pocket and went inside.

An electronic bulletin board in the foyer spelled out the words WELCOME INTERNATIONAL ASSOCIATION OF VETERINARIANS. I hadn't noticed it last night. Underneath the greeting was what appeared to be a schedule of events for Friday, Saturday, and Sunday. I noticed that on this evening, Saturday, the "annual banquet" was being held and the "keynote address" was being delivered in the Grand Ballroom. I guessed that the evening's festivities had recently ended, as a small throng of people wearing banquet-appropriate suits and dresses were lounging in chairs and on sofas in the lobby and in the bar area where I'd met Ken. They were talking in small groups, sipping drinks, reading pamphlets and catalogs, or looking up at the baseball game that was playing on the wide-screen television on the wall.

I found a bank of elevators on the other side of the lobby, waited for one to open, got in, and pressed the number three button.

A moment later I was deposited on the third floor. A sign on the wall indicated that rooms 300–345 were to the right. Sharon Nichols had told me that Ken's room was number 322.

The detritus of room service littered the corridor outside some of the rooms — trays holding lipstick-stained glasses, empty wine bottles, cups and saucers, plates smeared with mashed potato and spaghetti sauce, balled-up cloth napkins.

When I turned the corner to where I expected to find police swarming the corridor outside room 322, I saw nobody.

The door to room 322 was closed. I knocked on it.

A minute later, the door cracked open. Sharon Nichols looked out at me. Then she opened the door wide. "Oh, Brady," she said. "I'm so glad you're here."

I hadn't seen Sharon Nichols in over a decade. She looked pretty much as I remembered her. Blond hair, cut a bit shorter now. Wide-set blue-green eyes. Tall and slender. An attractive woman in her late forties who could have passed for thirty-something, although now her eyes were red and swollen, and her face seemed to have collapsed in on itself, and she was hugging herself as if she were trying to hold her body together.

"The police haven't arrived yet?" I asked.

"I didn't call them."

"I told you to call them."

"Well," she said, "I didn't. Please. Come in."

"No," I said. "You come out here. You shouldn't be in there."

"I've been in here for most of the evening already," she said. "Another few minutes won't do any harm. Come in, Brady. You should see it."

Sharon was wearing a pale blue jacket, and under it an off-white silk blouse and a dark skirt that stopped a few inches above her knees. There was a reddish blotch — a dried bloodstain, it looked like — on the

31

sleeve of her jacket.

I looked past her into the room, but it was dimly lit, and I couldn't see anything.

She stepped away from the door and held it open for me. I went in, and then I saw Ken. He was sprawled across the bed, as if he'd been sitting on the side of it and had fallen backward. He was wearing a maroon silk robe over a white T-shirt and gray suit pants. Black socks on his feet, no shoes.

There was a big splotch of dark blood on his chest and another just under his belt-line, and more blood had puddled on the bedcover. His healthy golfer's tan was gone. Now his skin was the color of lard. He looked smaller than he had the night before. Deflated.

This was the man who'd been drinking martinis with me and reminiscing about the old days just twenty-four hours ago.

"Jesus," I whispered. I turned to Sharon, who was standing there with her arms crossed over her chest. "Did you touch any-thing?"

"I touched him," she said. "I tried to see if he was breathing. He wasn't. He was dead when I got here."

"Come on." I grabbed her arm and led her out to the corridor. Then I took my cell phone out of my pocket and showed it to her. "I've got a lot of questions," I said. "I need to know everything. But first . . ."

I hit the speed-dial number for Roger Horowitz's cell phone. In Massachusetts all homicides except those committed in the cities of Boston, Springfield, and Worcester fall under the jurisdiction of the state police, and Horowitz was a homicide detective with the state police, one of the best. He was a crusty sonofabitch, but he was also my friend, and a solid cop, and I trusted him.

"Who's this?" he said by way of answering his phone.

"Brady Coyne," I said. "I've got a homicide for you."

"Oh, goodie," he said. "A homicide. Just what I wanted. What more could a guy ask for on a Saturday night. Hey, Alyse, honey. Guess what? It's your buddy Coyne, and he's got a homicide for me." He blew a quick breath into the telephone. "Jesus, anyway."

"I knew you'd be thrilled," I said.

"Thrilled and delighted," he said. "Alyse and I are here on the sofa in our living room watching an old Clint Eastwood movie on TV, eating popcorn, sipping hot cocoa. It's like the first evening we've had together in about a month. Clint's doing Dirty Harry, and I got my feet in Alyse's lap, and when the phone rang just now she was giving me a nice foot massage, and I was telling her, 'Honey,' I was saying, 'that feels awful good, and you shouldn't hold back on any impulse you might have to try it out on other parts of my poor old body, but wouldn't it be just perfect if Brady Coyne would call with a homicide for me and drag me away from here?' "

"I'm sorry," I said. "It was inconsiderate of this man to get stabbed to death on a Saturday night."

"Stabbed, huh?"

"Yes. Two stab wounds. Plenty of blood."

"There always is," he said. "Where are you?"

"Beverly Suites Hotel on Route 9 in Natick. Room 322."

"I know where that is," he said. "So who's the vic?"

"A veterinarian named Ken Nichols," I said. "Used to live in Wellesley. Ten years ago he got divorced, sold his business, and moved to Baltimore. There's a big vet convention here at this hotel this weekend. The IAV. International Association of Veterinarians."

"Never heard of 'em," he said. "And you're there why?"

"Nichols's wife called me. Ex-wife, I

should say. Sharon. She found him."

"She's your client?"

I glanced at Sharon. She was leaning back against the wall watching me. I gave her a quick smile and a nod, which I intended to be reassuring.

"Yes," I said to Horowitz. "She's my client. I've known her for a long time. We used to be neighbors. Both of them. Her and Ken. Our victim. I did the legal work for their business back when they were together and had the animal hospital in Wellesley. I was here last night, as a matter of fact. Had drinks with Ken."

"Drinks, huh?"

"That's right."

"And now he's dead."

"Yes."

"The wife," he said. "She do it?"

"Ha," I said.

"She called her lawyer," he said, "not the cops, though, huh?"

"That's right, and I called you."

"For which," he said, "again, hey, thanks a lot. Makes my day, as Clint would say. Okay. You and your client, don't touch anything. We'll be there in a few minutes." He disconnected without saying good-bye or thank you. Typical.

I snapped my phone shut and stuck it into

my pants pocket. "The police will be here," I said to Sharon. "So tell me. What time did you get here?"

"To Ken's room, you mean?"

I nodded.

"Nine o'clock," she said. "We'd planned for me to meet him here at nine, and I was right on time."

"Why?"

"Why did I come here, to Ken's room?"

I nodded. "The police will want to know."

She looked at me. "I was early, actually." Her eyes looked wet. She blinked a couple of times. "I waited in the lobby until it was nine o'clock. I didn't want to appear too eager. He had to go to the banquet. He was going to sneak out early." She blew out a breath. "It was a . . . a date. A rendezvous. I was meeting my ex-husband in his hotel room. I was excited and nervous. Keyed up, like a high school kid with a hot date. It was silly — but exciting. Did he mention it to you last night? That we were, ah, getting together?"

I shook my head. "No. He said nothing about it. He was discreet."

She nodded. "I'm glad." She hesitated. "Did he mention me at all?"

"Not really. We talked about golf mostly. Nothing very personal. Guy talk."

I glanced at my watch. It was a little after ten thirty. Sharon had been here with Ken — Ken's dead body — for about an hour and a half.

"He doesn't look like he just came from a banquet," I said. "Silk robe, no jacket or tie. No shirt, even."

She shrugged. "I suppose he changed. He said he was going to order a bottle of champagne from room service. It was a celebration. Maybe that's how you dress for a celebration." She cocked her head and looked at me, as if she expected me to challenge her.

"A celebration," I said.

She nodded.

"Of what?"

"Finding each other again after all these years, I guess." She shrugged. "It was Ken's word. When we decided to get together, he said it would be a celebration. I liked that, you know?"

I looked at Sharon. I wondered if she'd killed Ken. Means, motive, and opportunity. She had them all. Well, I didn't know about her motive yet, but she no doubt had one. All spouses — and especially ex-spouses — have motives for murder. That's why they make ideal suspects.

At this point, at least, Sharon was the only

suspect, although I remembered the bearded guy who'd pointed his finger at Ken in the lobby last night. Also, he'd had several calls on his cell phone that he didn't answer while I was there, but that had caused him to frown and glance around the room.

Still, Horowitz would focus on Sharon. She was the obvious suspect. As Horowitz liked to say, *The commonest things most commonly happen.* Spouses kill spouses on a regular and predictable basis, and there's no need for an investigator to complicate it. Occam's razor.

Sharon was looking at me with her eyebrows arched, and I had the feeling she knew what I was thinking. "So what happens next?" she asked.

"It's not unlike what you see on TV," I said. "Lots of people. Confusion. State cops and local cops and forensics techs and maybe a county sheriff and a DA or two. They'll want to ask you a lot of questions. I'll be with you. I'll decide whether you should answer their questions or not, and if so, which ones. You'll do what I say. Okay?"

"Why wouldn't I answer their questions?"

"You know the answer to that," I said. "It's why you called me in the first place."

"Because it looks like I might have done it."

I shrugged. "They'll want to know why you came here tonight, how you happened to be the one who found Ken's body, and why you called your lawyer instead of the police."

"Do you mean *you* want to know?" she asked.

"I need to know everything," I said.

"Of course you do." She looked at me and smiled. "Ken and I might've been getting back together after all these years. He sent me a birthday card in the fall. It came out of nowhere. I mean, we hadn't talked, hadn't communicated, for, I don't know, years and years. Then I get this warm and friendly card, and on it he wrote something about how nice it would be to see me again. I didn't think too much about it. You know, it's like when you say, 'How are you?' You're not really asking after anybody's health. You don't really expect an answer. You don't necessarily even care. It's just something you say. It doesn't mean anything. But then he sent a Christmas card, and on it he mentioned that he'd be coming up here for a conference in April and maybe we could get together. It made me curious. So I sent him a note saying sure, it would be nice to see him again. Then one evening he called me on the phone, and we talked for a long time, and it was as if we'd never split up. It was easy to talk to him. He called me again a week or so later, and it got to be that we talked on the phone two or three times a week, and pretty soon it began to feel, um, intimate. You know? I mean, here's this man I had children with, who I worked beside, who I shared a bathroom with, who I slept with for all those years. All the things that we had going for us, they were still there. I don't think they ever really went away. They were just, um, dormant, and talking with Ken reawakened all those things. The good memories. Why I once loved him. It was like a courtship, all those phone calls. It was kind of . . . it was sexy." She looked at me. Her eyes were brimming. She swiped her wrist across them. "I came here tonight to make love with my ex-husband in his hotel room. I felt like a teenager. I was very excited. I think he was, too." She stopped and stared. "What are you thinking?"

I shrugged. "Nothing."

"You believe me, don't you?"

"Sure," I said.

"You and Gloria," she said. "After you got divorced, did you ever . . . ?"

"No," I said.

"So should I tell the police what I just told you?"

I nodded. "You should tell them the truth. You'll have to explain why you came here tonight."

She hugged herself. "It's sort of embarrassing."

"Embarrassment is the least of our worries."

She nodded.

"Whoever did this," I said, "Ken must have let him into his room. Him or her."

"A woman, you think?"

I shrugged. "Maybe."

"Maybe that's what it was," Sharon said. "Maybe that's who did this. Some woman. I've been thinking about it. I don't want to delude myself. I guess I didn't really know Ken. People change a lot in ten years, regardless of what they might say on the telephone."

"We all do," I said.

We stood there awkwardly, leaning our backs against the wall, waiting for the police. After a few minutes, Sharon said, "It just occurred to me. You haven't asked me if I did it."

"Did what?"

"Killed Ken."

"You're right," I said. "I haven't asked."

She looked at me, then nodded. "Oh." She hesitated. "Well, I didn't, you know."

I smiled. "Good."

A minute or two later, as we stood there waiting for the authorities to arrive, a man turned the corner and started down the corridor. He was wearing a black sweatshirt with the hood over his head, so I couldn't really see his face, but I had the impression that he was white and young — late teens, early twenties. He struck me as out of place in this fancy hotel.

He took a few steps toward Sharon and me, and then he stopped. He hesitated for a moment, and I thought he was going to speak, but then he turned and began to run in the other direction.

"Hey!" I yelled at him. "Hey! Wait!"

He darted back down the corridor and disappeared around the corner.

I ran after him. When I turned the corner, I had the choice of an elevator, the stairwell, or a left or right onto another corridor.

I looked both ways down the corridor and saw nobody.

The numbers over the two elevators showed that one was descending from the seventh floor and one was stopped at the lobby.

When I opened the door to the stairwell, I heard the metallic echo of footsteps below me. The kid in the hoodie, I assumed, running down the stairs.

Already I was panting from my sprint down the corridor. I'd never catch him.

I turned and went back to where Sharon was waiting outside Ken's room. I leaned against the wall and tried to catch my breath.

"What was that about?" she asked.

I shrugged. "That guy panicked when he saw you and me standing here. I wanted to ask him why."

"You think . . . ?"

I shrugged again. "I think he was coming to Ken's room, but I could be wrong about that. Did you get a look at him?"

She shook her head. "No," she said. "You think he's the one who killed Ken?"

"Maybe," I said.

She looked at me. "But why?"

"Why would we think it was that man?"

"No," she said. "Why would he kill Ken?"

"Why would anybody?" I said.

FOUR

A pair of uniformed Natick police officers
arrived a few minutes later. One of them, a
young blond guy with a Marine Corps
haircut and a linebacker's build, went into
Ken's room. The other cop, a chunky fortyish woman named Lloyd, according to her
nameplate, stayed out in the corridor with
Sharon and me. All she said was "We're
here to secure the scene till the staties get
here." Then she stationed herself outside
the door with her hands clasped behind her,
staring straight ahead.

The blond cop came out a minute later.
Officer Lloyd arched her eyebrows at him.
He shook his head. Then they both stood
there with us in the corridor outside the
door to Ken's room, rocking back and forth
on their heels and toes, and nobody said
anything.

Eventually Roger Horowitz and his partner, a pretty female detective named Marcia

Benetti, showed up, and behind them an entourage of Massachusetts State Police officers and forensics technicians straggled in. Horowitz spoke briefly to the two Natick cops; then he and Benetti came over to where Sharon and I were standing.

He nodded at me and said, "Hey," and I returned his nod and said, "Hey," to him.

Marcia Benetti gave me a quick smile, then went over to Sharon. "I'm Detective Benetti," she said. "I need your jacket."

Sharon looked at her. "Excuse me?"

"Your jacket," said Benetti. "For evidence. That appears to be a bloodstain." She pointed at the sleeve.

Sharon shrugged, slipped her jacket off, and handed it to Marcia Benetti, who dropped it into a big plastic bag and carried it over to a tech who was standing outside Ken's hotel room.

Horowitz turned to Sharon. "Mrs. Nichols, is it?"

She nodded. "Yes. Sharon Nichols. I kept my married name."

"We're going to need to talk with you. I assume you'll want your lawyer" — he jerked his head at me — "with you?"

"Yes, she will," I said.

"Brady's an old friend," said Sharon.

"That's swell." Horowitz looked at me and

45

gave me one of his cynical smiles. "Okay," he said to Sharon. "Officer Lloyd here will stay with you until we're ready. You folks want some coffee or something?"

"Coffee would be nice," said Sharon. "Milk, one packet of sweetener. Sweet'N Low, if you have it."

"Me, too," I said. "Black."

"You bet," Horowitz said. "We aim to please." He went over to talk to a cluster of people, a few in uniforms but most in plain-clothes, who were milling around outside Ken's room.

Ten minutes later somebody brought over a couple of folding chairs for Sharon and me, and a short time after that, a uniformed officer handed us foam cups of coffee.

People kept going into and out of the hotel room. After a while, a gray-haired man, accompanied by a younger Asian man carrying a big camera bag, showed up. Both of them nodded to me. The medical examiner and his assistant. I'd run into them before. They talked with Horowitz for a few minutes. Then the three of them went into Ken's room, too.

My coffee cup was nearly empty when Horowitz came out of the room. "Coyne," he said, crooking his finger at me, "you want to come with me?"

I got up and followed him into the hotel room. He stopped in the little foyer just inside the door and turned to me. "I suppose you and your client have contaminated everything with your fingerprints and whatnot."

I shrugged. "Probably. Sorry."

"Well, put your hands in your pockets. Let's try to keep the damage to a minimum." He turned and continued into the room.

I followed him. Three young men and one woman wearing Massachusetts State Police windbreakers were conferring outside the bathroom. The ME appeared to be examining Ken's body. His assistant was taking flash photographs.

Horowitz went over to a closet. He opened the door and shined his flashlight inside. "C'mere, Coyne," he said. "Take a look at this."

I moved up beside him and looked into the closet. It was empty except for a red-and-black gym bag on the floor in the corner. Horowitz knelt down beside the bag, and I stood right behind him and looked over his shoulder.

The gym bag was unzipped. He pulled open the top and pointed his flashlight at the contents. It was full of small glass bottles. They were about the size that cough medicine comes in. Ten or twelve ounces, I guessed. "This bag was here," Horowitz said. "Just like this, except it was zipped up. I'm wondering if your dead buddy here might've said something about this when you saw him last night."

I shook my head. "What is it?"

He reached into the bag with his latex-gloved hand, took out one of the bottles, and showed it to me. It contained a clear liquid. KETASET was the word on the label. Obviously a brand name.

"Ketaset," I said. "What is this stuff?"

"Brand of ketamine," said Horowitz. "Common anesthetic used in animal surgery."

I shrugged. "Ken Nichols was a veterinarian who probably performed a lot of animal surgeries, and here he is, at a convention of veterinarians."

Horowitz smiled bleakly. "Ketamine is also a Schedule III drug that's sold illegally and abused by humans. It's a psychedelic. What we call a dissociative. Commonly used for date-rape purposes."

"Date rape," I said.

"Among other things," he said. "Dances, concerts, parties. Wherever boys and girls gather. It loosens you up, helps you groove on the music. Diminishes anxiety and stimulates your libido. It can give you a psychedelic, out-of-body experience, a trip to what they call K-land, which you'll probably forget when you come down. They call it K, or Special K, or Ket. A bad trip can be pretty awful, I'm told. Then, as they say, it lands you in the K-hole. Special K was fairly popular back in the nineties."

I shrugged. "Never heard of it."

"Well, you ain't a cop," he said. "Ketamine fell out of favor for a while, but lately it's been making a comeback. What they do is, they dry this liquid in a microwave and sell the powder in little plastic bags. The users, they either snort it or dissolve it and inject it."

"And Ken, being a vet, had access to this stuff," I said.

"And Ken," said Horowitz, mocking my tone, "having access to this stuff, might also have been using it. Or selling it. We've been seeing an increase in the number of break-ins at animal clinics and vets' offices in the past year or so. Ketamine is one of the things they're looking for. It's a fun drug again."

It occurred to me that Ken Nichols, expecting Sharon to show up in his hotel room, might've had a logical reason to want

49

to give his libido a boost. "Will it show up in the ME's tox screen?"

"We'll tell him to test for it," Horowitz said.

"You think Ken was selling this stuff?" I asked.

He shrugged. "Why else bring a big bag of it with him from Baltimore? One bottle would be enough to take care of his personal needs and that of a few friends for a week-end."

"So are you saying this ketamine is your motive for murder?" I asked.

"I'm saying no such thing," said Horowitz. "We already got a perfectly fine suspect with many good motives."

"You don't really think Sharon did this," I said.

"Sure I do," he said. "She's the spouse."

"No, you don't." I snapped my fingers. "Shit. I meant to tell you. After I called you, when Sharon and I were waiting in the corridor for the troops to get here, this guy came around the corner, took one look at us standing there, and turned and started running. I went after him, but I couldn't catch him."

"You being old and out of shape."

I nodded. "I thought the guy was acting guilty, turning and running like that."

"Now you tell me."

"Sorry," I said. "It slipped my mind."

"Yeah," Horowitz said. "In all the excitement."

"I said I was sorry."

"One of your animal doctor's customers, maybe," said Horowitz, "looking to buy himself some Special K. That what you think?"

I shrugged. "Could be, huh?"

"Could you ID this guy?"

I shook my head. "He was wearing a black sweatshirt with the hood over his head. His face was in shadow. I didn't get much of a look at it. I had the impression he was white, male, and young. Late teens, early twenties. A smallish guy, kind of skinny, five-eight or -nine, maybe one forty. Like I said, I didn't really get a look at his face. I could pick his sweatshirt out of a lineup, maybe, but not him. He could run fast, I can testify to that. Wearing baggy blue jeans and white sneakers."

"He ran fast," Horowitz said, "and you ran slow."

"I've lost a step in the past few years."

"I wish you'd mentioned this earlier."

"I said I was sorry," I said.

Horowitz went over and spoke to Marcia Benetti, who was conferring with the ME beside Ken's body. When he finished, she nodded, said something to the medical examiner, and left the room.

Horowitz came back. "We'll get some people looking," he said, "but I'm not holding my breath. I'd be shocked if your friend in the hoodie isn't long gone by now. Too bad." He jerked his head toward the door. "You got anything else I should know?"

"I told you I had a drink with Ken last night," I said. "While I was there, he had an encounter with a guy."

"What kind of encounter?"

"I didn't hear what they were saying," I said. "I thought at the time that they must've been friends, but reading their body language, there might've been some anger going on between them. This other guy pointed his finger at Ken like his hand was a gun."

"Could you identify this guy?"

I nodded. "Sure. I got a good look at him. He was fiftyish, dark, neatly trimmed beard with some gray in it, big forehead, balding on top. Wearing a suit and tie. I assume he was another vet."

"You didn't get a name, did you?"

I thought for a minute, then said, "Clem. Ken called him Clem."

"Clem what?"

"I don't know."

"First name? Last name?"

I shrugged.

"We can check the registration," he said, "see if there's a vet named Clem in attendance. Mr. Nichols didn't say what they were angry about, huh?"

"I didn't ask, he didn't say. I'm not sure it was anger. He did seem kind of upset, though. Implied he had a lot of problems. Now that I think of it, he was pretty jumpy the whole time I was there. Looking around the room, checking his watch. His cell phone rang several times, but he only answered it that once, when the bearded guy called from the other side of the room."

"Clem."

I nodded.

"What'd you talk about?" asked Horowitz. "Any hints about what was bothering him?"

"No, nothing like that. We talked about the old days. I hadn't seen him in about ten years."

"You were with him how long?"

"Hour, maybe an hour and a half. Then he had to go to some committee meeting."

"Did he talk about his wife?"

"His ex-wife, you mean?"

He nodded. "Your client."

"No," I said.

"And if he did, you wouldn't tell me."

I shrugged. "She's my client."

"Well," Horowitz said, "we'll check out his phone, see if we can catch up with those two you mentioned. The kid in the hoodie and Clem with the beard. You got anybody else we should check out?"

"That's all I can think of," I said. "Just those two. Look. What are you planning to do about my client?"

"Question her, of course."

"When?"

"Tonight. Soon. Okay?"

"Please," I said. "It's getting late. She's had a very traumatic experience."

"She gonna be cooperative?"

"I don't see why not," I said.

I went back over and sat on the folding chair beside Sharon.

She said, "Is everything all right?"

"In your conversations with Ken," I said, "did he ever mention ketamine?"

She frowned. "Ketamine?"

"It's a recreational drug," I said. "Vets use it as an anesthetic for animal surgery."

"I remember now," she said. "It's been a while since I worked in a vet's office. What about ketamine?"

I shrugged. "There was a bag of it in his room."

"What do they think," she said, "that he was selling it or something?"

"It kinda looks like it. Or else he was using it himself."

She shook her head. "That just shows how much I didn't know him anymore."

"Does the name Clem ring a bell?"

She frowned and shook her head. "Should it?"

"A guy Ken talked with when I was there, that's all. No reason you'd know him."

She tilted her head. "So now what happens?"

"They're going to want to question you," I said. "We don't have time to go over all the things they might ask you. They'll want to know everything you can tell them about Ken. About his business, his finances, his personal life. His friends and enemies. You should just answer their questions as well as you can. Tell them the truth. If they ask you something you think is out of line in any way, consult with me. I'll be there with you, and if I don't like a question, I'll tell you not to answer until we talk about it. Okay?"

"I don't really know much about him," she said. "We've been apart for over ten years. Just what he might've mentioned on the telephone."

" 'I don't know,' " I said, "is a perfectly

valid answer. Don't hesitate to use it."

"They think I did it, don't they?" she said.

"They'll ask you a lot of questions about yourself," I said, "treat you like a suspect, sure. Don't take it personally. It's how they think. They consider everybody a suspect until they can eliminate them."

"Especially the spouse. Or the ex-spouse."

"Yes," I said. "Especially the spouse."

Sharon shook her head. "I was falling in love with him all over again," she said. "Why would I want to kill him?"

It was a rhetorical question, and I didn't bother answering it.

FIVE

After a while, Officer Lloyd came over. "Mr. Coyne, Mrs. Nichols, would you come with me, please?"

We both stood up and followed Officer Lloyd to the elevators. We took one of them down to the first floor, where she led us to a small conference room off the lobby. It was wood-paneled and empty except for a rectangular table with about a dozen leather-cushioned chairs arranged around it.

"Have a seat, please," said Officer Lloyd. "The detectives will be here in a minute. Can I get you something?"

"Another coffee for me," I said.

"Just a glass of water, please," said Sharon.

Officer Lloyd nodded and left the room, closing the door behind her.

Sharon and I sat side by side at the table. I looked at my watch. It was a few minutes before one in the morning.

Officer Lloyd came back with a cup of coffee for me and a bottle of water for Sharon. We thanked her, and she left again.

I'd drunk about half of my coffee when the door opened and Horowitz and Marcia Benetti came in. They sat across from us.

"I'm Detective Horowitz," he said to Sharon. "This is Detective Benetti."

They all nodded to each other.

Horowitz looked at me. "We're gonna be here all night. There are two hundred and seventeen visiting veterinarians attending this convention. Tomorrow they'll all go home. They come from all over the world. Japan and Argentina and Denmark and Egypt. We got to interrogate and clear every one of them." He shook his head. "Not even to mention about fifty hotel employees on duty tonight and all the other hotel guests."

"Poor you," I said.

"My sentiments exactly." He put his forearms on the table, leaned forward, and looked at Sharon. "We hope you can help us understand what happened here tonight," he said. "You won't mind answering some questions for us?"

"I don't mind," said Sharon.

"Okay, good," said Horowitz. He jerked his head in the direction of his partner. "We're going to record this. Save us the trouble of taking notes." He looked at me. "Okay?"

I nodded. "Sure."

Benetti reached into her big shoulder bag and took out a battery-run digital recorder. It was about the size of a television remote. She pressed a button on its side, said, "Just testing," flipped another button, and we heard, "Just testing," loud and clear.

She put it in the middle of the table between us and said, "Okay. We're good to go."

Horowitz said, "We're here at the Beverly Suites Hotel in Natick. This is Detective Roger Horowitz. Detective Marcia Benetti is here, along with Sharon Nichols and attorney Brady Coyne. It's, um, April twenty-one" — he glanced at his wristwatch — "no, it's after midnight — 12:42 A.M. on Sunday, April twenty-two." He looked at Sharon and me and shrugged. "Okay, then. Mrs. Nichols. Our victim, Kenneth Nichols, he was your ex-husband, right?"

"Yes, that's right," said Sharon.

"And you were here tonight . . . why?"

"We hadn't seen each other in a long time. It was a kind of . . . a get-together. A chance to get to know each other again."

"Like a date."

"Sort of, yes."

"In his hotel room."

Sharon nodded.

"Answer for the recorder, please," Horowitz said.

"Yes," she said. "We'd planned to meet in Ken's hotel room."

"Why in his room?"

"It was a kind of celebration. He was going to order champagne."

"A celebration of what?" asked Horowitz.

"Of our . . . of being interested in each other again."

Horowitz hesitated, then said, "You were planning on, um, having sex with him? Is that what you mean?"

"I thought that might happen, yes," said Sharon.

Horowitz leaned back in his chair and looked at Marcia Benetti.

"So you're saying that's why you went to your ex-husband's room," Benetti said to Sharon. "To have sex with him."

"Maybe," Sharon said.

Horowitz leaned forward. "You've been divorced for how long?"

"Ten years. It'll be eleven next September."

"Why?"

"Why what?" asked Sharon. "Why did we get divorced?"

Horowitz nodded.

Sharon shook her head. "We didn't love each other anymore. We were unhappy." She shrugged. "No dramatic reason, if that's what you're looking for."

"I wasn't looking for anything," Horowitz said.

"It was mutual," she said. "Nobody's fault."

"Mr. Coyne here was your divorce lawyer?"

"No," Sharon said. "Mr. Coyne handled our veterinary business. My husband's and mine. When we were married. Brady did not do my divorce, but he's my attorney now."

"Kids?"

She frowned. "Excuse me?"

"You and your husband," he said. "Ex-husband, I mean. Did you have children?"

"Yes," she said. "Two. A girl and a boy. Ellen and Wayne."

"How old?"

"Then or now?"

"Now."

Sharon frowned for a moment, then said, "Ellen's twenty-five. Wayne's twenty-two."

"And where are they now?"

"Both in school," she said. "Ellen's getting her master's at BU. Wayne's a junior at Webster State College in New Hampshire."

61

"So how did they get along with your — with their father?"

She shrugged. "They had the normal issues, I guess."

"Normal?" asked Horowitz.

"They resented him," she said. "They resented both of us, really. For splitting. For wrecking our lovely little family. They were angry."

"Did they keep in touch with him?"

"Ken, you mean?"

Horowitz nodded.

"I don't honestly know about that," Sharon said.

"How about you?"

"I haven't talked with Wayne for a while. Ellen and I have remained close."

"How long is a while?"

Sharon glanced at me, then looked at Horowitz. "A couple of years."

Horowitz's eyebrow went up. "You haven't communicated with your son for two years?"

Sharon nodded. "Maybe a little longer than that, actually."

"Can you tell us how to reach Wayne and Ellen?"

"You consider my children to be suspects?" Sharon asked.

"Everybody's suspects," said Horowitz.

"I can give you their phone numbers and

62

addresses, sure," she said.

"Give her something to write on," Horowitz said to Marcia Benetti.

Benetti slid a pad of paper and a pen across the table to Sharon, who took an old-fashioned hand-sized address book from her purse and copied out some information on the pad of paper, which she then pushed back to Benetti.

"Thank you," said Horowitz.

Sharon shrugged.

"Okay, good," said Horowitz. "So, back to your husband — your ex-husband, I mean, Kenneth — he was living in Baltimore? That right?"

She nodded. "His office was in a suburb just outside the city."

"His veterinary office."

"Yes."

"How would you characterize your relationship with your ex-husband for the past ten, almost eleven years?"

"We were divorced," she said. "We lived in different states. We had occasional long-distance telephone conversations or an exchange of e-mails, mostly about our children. Otherwise, until last fall, Ken and I didn't have any kind of relationship."

"What happened last fall?" Horowitz asked.

Sharon turned and looked at me.

I nodded.

"We began talking on the telephone," she said. "We discovered that we still liked each other. Or I should say, we liked each other all over again. We were talking about getting back together."

"Neither of you had remarried?"

"No."

"Or was in a relationship?"

"No," said Sharon. "Well, I wasn't, and Ken said he wasn't."

"But you don't know if he was telling you the truth?"

"No, I suppose I don't," she said. "I believed him, but I don't know it for sure."

"He could have been lying to you," said Marcia Benetti. "By way of seducing you. To get you into his hotel room tonight. Is that what you mean?"

Sharon looked at Benetti for a moment. The hint of a smile played on the corners of her mouth, as if she were acknowledging her bond with this other woman, their gender's ancient understanding that men were manipulative pigs. "Yes," she said. "I suppose I wanted to believe him. I might have been deluding myself. He seemed sincere, but I guess he could have been lying. I didn't know him well enough anymore to tell."

Marcia Benetti nodded and leaned back in her chair.

Horowitz had been smiling as he followed this exchange between the two women. He cleared his throat. "In all of your telephone conversations," he said, "did Mr. Nichols ever mention anybody he was having problems with? Any kind of enemy?"

Sharon frowned for a moment, then shrugged. "Not that I remember."

"Would he have been likely to tell you if there was such a person in his life?"

She glanced at Benetti. "I think he would have, yes," she said. "We talked about everything."

"What about a man named Clem?" asked Horowitz.

Sharon looked at me.

"I asked her already," I said.

He shrugged. "So'd I."

Sharon shook her head. "Like I told Brady, I don't remember Ken mentioning anybody named Clem."

"What about the man in the hood?" Horowitz asked. "Who you saw tonight. Did you recognize him?"

"No," Sharon said. "I did not."

"Did your husband — your ex-husband

65

— ever talk about selling illegal drugs?"

Sharon turned to me, bit her lip.

I shrugged. "Just answer his question."

"No," she said to Horowitz. "He said nothing about that to me."

"So as far as you know, he had no problems," Horowitz said.

"Oh, he had problems," Sharon said. "I don't know anything about drugs, but Ken had plenty of problems. He was lonely, for one thing. He didn't like Baltimore very much. He didn't get along very well with his partner at the veterinary clinic. There was always the pressure of money. I think he was having financial problems. I don't think he was very happy."

"Did he talk to you about his financial problems?"

Sharon shook her head. "Not really. We didn't talk about problems. It was kind of implied, that's all."

"Implied how?"

Sharon lifted her hands, let them fall. "I can't really explain it. Nothing specific. Just an impression I got."

Marcia Benetti cleared her throat. Horowitz glanced at her, then nodded and sat back in his chair.

"So, Mrs. Nichols," said Benetti, "what'd you do with the knife?"

Sharon frowned. "Knife?"

"The murder weapon. How did you dispose of it?"

Sharon turned and arched her eyebrows at me.

"Don't say anything," I said to her. I looked at Benetti. "You want to rephrase that question?"

Horowitz had his arms crossed over his chest and a big smile plastered on his face.

Benetti glowered at me for a moment, then looked at Sharon and said, "Mrs. Nichols, did you notice a knife in the hotel room where you found your . . . Mr. Nichols's body?"

"No," said Sharon. "I didn't see any knife."

"It would've been a steak knife," Benetti said, "such as would be included in a room-service delivery along with a fork and a spoon. A serrated steak knife with a blade about five inches long."

Sharon shook her head. "I didn't see any kind of knife."

"When people finish their room-service meal," said Benetti, "they put the tray with the dirty dishes outside their door. You could have taken a steak knife from one of those trays."

"I guess anybody could have done that,"

said Sharon, "but I didn't."

Benetti flashed a quick, humorless smile. "The medical examiner tells us that your husband was stabbed twice with a serrated knife," she said. "Once in the abdomen and once under the rib cage. The wound in his chest penetrated his heart and caused him to die instantly. The wound to his abdomen punctured his liver and bowel and would've probably killed him eventually."

Sharon was staring at Benetti. Her eyes were brimming.

"So what about the knife?" asked Horowitz.

"My client already answered the question about the knife," I said. "Is there anything else? Because it's really late and we are exhausted."

"One more thing," said Horowitz. "Mrs. Nichols, you said you came here tonight to, um, meet with your husband, is that right?"

"He was my ex-husband," Sharon said.

"Right. Excuse me."

"We had planned to get together tonight, yes."

"In his hotel room."

Sharon nodded. "That's right. I already explained that."

"Not down in the lobby or in one of the bars or coffee shops or restaurants in this hotel or somewhere nearby. In his room."

Sharon nodded. "In his room, yes."

"Why in the room?" asked Horowitz.

"I told you. We were probably going to have sex."

"You hadn't seen each other in, what, ten years?"

"Since the divorce," she said. "Almost eleven years."

"And what time did he expect you to arrive in his room?" asked Benetti. "To have sex."

"Nine o'clock," said Sharon. "We agreed to meet there at nine. There was a banquet tonight, and afterward there were going to be speeches. He felt he had to be there for part of it, but he was planning to sneak out early."

"To meet you."

"Yes."

"In his hotel room."

Sharon nodded.

"To have sex."

"Maybe."

"You look nice," said Benetti. "You dressed for the occasion."

Sharon looked at me. "How am I supposed to answer that?"

"It wasn't a question," I said. "No answer required."

Sharon turned back to Marcia Benetti and smiled. "Thank you. I wanted to look nice for him."

"So what time did you arrive here at the hotel?" asked Benetti.

"A little before eight thirty."

"Even though you weren't meeting him until nine."

"That's right," said Sharon. "I was early."

"So did you go straight to the room?"

"No," Sharon said. "I didn't want to appear to be too . . . too eager. Plus, I didn't know if he'd be back from the banquet. So I sat in the lobby until nine o'clock. It was maybe five after nine when I got to his room."

"Did you talk with anybody while you were in the lobby?" asked Benetti.

Sharon shrugged. "No, I don't think so. I just sat there in one of the chairs and read a magazine."

"Because," said Benetti, "it would help if you could account for your time before nine o'clock."

"Somebody might've noticed me," Sharon said, "but I couldn't tell you who. I just sat there by myself reading my *Newsweek* and waiting for nine o'clock to arrive, and it seemed to take a long time. Then I went up to his room. The door was ajar, so I pushed it open and went inside, and that's when I . . ." She shrugged.

"You were eager," said Benetti.

"I was pretty excited," Sharon said.

"According to the ME," said Horowitz, "Mr. Nichols died somewhere between six thirty and eight thirty tonight. We have witnesses who are willing to testify that he was still at the banquet at seven fifteen, when they began clearing the tables, and that he was gone before eight o'clock, when the speeches began. So we've got that hour between eight, when he was gone from the banquet, and nine, when you said you went to his room." He looked at Sharon and pursed his lips.

"Well, I already told you, I didn't go to his room until nine," said Sharon. "So I guess I couldn't have done it."

"But," said Marcia Benetti, "you could have gone to his room, say, at eight, and you could have stabbed him with a room-service knife, and then you could have ditched the knife and gone down to the lobby at, say, eight thirty, then back up to the room again at nine."

"I could have," said Sharon, "but —"

"Whoa." I put my hand on Sharon's arm. "This is getting out of line. My client is answering your questions fully and honestly.

71

She told you where she was and what she was doing at the times you asked her about." I looked at Horowitz. "I think that's enough for tonight."

He glanced at Benetti.

"I've got one more question," she said.

"One more question," Horowitz said. "Okay?"

I looked at Benetti. "Be nice."

She smiled quickly, then turned to Sharon. "When you went to your husband's room, you told us that you found the door ajar, isn't that right?"

"That's right," said Sharon. "He was my ex-husband."

"Yes, sorry." Benetti cleared her throat. "So you just pushed the door open and went inside."

"I knocked and called Ken's name first," Sharon said. "When he didn't answer or come to the door, I pushed on it and it opened. So I went in."

"You didn't have a key card?"

"No."

"Mrs. Nichols," said Benetti, "I tried to leave that door unlatched. I tried to see if I could leave it open a crack. You know what?"

Sharon shrugged.

"I couldn't do it," said Benetti. "That door is heavy, and the way it's hung, if you try to leave it ajar, it just swings shut and the latch engages and it automatically locks."

Sharon was shaking her head. "I'm not sure what you're getting at."

"What I'm getting at," said Benetti, "is that you couldn't have found that door ajar. It had to've been locked. So there were only two ways for you to get inside. One, you had a key card and let yourself in, or, two, Mr. Nichols let you in. Since you say you didn't have a key . . ."

"I didn't mean the door was ajar, exactly," said Sharon. "It was all the way shut but not latched. When I pushed on it, it swung open."

"It wasn't ajar."

"No. It was shut but not latched."

"You told us it was ajar. Which was it?"

"Shut but not latched," Sharon said. "That's what I meant to say."

"It couldn't have been," said Benetti.

"Well, it was," said Sharon, "because all I had to do was push it open. And Ken was dead when I went inside."

"You mean," said Benetti, "that he was alive when you went in. But then he was dead when you left."

Sharon turned to me.

"Okay, that's it," I said to Sharon. "Don't

say anything else." I looked at Horowitz. "Unless you intend to charge my client with a crime, we're done for tonight."

He shrugged. "We're not charging anybody with anything right now."

"Then we're out of here," I said.

"Yeah, okay," Horowitz said. "I guess we're done for now anyway." He looked at Sharon. "We'll want to talk to you again." He smiled. "You've been very cooperative, and we appreciate it."

She nodded. "I want to cooperate. I want you to catch whoever did this to Ken."

"We'll talk again," he said. "You should bring your lawyer."

"Count on it," I said.

Six

We all left the conference room. Horowitz and Benetti went over to the elevators. Sharon and I headed for the front lobby.

"Did I do okay?" she asked.

"You did fine," I said. "You kept your cool. You didn't let yourself be bullied. You seemed entirely truthful. You were very credible."

"I *was* entirely truthful," she said.

I smiled. "I didn't mean to imply otherwise."

"I don't think they believed me, though," she said. "When I said why I went to Ken's room. That I thought we might have sex."

"People who've never been divorced don't understand how complicated it can be."

"The relationship between former spouses, you mean," Sharon said.

I nodded. "People seem to expect us to hate each other. They always seem surprised to know that we don't. That we might actually like each other. That there might still be something like love between us."

"You and Gloria, you mean."

I nodded. "You and Ken."

"You believe me, then."

"Sure I do."

When we stepped outside, I remembered that the police had taken Sharon's jacket. It was a chilly April evening, and a soft rain was still falling, and she was standing there in her thin silky blouse hugging herself. I took off my jacket and draped it over her shoulders.

She looked up at me. "Oh. Thank you, Brady."

At that point a young man wearing jeans and sneakers and a green windbreaker approached us. "Mrs. Nichols?" he said. "My name's Josh Neuman. I'm a reporter with the *Boston Herald,* and I —"

"She has nothing to say," I said quickly.

He ignored me and stepped closer to Sharon. "Are you a suspect in your husband's murder? You found the body, isn't that right? Did you —"

I stepped in between him and Sharon. "Go away," I said.

"You're Brady Coyne, right?" he asked. "Her lawyer? Come on, Mr. Coyne. Let me do my job here."

"I'm sure the police will have a statement for you," I said, "but we don't. Mrs. Nichols is tired and upset, and we're both leaving now."

"Can I talk with her tomorrow?" Josh Neuman asked me. "Will you allow her to give me an interview? Or will you talk to me?"

"You can call me on Monday," I said. "No promises. Now leave us alone."

"You got a card? What's your number?"

"Look it up," I said.

"Okay. I'll call you." He gave Sharon a little bow, turned, and went back into the hotel.

I turned to Sharon. "Sorry about that."

"Thanks for handling it."

I nodded. "Do you need a ride home?"

"I've got my car," she said.

"Did you have a valet park it?"

"No. I left it in the lot. It's right over there." She pointed toward a sea of vehicles in a well-lit parking area. "Why?"

"A valet might be able to corroborate the time you got here," I said.

"Well," she said, "too bad. That would help, huh?"

I shrugged. "It would help, sure. No biggie, though."

We were standing under the portico in

77

front of the main entrance to the hotel. The misty spring rain made halos around the lights that illuminated the brick pathways.

"I don't understand about the door," Sharon said. "It *was* unlatched. I guess I said ajar, and that's not precisely what I meant. It was closed, but I was able to push it open. So maybe they couldn't make the door do that. I can't explain that. That's how it was. I wasn't lying."

"There are always things like that," I said. "Anomalies. Details that don't fit, that can't be explained. With murders, things are never neat and tidy. The police know that. When everything is orderly and logical, they begin to worry. That's a sure sign that something is seriously off."

"I can see how it looks," she said. "About the door, I mean. It looks like Ken had to have been alive when I got there. If the door wasn't unlatched, the only way I could've gotten in was if he let me in."

I shrugged.

"But it was unlatched."

I nodded.

"They were playing good cop, bad cop," she said. "Except the sweet-looking female was the bad cop, and the crabby man was the good one."

"Actually," I said, "they're both good cops."

"Well, Detective Benetti was pretty hostile, I thought." She turned to me and gave me a hug. "Thanks for being here for me."

I patted her shoulder. "That's what lawyers are for. Will you be all right?"

"Oh, sure." She smiled quickly. "Of course, my ex-husband, who I was falling in love with all over again, got murdered tonight, and I was the one who found his bloody body, and the police think I'm the one who killed him. But, yes, actually, I am. I'm okay." She shrugged. "Maybe it just hasn't hit me yet."

"Do you have somebody who can stay with you?" I asked. "It might be better not to be alone tonight."

"It's pretty late," Sharon said, "but maybe I'll call Ellen. Even if she can't come over, it will help if I can just talk to her." She put a hand on my shoulder, went up on her tiptoes, and kissed my cheek. "Thanks, Brady Coyne. I'm sorry to drag you away from whatever you were doing tonight. I'm so grateful to you for being here for me."

I patted her shoulder and did not return her kiss. "I'm glad I could do it," I said.

"Thank you for your jacket, too. I'll return it next time I see you, if that's okay." She gave me a quick smile. "I expect we'll be seeing each other again."

I nodded. "I'm sure we will. Don't worry about the jacket."

"Well, good night," she said, and then she turned and began walking through the misty rain in the direction of the parking lot.

I hurried after her. "Wait," I said. "I'll walk with you."

"No need," she said. "I'm perfectly capable."

"I know," I said, "but in my head I hear the voice of my mother, reminding me that I should always walk the young lady to her door."

Sharon turned and smiled at me. "How extraordinarily old-fashioned." She hooked her arm through mine. "It's really quite sweet. Thank you."

It took a little more than half an hour to navigate the wet, empty city streets from the hotel on Route 9 in Natick to my parking garage on Beacon Hill in Boston, and another fifteen minutes to walk the length of Charles Street to my townhouse halfway up Mt. Vernon Street. It was three thirty in the morning when I stepped into the house.

Henry greeted me at the door with a lot of happy whining. I knew what he'd been thinking: *This time he's never coming home, and who's going to feed me?*

His entire hind end wagged when I knelt down to rub his ears and scratch his forehead.

Who loves you like a dog?

I let him out into the backyard, and then I used the kitchen phone to check my voice mail.

I had two messages.

The first was from Billy. He'd called at 11:06 P.M. "Hey, Pop," he said. "Hope your lawyer thing went all right. As for us, we ended up having a great dinner at Mosca's. Good choice of restaurants, man. The osso buco was outstanding. I bet that's what you'd've ordered. It came with a nice garlicky risotto, and . . . Well, hell. It was too bad you had to leave. So anyway, um, listen. You remember how me and Gwen, we wanted to talk to you and Mom, right? Well, I'm sorry, but we ended up telling her, um, what we had to say. But I want to talk to you. Gwen and I do, I mean. Not on the damn phone. Look. We're going to be around for a few more days. Just let me know when's good for you. We can come to your place just about anytime — well, not tomorrow, but some day this coming week — have a beer, or maybe grill something, like the good old days at your condo on Lewis Wharf. You provide the grill, me and Gwen'll bring the meat. How'd that be? Or if you'd rather, we could meet somewhere and get something to eat. Whatever. Let me know, 'kay?" He paused, then said, "Well, okay. That's it. Call me. You've got my cell number. Love you, man."

The second message came at 1:14 A.M. "Hey, Brady?" It was Alex Shaw, calling from her house in Garrison, Maine. "Are you okay? I sorta expected to hear from you tonight. It's Saturday night, right? I know you were out with Billy and his lady friend and, um, Gloria, but I thought . . . Well, whatever. Look, it's around one fifteen, and I'm tucked in here for the night, all snuggly in that Red Sox T-shirt you gave me, and I'm going to read for a while and I'll probably fall asleep after like two pages, but I wouldn't mind if you called and woke me up, you know? I mean, if you don't mind me being all sleepy-voiced and fuzzy. I don't care what time it is. Call me, 'kay?" She yawned loudly. "Sorry, hon. Well, I hope everything's all right. Good night for now."

I smiled. I was picturing Alex in her extra-large Red Sox T-shirt, which, of course, was her intention. I knew for a fact that she wore nothing else to bed. When she stood up, the

T-shirt molded her body and fell to midthigh. In bed it would ride up over her hips. She liked to lie on her side, facing away from me, and then push her butt back up against me, and she'd grab my hand and hold it against her breast . . .

Well, her message was having exactly the effect she intended.

Henry was whining at the back door. I hung up the phone and let him in. When I gave him a Milk-Bone, it reminded me that Sharon's call had taken me away from the restaurant before I'd eaten anything except a couple of olives and a hunk of Italian bread and half a glass of Chianti. I realized that I was starved.

I found a slab of leftover pork loin in my refrigerator. I sliced it, slapped Dijon mustard on four slices of bread, and made two sandwiches of pork slices, with potato chips and dill pickles on the side.

I wolfed down the sandwiches with a bottle of beer at the kitchen table, with my television tuned to ESPN so I could watch some baseball highlights from the previous day. Henry sprawled under the table so that he'd be in position to snag stray crumbs, not to mention any pieces of pork sandwich I might hold down for him. Henry liked potato chips, too, but he wasn't fond of dill pickles.

After we ate, Henry and I went upstairs. I brushed my teeth and went to bed. He curled up on the rug beside me. It was after four in the morning, but I was wide-awake, with a stomach full of pork sandwich and dill pickle and a head full of questions.

I took the phone from my bedside table, rested it on my chest, and called Alex.

She picked up the phone on the fifth ring. There was a long silence before her distant, muffled voice said, "H'lo? . . . Brady? Honey? That you?"

"It's me, babe," I said. "Look. Why don't you just hang up and go back to sleep. We can talk tomorrow. I just wanted to tuck you in, say good night."

"No, no," she said. "I'm already tucked in. All alone here in my warm cozy bed. Why are you there and me here, huh? Wanna come snuggle with me?"

"I'd love to. But not tonight, I don't think. Let's make it next weekend. Your place or mine, it doesn't matter. How's that?"

"Mm," she said. "I can't wait." She sighed. "I'm pretty sleepy. You okay? Everything okay?"

"Everything's fine," I said. "I got called away on a new case. That's where I was when you called. I'll tell you all about it. Now here's a hug and a kiss. Go to sleep."

She made a kissy sound. "You, too, baby. 'Night, swee'ie. Talk tomorrow."

I think she was asleep before the phone disconnected.

Not me. I lay there wide-awake for a long time, with images of Ken Nichols's pale, lifeless body and questions about Sharon tumbling around in my head. Even a couple of chapters of *Moby-Dick*, my never-fail soporific, failed to make my eyelids droop, and I didn't drift off to sleep until sometime after the purple outside my window had faded to silver and the fresh breeze of a new April day had swept the clouds out of the sky.

SEVEN

Henry woke me up, whining to go outside. I asked him nicely if he couldn't hold it for a while, but he made it clear that an accident was imminent if I didn't get up and let him out.

It was about quarter past nine on this Sunday morning. I figured I'd had less than four hours of sleep.

I pulled on a sweatshirt and a pair of jeans, followed Henry downstairs, and let him out into our walled-in patio garden. I put together a pot of coffee in my electric coffeemaker, and pretty soon the aroma filled the kitchen. I poured myself a mugful, took it out back, and sat in one of my wooden Adirondack chairs. Henry wandered over and lay down on the brick patio beside me.

It was a warm late-April morning in Boston. The sun bathed my little backyard in its warmth, and the spring bulbs were blooming — tulips and daffodils, crocuses and hyacinths — and the irises and other perennials were poking through the earth.

Evie had always been in charge of the flower beds. She'd planted them when we first moved here, and she was the one who'd tended them. This was the garden's first spring without her. I liked flowers, but I had little knowledge and less enthusiasm for taking care of flower gardens. I figured they'd make it through this one season all right if I remembered to keep them weeded and watered. After that, they'd need serious attention. With perennials, you had to dig up, thin out, cut back, fertilize, separate, replant, reorganize. You couldn't ignore perennials. They kept coming back at you, year after year.

Evie had liked gardening, and I'd liked the fact that she liked it, because it meant that I didn't have to do it. I used to enjoy coming home from court, after a day of explaining reality to angry clients and arguing points of law to skeptical judges, and finding her on her knees in our garden digging and troweling and grubbing around in the earth. I'd bring out beers for both of us and urge her to take a break, and we'd sit at the picnic table, Evie in her cutoff shorts and baggy T-shirt and gardening gloves, smudges of dirt on her face, her auburn hair tucked up under one of my old Red Sox caps, and me in my pinstripe suit with my necktie pulled loose.

Sometimes she'd slither onto my lap and nuzzle my throat and unbutton my shirt and get my clothes dirty, which I didn't mind at all. That's why God invented dry cleaning.

Well, Evie was gone, and she wasn't coming back. Once in a while something — like seeing the spring bulbs that she'd planted two autumns ago now rioting in our flower gardens — would remind me of her, and I'd remember something specific, like how she'd stick that excellent butt of hers up in the air when she kneeled in the garden to pull weeds, or how the skin at the nape of her neck tasted when she was sweaty after gardening on a warm afternoon in July . . . and then, for a few minutes, I missed her.

But mostly I didn't think about her. She'd been gone for a long time. Almost a year.

Sometimes for no apparent reason Henry would suddenly scramble to his feet and trot over to the front door and press his nose against it, and nobody would be there. He'd stand there for a while, staring at the door, whining softly, and it would seem to me that he was missing Evie and hoping — maybe expecting — that she was about to open the door and come back home.

After a while, he'd kind of sigh, and then he'd wander into some other part of the house and curl up and go to sleep.

When my mug was empty, Henry and I went inside. I fetched the Sunday *Globe* from the front stoop and took it to the kitchen. I dumped some dog food into Henry's bowl and put it down on the floor for him. Then I filled a bowl of my own with Cheerios. I sliced a banana on top, added half a handful of blueberries, sprinkled on some brown sugar, and ate it that way, crunchy, without milk.

While I ate I skimmed the news sections of the paper. Ken Nichols's murder had apparently happened too late on Saturday night to make the Sunday papers. I was curious to see how the press would handle it, how Roger Horowitz would be quoted, how Sharon's role would be described, if Ken's gym bag full of ketamine would be mentioned.

I remembered Josh Neuman, the persistent young *Herald* reporter. I was a big believer in the free press, and an informed public, and the inalienable right to express opinions without fear — but no way was Sharon going to talk with this guy, or any other reporter. It could do her no good and possibly a lot of harm.

It was early in the afternoon, and I was in my backyard raking last fall's leaves out from under the bushes and packing them in big plastic trash bags — not my idea of a fun way to spend a Sunday in April, but it had to be done. Anyway, the sun was warm on the back of my neck, and the Red Sox were playing the Orioles on my portable radio, and I had a half-empty bottle of chilled Sam Adams lager sitting on the picnic table, so it wasn't so bad.

I was taking a break, sitting at the table sipping my Sam, when my cell phone vibrated in my pocket.

It was Sharon Nichols.

"How are you doing today?" I asked.

"Not that great," she said. "I think I had some kind of delayed reaction. When I got home last night, I thought I was fine. I called Ellen, woke her up, and I started telling her how her father was, um, was dead, how he'd been . . . murdered, and suddenly I started shaking, and my throat got all tight, and I was seeing all that blood, remembering how it smelled in that room, and poor Ellen on the other end of the line, she kept saying, 'Mother? Are you all right? Mother? What's the matter?' Like that.

90

Anyway, she came over, and we stayed up until after the sun rose, drinking wine and crying and reminiscing, and eventually, talking with Ellen, I started to get it together again. I'm better now. Still kinda shaky, I guess. But better. I just woke up, can you believe it? I mean, it's after one in the afternoon."

"This is all to be expected," I said. "You held it together for a long time last night. You did very well. That was all pretty traumatic."

"Yes, it was." She was silent for a minute. "So how are you?"

"Me?" I asked. "Oh, I'm good. I've been through things like this before."

"Murders, you mean. Dead bodies. Blood. Hysterical women."

"Yes. All of the above."

"I'm so sorry for . . . for messing up your weekend."

"I'd say your weekend was messed up worse than mine," I said.

"Mm." She chuckled softly. There wasn't any humor in it. "Well, the reason I called . . . last night you said if I needed anything?"

"Sure," I said. "What can I do?"

"Well," she said, "like I said, Ellen came over, so she knows about it. What happened to Ken. I haven't been able to reach Wayne yet, but I'll keep trying. It's Ken's father that I'm worried about."

"Ken's father's still alive?"

"Yes. He has outlived his only child. Isn't that sad?"

"It is," I said. I thought of my sons, Billy and Joey. I hoped I wouldn't outlive either of them. "So you want to tell him, is that it?"

"I think I should," Sharon said. "Before somebody says something or he hears about it on the news." She hesitated. "His name is Charles. Charles Nichols. He's in an assisted living facility. It's a really nice, um, very expensive place out in Ashby. Charles is quite frail, and he's been fading for the past year or so. Probably doesn't have a lot of time left. He's somewhere in his mid-eighties. Eighty-five or -six. He's got congestive heart failure and diabetes among other problems, and I'm afraid this news could, you know . . ."

"I'll go with you," I said.

"Oh, I couldn't ask you to do that."

"You didn't," I said. "It was my idea."

She laughed softly. "Well, of course, it *is* why I called you. Really, though, it's a Sunday afternoon. You must have plans. I honestly don't want you to —"

"No plans," I said. "I'll go with you. It's what we lawyers do."

She laughed softly. "Somehow I doubt that."

"It's what this lawyer does," I said.

"Would you? Thank you, Brady. I could really use some moral support. It'll make me feel much better if you're with me. I don't know how Charles will handle it. He and Ken had their issues, and I don't think Ken visited him very often, but still, Ken was an only child, and Charles's wife is gone, so Ken was all he had left."

"Aside from you and his grandchildren, you mean," I said.

"Well," said Sharon, "Charles and I always got along just fine, but I'm not family. Not now, anyway, not after the divorce. I haven't seen him for a long time. But still. I think I'm the one who should tell him what happened."

"You want to do this today?"

"Yes," she said. "The sooner the better, don't you think?"

"I do," I said. "I'll pick you up in about an hour. How's that?"

"You're my hero," she said.

EIGHT

When they ran their veterinary clinic and
kennels in Wellesley, Ken and Sharon Nichols lived with their two kids in a gorgeous
old Victorian on five or six acres abutting
some conservation land off a country road
on the west side of town.

Now Sharon was living in a third-floor
condo unit in a boxy brick building on
Route 2A in Acton about a mile west of the
Concord prison. A different lifestyle, usually a less lavish one, was the price of
freedom, and more often than not, both parties in a divorce ended up paying it.

Condominium buildings had popped up
like mushrooms along 2A in Acton during
the real estate boom of the late seventies
and early eighties. Speculators bought six or
eight units at a time, and sometimes entire
buildings, with the intention of renting them
out while the market continued to grow and
then flipping them for big profits. Then

pretty soon the boom busted, and a lot of smart investors were suddenly stupid and ended up stuck with big mortgages and depressed rents and scarce tenants and high maintenance fees and no buyers.

I parked in the lot behind Sharon's building, told Henry to wait in the car, went to the back door, and pressed the button beside her number.

A minute later her voice came to me from a speaker beside the door. "Brady? Is that you?"

I leaned to the speaker and said, "I'm here."

"I'll be right down," she said.

"Take your time," I said.

I went over to my car and let Henry out. He proceeded to investigate the weeds that grew amid the trash along the chain-link fence that bordered the parking lot, and he was still at it when Sharon emerged from the back door about five minutes later.

She waved at me and came over to where I was leaning against my car. She was wearing a pair of snug-fitting jeans and a red-and-white-striped long-sleeved jersey. Her blond hair was artfully tousled, and she'd done some neat tricks with makeup to hide evidence of the previous night, when she'd found the murdered body of her former husband, answered the hard questions of suspicious police officers, and then drunk wine and cried and stayed up till after sunrise with her daughter.

She looked, in other words, spectacular.

She put her hand on my shoulder, tiptoed up, kissed my cheek, and gave me a quick one-armed hug.

I returned the hug but not the kiss. "You look nice," I said.

She smiled. "Thank you." She had the jacket I'd loaned her folded over her arm. She handed it to me. "For this, too. Again. It was very gallant of you."

"Gallant," I said. "That's me, all right." I whistled to Henry, who came trotting over. "This is Henry," I said to Sharon.

"Hey, Henry," she said. She bent over and scratched the special place on his forehead, and her ease with Henry reminded me that she used to work with Ken at their veterinary hospital. She obviously understood and liked animals.

"That's his G-spot," I said. "Right there in the middle of his forehead."

Sharon straightened up and smiled. "Everybody's got one, even dogs."

I opened the back door for Henry, and he jumped in. Then I went around and held the passenger door open for Sharon.

"Oh, thank you," she said as she slid in. "*Gallant,* as always." She pronounced it with the accent on the second syllable, making it the French word. "Chivalry is not dead."

"My mother again," I said, "reminding me to hold the door for the lady." I shut her door, went around to the driver's side, and got in. "Ashby," I said. "I assume you know how to find the place?"

"It's not that far from here," she said. "I feel terribly guilty that I haven't visited Charles more often since he's been there. I mean, Ashby is only about an hour up the road from Acton. He's been there four or five years now, and I can count the times I've visited him on one hand, mostly the first couple of years he was there, to bring him Christmas presents. Good dutiful Ellen came with me each time. Ellen still visits him once in a while. I'm ashamed to say, I don't. Charles never did make me feel overly welcome, but that's no excuse."

"He's not your father," I said.

"No," she said, "and he's never been a very loving — or lovable — father-in-law. Still, he is my children's grandfather, and he helped Ken and me out when we were getting started."

"With money, you mean?"

"That's right," she said. "We couldn't have

done what we did without Charles's help. Buying the house and the land, building the kennels and the hospital, getting the business up and running. We all pretended it was a loan, and maybe we would've eventually paid him back, but then we got divorced and money was a different kind of issue, and I'm sure Ken didn't give Charles a penny of what we owed him. Not that he needs it."

The village of Ashby, Massachusetts, was a straight shot northwesterly on Route 119 from Sharon's place in Acton. Ashby was the last town before the New Hampshire border, and it had the feel of a rural New Hampshire village.

Charles Nichols's assisted living place was a big rambling two-story redbrick structure at the end of a long country road. It sat on the edge of a meadow that sloped up to a woody hillside. To the north a range of round-topped mountains pushed into the sky. A pretty little rocky stream meandered alongside the building, and there were paved walkways and patios along its banks so that wheelchair-bound residents could sit out there and listen to the water music and bask in the sunshine.

The stream looked like it would hold trout, and seeing it reminded me that springtime had come to New England, and soon the trout would be rising to mayflies, and that reminded me once again that it was time to call Charlie McDevitt and J. W. Jackson and Doc Adams and make some fishing plans.

A sign directed us to the visitors' parking area, and from there another sign pointed to the entrance.

A fortyish woman sat behind a desk in the foyer. When we walked in, she looked up, smiled, and said, "May I help you?" She wore a plastic nameplate over her left breast. Her name was Joan Porter. Her smile was well practiced and automatic.

"We're here for Charles Nichols," Sharon said. "I'm his daughter-in-law."

Joan Porter looked Sharon up and down, glanced at me, then turned back to Sharon and gave her that professional smile. "Charles is in the dayroom. Do you know where it is?"

Sharon shook her head.

"Down that corridor and around the corner on your right," she said with a vague wave of her hand. "They're watching the Red Sox game."

"How is he?" Sharon asked.

"Charles is a lovely gentleman," said Joan Porter, "and he rarely complains. He's recovering from his accident."

"Accident?" asked Sharon.

"You didn't know?"

Sharon shook her head.

"He fell and broke his wrist a couple of weeks ago," said Joan Porter. "He's been having some pain, not sleeping well, and of course a man his age, he heals slowly."

"Why did he fall?" asked Sharon.

Joan Porter frowned. "Excuse me?"

"I meant, how did it happen?"

"He was alone in his room. People Charles's age, they tend to lose their balance."

"Nobody was with him when it happened?" asked Sharon.

Joan Porter shook her head. "It was in the evening. He was alone. In his own room. In the independent living wing."

Sharon nodded. "This is my friend Brady Coyne, by the way," she said. "He's a lawyer."

Joan Porter held out her hand and smiled. "It's nice to meet you."

I gripped her hand.

"Please don't sue me," she said.

I smiled quickly.

"Oh," she said. "I bet everybody says that to you."

"Just about everybody," I said.

"Down this corridor, is it?" asked Sharon.

Joan Porter nodded. "Before you jump to conclusions," she said, "you should talk to Charles's physician."

Sharon turned and looked at her. "What do you mean?"

"You're his daughter-in-law?"

Sharon nodded, although technically she was the old guy's *ex*-daughter-in-law.

"Do you know about Charles's . . . condition?"

"Condition?"

"Well," Joan Porter said, "I know Charles's son has been informed, and I believe Charles himself told his granddaughter. She was here a week or so ago. Neither of them has shared the news with you?"

Sharon shook her head.

Joan Porter hesitated, then said, "Mr. Nichols — Charles — he has recently been diagnosed with a brain aneurysm."

Sharon blinked. "Oh," she said. "Oh, dear. What will they . . . ?"

"There's apparently nothing they can do for him."

"No operation?"

"Evidently not. You might want to talk with his physician, get a professional opinion, but as I understand it, a man Charles's age, with all his other infirmities . . ."

"That's why he fell, Ms. Porter?" Sharon asked. "The brain aneurysm? He passed out or got dizzy or something?"

Joan Porter shrugged. "That's what the doctor thinks. Charles doesn't really remember what happened. It may never happen again. There's no telling with aneurysms."

"It could, um, burst anytime?" asked Sharon.

"As I understand it."

"Which would kill him."

"Oh, my, yes," said Joan Porter.

"Can he continue living here?"

"Certainly," Joan Porter said. "This is his home. If he falls and hurts himself again, we'll have to think about moving him to the assisted living side. Charles would hate it, of course. We're hoping we won't have to go that route."

Sharon looked at Joan Porter for a moment, then said, "Well, thank you for telling me. Thank you for your candor." She held out her hand.

Joan Porter took Sharon's hand in both of hers, and I read genuine kindness in the woman's eyes. "You're one of his relatives," she said. "You have a right to know. Knowing Charles, I'm not sure he would tell you."

Sharon hooked her arm through mine. We started down the wide corridor, turned a corner, and came to a big open area furnished with comfortable chairs and sofas and a giant wide-screen television showing a baseball game. A few white-haired people were sitting on the furniture, and some others were parked in wheelchairs, facing the TV, where a pitcher in a Blue Jays uniform was peering in to get the sign from his catcher, and a Red Sox runner was taking his lead from first base.

Sharon stopped and looked around for a minute. Then she said, "There he is."

I followed her over to a man sitting in a wheelchair in the back of the room. He had wispy white hair and a little white mustache and transparent skin. A cast covered his right arm from his fingertips up past his elbow. It hung from a sling around his neck. His lap and legs were covered with a brown blanket. He was wearing a green cardigan sweater over a white dress shirt that was buttoned to his throat.

As we approached him, I heard him say quite loudly, "Try a bunt, for Christ's sake. They *never* bunt. What's wrong with a bunt now and then?" Nobody else in the room was paying any attention to him. He seemed to be addressing the television set. "It's a perfect spot for a bunt. God damn prima donnas. Nobody makes them practice the fundamentals. They don't get those big contracts for laying down a nice bunt. Ha. Come on. Play the game right."

NINE

Sharon walked up beside Charles Nichols, put a hand on his shoulder, and said, "Charles?"

His head snapped around. He looked up at Sharon and frowned. "What do you want?"

"Charles, it's me. It's Sharon."

He blinked at her. Then he said, "Oh. Sure. What are you doing here?"

"I came to visit with you," she said. She bent down and kissed his cheek.

He neither resisted her kiss nor reciprocated it. He returned his attention to the television.

"This is my friend Brady Coyne," Sharon said. "Brady, Charles Nichols."

I stepped up and held out my hand.

Charles looked at it and shrugged. "I can't shake hands." He tapped the cast on his right arm with his left hand. "I can't cut my food or hold a newspaper or get dressed. I can't even unzip my fly and take a leak. Whaddya think about that?"

I patted his shoulder. "I'm sorry. When do you get the cast off?"

He frowned at me. "Who're you, the boyfriend? She dumped my son for you, is that it?"

"I didn't dump Ken," said Sharon. "It was . . . mutual. Anyway, that was ten years ago."

"Actually," Charles said, "I don't care. If you dumped him, I wouldn't blame you. So how come you picked today to visit me after all this time?"

"Is there someplace more private where we can talk?" Sharon asked.

"Why talk?" Charles asked. "Let's watch the ball game."

"We've got to talk," Sharon said, "whether you want to or not." She grabbed the handles of Charles's wheelchair, released the brakes, and pushed him out of the room. I followed along behind.

"You could've waited till the end of the inning, at least," he grumbled.

"It's nice," Sharon said, "you're still so interested in baseball."

"I'm really not. Never was." He turned his head and looked at me. "Baseball is boring and irrelevant. But it's what there is. As you can see, there isn't much else around here. Am I right?"

I shrugged. "I like baseball."

There was a balcony off the corridor on the other side of some glass doors. "How about out here?" Sharon asked.

"I don't care," Charles grumbled. "I want to get back to my ball game. If you'd been considerate, you would've come when there wasn't a ball game on the TV. When there isn't a game, I'm bored out of my skull."

I opened the doors, and Sharon wheeled Charles onto the balcony, where there was a round glass-topped table with a big umbrella sticking out of it and four aluminum chairs. It overlooked the trout stream, and we had it to ourselves.

"This is nice," Sharon said. "Doesn't the sun feel good?"

"I'm chilly," said Charles.

"Oh, no," she said. "It's quite warm out here, this nice sunshine, and sheltered from the wind."

"Yeah," he said, "well, I'm always chilly. It's my circulation. It's why I'm in this damn wheelchair. I can't feel my legs. They're numb, like hunks of wood. The numbness is moving up my body. They tell me when it gets to my vital organs, they'll stop working the way my legs have stopped.

Then I'll need more than a damn wheelchair. Of course, this thing in my head will probably blow up first." He looked up at me and winked, as if he and I were sharing some kind of secret.

I winked back at him.

Sharon sat in one of the chairs so that she was facing Charles. "I'm sorry I haven't visited you more often," she said.

He shrugged. "I don't expect you to. It's not like I wake up every morning and say, 'I wonder if today is the day Sharon will come for a visit?' Nobody visits me. Except Ellen. I don't know why she keeps coming to see me. She was here just a few days ago. She came when there wasn't a ball game on TV. She's a nice girl, Ellen is. But she's the only one. I don't care. I don't expect visitors." He narrowed his eyes at her. "So this isn't just your basic visiting-old-Charles-on-a-Sunday-afternoon. You're here for a reason. You said you wanted to talk with me. What is it?"

Sharon glanced at me, then looked at Charles. She reached out and gripped his left hand, the one not covered with a cast, in both of hers. "It's Ken," she said. "I'm sorry . . ." She shook her head. Tears welled up in her eyes.

"What?" asked Charles. "What about him?"

She cleared her throat. "He's . . . he died, Charles. I'm sorry."

He glared at her. "What? What did you say?"

"Ken died last night," she said.

Charles snatched his hand away from Sharon's grip. He put it over the lower half of his face and moved it up and down, as if he were trying to rub feeling into his cheeks. He was looking at her out of his pale, watery eyes. "He died, you said?"

She nodded. "Yes."

Charles swiveled his head and looked at me. "What's this got to do with you?"

"I'm Sharon's friend," I said.

"Okay." He returned his eyes to Sharon. "Last night, huh? So what happened? What did my son die of? He's not that old, for Christ's sake. I'm the one who's supposed to die, not him."

"He was murdered," said Sharon.

"Huh? Murdered?" Charles frowned. "Why?"

"They don't know. The police are working on it."

Charles looked at me again. "What're you, a cop? Is that it?"

"No," I said. "I'm just a friend."

"You fucking her?"

"Charles," said Sharon. "Please."

"Well?" he said to me.

"No," I said. "I'm not."

"Great-looking woman, isn't she?"

I smiled. "She is, yes."

"Maybe she was my son's wife," he said, "but I used to think, *Oh, I wouldn't mind a piece of that. No sir.*"

"Charles, come on," said Sharon. "Did you understand what I told you?"

"You said my son was murdered," he said. "Maybe my body parts have stopped functioning, but I haven't lost my mind yet, unlike most of the inmates in this place. I understand fine. I haven't seen Ken in . . . I can't remember the last time. Haven't even talked to him. After a while, a person becomes an abstraction, even if he's your son. Like he doesn't even exist. Weeks go by, Ken doesn't even pass through my mind. I know he's got his own life, but he's my only son and my heir, and you'd think . . ." He waved his left hand in the air.

We sat there looking out at the trout stream and the woods, and nobody spoke for a while.

After a few minutes, Charles said, "Murdered, you said?"

Sharon nodded. "Yes."

"They don't know who did it, or why, is that it?" I noticed that Charles's eyes were watery.

"That's right," said Sharon.

"Do they have a theory?"

Sharon cleared her throat. "One of their theories is that I did it."

Charles looked at her and smiled. "You, huh?"

She nodded. "I found his body."

"Why would you kill Ken?"

"I wouldn't," she said. "I didn't."

He wiped his left hand across his eyes. "It's a silly theory," he said.

"Yes, it is," she said.

"They haven't arrested you."

"Not yet."

"You got a lawyer, I hope."

Sharon glanced at me. "Yes. A good one."

Charles turned and looked at me. "You, huh?"

I nodded.

"You gonna get her off?"

"Sure," I said.

"Did she do it?" he asked me.

"No," I said. "She's innocent. Don't worry about her. She's going to be fine."

"I wasn't worried about her," he said. "I was just worried she might not come and visit me anymore. Look at her, will you? I

111

always thought Ken was a dodo, letting her go."

Sharon looked at me and rolled her eyes.

I smiled.

"Charles," she said, "it's possible that the police might come to talk to you. Isn't that right, Brady?"

"It's likely," I said. "Generally they try to talk with all of the victim's relatives and friends."

"I didn't want you to hear about Ken that way," Sharon said.

"I get it," he said. "Thank you."

"Look," she said, "if there's anything you need, anytime, please just call me. Will you promise to do that?"

"I won't need anything," he said. "Unless you can dig up a new body for me." He slapped the arm of his wheelchair with his functional hand. "Let's go. Take me back to my ball game, will you?"

The afternoon sun was low in the sky when I pulled into the lot behind Sharon's building.

"Why don't you come up, have a drink?" she asked.

"I don't think so," I said. "Thanks. I should get going."

"Got a busy evening ahead of you, do you?"

I turned and looked at her. She was smiling.

"No," I said. "I just don't think it's a good idea to mix pleasure with business."

"Having a drink with me would be pleasure?"

I nodded. "I think it could be, yes."

"I really didn't mean anything," she said. "Sometimes a drink is just a drink."

I shrugged.

"Are you involved with somebody, Brady?"

"I'm kind of between involvements," I said, "but I'm, um, working on it. How about you?"

She shook her head. "I wouldn't mind. It's just I haven't met anybody. It can be hard for a woman of my age. There was a man a few years ago. It didn't turn out well."

"What happened?"

She shrugged. "We had fun, and he was very good to me, very generous, but after a while I realized I didn't love him, that I never would love him, that I was just kind of indifferent toward him. There was no future in it. I wasn't interested in a relationship with no future. When I told him, he took it badly."

"Badly how?"

"He wouldn't take no for an answer. He kept sending me flowers, calling me at all hours of the day and night, and when I stopped answering the phone, he'd fill up my answering machine with his messages."

"He was stalking you," I said.

She nodded. "I guess that's what it was."

"Did you go to the police?"

She shook her head. "He didn't threaten me. I wasn't afraid. I was just annoyed. Well, it was worse than that. I was furious. The man was wrecking my life."

"You could've gotten a restraining order."

"Well," she said, "I didn't need to. Eventually he went away."

"You were lucky," I said. "Stalkers generally don't just go away."

Sharon smiled. "He was, um, encouraged to go away."

"Encouraged how?"

"Ellen was home from school — Wayne was a senior in high school, I think — and we were eating out, my kids and I, having a nice Italian dinner at Papa Razzi there by the Concord rotary, the three of us, Wayne and Ellen and I. We all got along with each other back then. So we were sitting there at our table at Papa Razzi and Gary appeared. I looked up, and there he was, leaning his elbow on the bar, and when he saw me, he smiled and lifted his glass to me. I just about hit the roof. My kids, naturally, wanted to know what was going on, so I told them. Well, Wayne excused himself, got up, and went over to Gary, and I don't know what was said, but after a few minutes, Gary turned around and walked out of there, and Wayne came back to the table and said I wouldn't have to worry about that guy anymore, and sure enough, it's been four or five years now, and I haven't seen Gary or heard a peep from him since then."

"Wayne must be a persuasive guy," I said.

"I asked him what he said," Sharon said, "but he wouldn't tell me." She reached over and squeezed my arm. "Sure you won't come up?"

I patted her hand. "Thanks. Maybe another time."

She nodded. "Okay. Another time." She hesitated. "Look, Brady. I can't tell you how much I appreciate your coming with me this afternoon. I don't know as I could've managed it without you."

"You would've done fine," I said. "I didn't do anything."

"You were there for me," she said. "I know it's way above and beyond the call of duty. Not many lawyers would do that on a

Sunday afternoon."

"Friends would," I said.

She leaned over, touched my cheek with her fingertips, and kissed the corner of my mouth. "Well, thanks, friend," she said.

Ten

In the middle of the morning on Monday I was in my office working on my third mug of coffee and plowing through a stack of paperwork that Julie, my long-suffering secretary, had dumped on me, as she did on a regular basis in her role as the boss of my law practice, when the console on my desk buzzed. "It's Detective Horowitz," Julie said when I picked up.

"Okay," I said. "Got it." I hit the blinking light and said, "Roger."

"Nobody named Clem, Clement, Clementine, whatever," he said without preamble, "registered at the damn veterinarian convention. You sure you got that name right?"

"Yes," I said, "it's a lovely day, and I'm doing very well, thank you for asking. How are *you?*"

"Don't push me, Coyne," he growled. "I'm trying to capture murderers here. You sure that name was Clem?"

"I'm quite sure that's what Ken called the guy," I said. "Clem."

"No idea, first name, last name, nickname, huh?"

"Sorry," I said.

"Well, we're striking out on it."

"I asked Sharon," I said. "It rang no bells with her."

"Try again," he said, and with that he disconnected.

After Horowitz hung up on me, I called Sharon's cell phone, and when her voice mail clicked in, I said, "It's Brady. Hope you're doing okay. I wanted to ask you to rack your brain again, see if that name Clem means anything to you. If you think of anything, let me know, please. The police are pretty interested in him, and we should both be happy to help them focus on suspects other than you."

I returned to my bottomless stack of papers, and an hour or so later there came a soft one-knuckle rap on my door.

"It's unlocked," I grumbled. "Just come in."

The door opened, and Julie stepped in.

"What?" I asked.

"You don't have to be crabby," she said.

"Paperwork makes me crabby," I said. "It's your own fault."

"You want to make any money," she said, "you've got to do paperwork. You've got a visitor."

"A visitor," I said.

"A young woman. She wants to see you. She doesn't have an appointment. I told her she had to make an appointment, that you were busy all day. She said she'd just wait, if that was okay, and maybe a minute would open up when you could see her. I don't think she intends to leave."

"Who is it?" I asked. "What's she want?"

"She says her name is Ellen Nichols. She wouldn't tell me what she wanted. She seemed to think you'd know."

"Oh, shit," I said.

"What?"

"I didn't tell you about our new client."

"We have a new client?"

I nodded.

Julie shook her head. "You did it again? You took on a new client without telling me?"

"Well," I said, "she's not exactly a new client. She's an old client with a new problem. We used to handle the legal work for the animal hospital she and her husband ran before they divorced. That was about ten years ago. Her name is Sharon Nichols?" I made it a question.

Julie frowned for a minute, then nodded. "Yes, I remember them."

"Well," I said, "Sharon's ex-husband, Kenneth Nichols, was murdered Saturday night, and that's their daughter out there. I'm sorry I didn't mention it before." I stood up. "I need to talk to her."

Julie followed me out into our reception area. Ellen Nichols was sitting on one of the sofas with her chin propped up on her fists and her elbows on her knees and a pair of big round glasses perched on the end of her nose. She was frowning at a laptop computer that was open on the coffee table. She was a younger, darker-haired version of her mother — the same flashing eyes and generous mouth and slender body.

I started over to her, and she looked up and said, "Mr. Coyne?"

"It's Brady," I said. "Do you want to come into my office?"

"I know you're busy . . ."

"It's okay," I said. "Come on in."

Ellen Nichols shut her laptop, stuck it into her backpack, hooked the backpack over one shoulder, and followed me into my office. She sat on the sofa in the conference area by the big window that looked out on Copley Square.

I took the upholstered chair across from her.

Julie had trailed along behind us. "Can I bring you some coffee? Tea? Water?"

"Nothing for me, thank you," Ellen said.

"I'm good," I said. "Thanks."

Julie left.

"Do you remember me?" Ellen asked.

I shrugged. "You were a lot younger when I did legal work for your parents."

"I was just a kid," she said. "My brother and I used to hang out with Billy and Joey."

"Back in the neighborhood," I said.

She nodded. "I guess I shouldn't have come barging in like this," she said. She used her forefinger to push her glasses up onto the bridge of her nose. "I've got classes later this afternoon, so I was in the neighborhood, and I wanted to see you. If it's not convenient . . ."

"No," I said, "it's all right. You're at BU?"

"That's right. I'm in a master's program. Elementary ed. Specialty in reading."

"I'm glad you stopped in. I wanted to talk with you anyway. I'm very sorry about what happened to your father."

"Thank you," she said. "I'm kind of numb about it. Actually, the reason I'm here is my mother. I'm really worried about her. I mean, is she really a suspect? Are they going to arrest her?"

"She's a suspect, yes," I said, "but the fact that it's been two days and the police haven't done anything makes me believe that they're not going to charge her, that they don't think they have enough evidence for an arrest."

"I'm worried about how she's doing, too."

"Her peace of mind, you mean?"

"Yes. Her . . . sanity." Ellen leaned forward and squeezed my forearm. "She's never been all that emotionally strong. She had a hard time of it when my dad moved out, and since then, she's had one bad relationship after the other. Not to mention all the heartache my brother's caused her."

"Wayne," I said. "Has anybody told Wayne what happened?"

"My mother said she couldn't reach him. I tried, too, but just got his voice mail. I left him a message, but he hasn't called me back."

"If you can give me his phone number," I said, "I'll see what I can do. I need to talk with him anyway."

"Sure." Ellen fished a BlackBerry out of her purse, poked some buttons on it, then asked, "Got a pencil?"

I went to my desk, picked up a yellow legal pad and a ballpoint pen, and said, "Shoot."

She recited a cell phone number and a street address with an apartment number in Websterville, New Hampshire.

I wrote them down. "He's going to Webster State, is that right?"

Ellen nodded. "Neither my mother nor I have heard from him for a long time. She worries about him."

"I can understand that," I said.

"I'm not worried," she said. "That's just how Wayne is. In his own world. I love my brother, but he's awfully inconsiderate."

"How did Wayne and your dad get along?" I asked.

"Last I knew, not so good," she said. "He blamed our dad for wrecking our family."

"So he's estranged from all three of you."

She frowned. "Our family's kind of a mess, Mr. Coyne. Even so, Wayne still deserves to know what happened."

"Did you and your father have a good relationship?" I asked.

"It was hard for all of us," she said. "I'm older than Wayne. I saw it differently. When my parents split, I was sad about it, but I didn't blame anybody. My dad and I kept in touch, and we got together now and then."

"In Baltimore?"

She nodded. "I went down and visited him

a couple of times. Sometimes he'd come to Boston on business, and we'd make it a point to get together, have dinner or something."

"What about this past weekend?" I asked. "He was at a conference up here. Were you going to get together with him?"

She shook her head. "I didn't even know about it. He didn't tell me. When my mother told me about it, it kind of hurt my feelings, that he'd tell her, make a plan to see her, but not me." She gave me a quick smile. "She said they were thinking about getting back together."

"How would you feel about that?"

"If it was true, you mean?"

"Why wouldn't it be true?"

Ellen rolled her eyes. "I always thought they hated each other. It's how I understood their divorce. So it didn't make any sense."

"People change," I said.

"I guess so," she said. "I mean, if it was true, if they both felt that way, well, it would've been awesome." She shook her head and blinked, and I saw that tears had welled up in her eyes. "Well, anyway," she said, "that's never going to happen now."

She took off her glasses and wiped her eyes on the back of her wrist. I handed her the box of tissues I keep handy for such occasions, and she took one and dabbed at her eyes with it. Then she blew her nose. She smiled at me. "Thank you. I'm okay. Sorry." She fitted her glasses back onto her face.

"I wanted to ask you," I said, "if you knew of anybody who had a problem with your dad."

"What do you mean?"

"Did he ever mention owing money to somebody," I said, "or someone owing him, or his being threatened, or having any kind of conflict or disagreement with somebody?"

"You mean, like who'd want to kill him?"

I nodded.

"I haven't a clue," Ellen said. "He had a whole life down in Baltimore that I didn't know anything about. I mean, like I said, I did visit him down there a few times over the years, but I never had any sense of what his life was like. I never met any of his friends or business acquaintances, and he never talked about things like that with me. I don't know if he had girlfriends, of if there was somebody special in his life, or anything along those lines."

"He was killed up here," I said, "not in Baltimore."

"Well," she said, "I just don't have any

idea. I'm sure it wasn't my mother. That's all I know."

"Do you know anybody named Clem?"

She frowned. "Clem?"

"Middle-aged man, friend of your father."

Ellen shrugged. "No. Sorry. Clem doesn't ring a bell."

"Did your father ever talk to you about business problems," I said, "or schemes he might've had for earning money, or investments he made?"

Ellen smiled. "My dad was a vet, Mr. Coyne. He liked animals. That's what he was good at. I don't think he was very good at business, or had much interest in it. He was just a nice, uncomplicated man."

"I expect the police will want to talk to you," I said.

She nodded. "Sure. Okay."

"They'll probably ask a lot of questions about your mother, and about your parents' relationship."

"My mom being a prime suspect."

"Right now she is, yes," I said. "So I'd like to know of anything at all that you might say to them that could incriminate her."

Ellen shook her head. "My mother couldn't hurt anybody, regardless of how justified she might be."

"Do you mean you think she'd be justified to, um, to murder your father?"

"No, I didn't mean that."

"Well —"

"I only meant," she said, "that my mother suffered a lot when they split. She was angry and hurt. In her mind, it was all his fault."

"In her mind."

"That's how she saw it. It's still how she sees it. My mother has never faced up to her own responsibility for what happened. Oh, if you ask her, she'll say it was nobody's fault — but deep down, she's always blamed him. That's all I meant."

"She's been angry with him."

"Oh, sure. Furious. Ever since it happened."

"And that's what you'll tell the police."

Ellen looked at me. "Oh. I see what you mean. Well, what should I do?"

"It's easy," I said. "Just tell the truth."

"Well, sure. Except my mother . . ."

"People who are divorced from each other do tend to be angry and blame each other. It's normal."

"Except," she said, "my father got murdered."

"He invited her to his hotel room," I said. "That doesn't sound like angry people to me."

She shrugged. "If it's true."

127

"You think your mother's been lying to us?"

"Oh, no," said Ellen. "That's not what I meant. I'm sure she felt that way. I mean, I think she believed it. All I meant was I wonder if my father felt the same way."

"Do you have any reason to doubt it?"

"Look, Mr. Coyne," she said. "I don't want to take sides here. I've never taken sides. I've always tried to show my parents that even if they didn't love each other, I loved them both, and that they could be good parents even if they weren't together. So please, don't ask me to speculate about either of them. It's hard to be objective about your parents, and particularly if one of them's just been murdered and the police suspect the other one of doing it. I only came here to be sure that my mother was being taken care of. She has a lot of faith in you. You will take care of her, won't you?"

"Yes," I said. "Of course."

"The legal stuff, I mean."

I nodded.

"Thank you." She stood up. "I won't take up any more of your time, then."

"Why don't you leave me your phone number, in case I need to talk to you again."

"Sure." She told me, and I wrote it down. "Will you keep me posted?"

"If your mother wants me to," I said.

"Oh, right. She's the client, not me. Sure. That's fine."

"If you think of anything that might have some bearing on this . . . this situation," I said, "please give me a call."

"Like who'd've wanted to murder my father?"

"Well, sure. Or just anybody you might remember your father mentioning, friend or foe, or any problem or worry or issue he might've alluded to. Anything at all, even if you think it might be irrelevant. Okay?"

"Sure. Okay."

I scratched my home number on the back of one of my business cards and handed it to her. "Call anytime, day or night."

She took the card, glanced at it, and stuck it into her purse. Then she held out her hand. "Thanks for seeing me."

I took her hand. "Thank you for dropping in. I'm glad we talked. We'll be in touch."

After Ellen left, the console on my desk buzzed. I picked up the phone, and Julie said, "You had a couple calls. Don't know if you want to take them."

"Who?"

"A reporter."

"Josh Neuman?" I asked. "The *Herald*?"

"That's the one," she said. "What's he want?"

"It's about the Nichols case. I've got nothing to say to him."

"He called twice," Julie said. "He seems quite persistent. He made it pretty clear that he intends to keep calling until he's satisfied. I suppose I can keep putting him off if you want, but . . ."

"You think I should talk to him, huh?"

"Get it out of the way," she said. "He could become very annoying."

"You're probably right," I said. "Okay. If — when — he calls again, I guess you better put him through."

Half an hour later my phone rang. "It's that reporter Josh Neuman again," Julie said. "Line two."

"Got it." I pressed the blinking button, heard the click, and said, "Mr. Neuman. How're you doing?"

"Not that good," he said. "We got a brutal murder in an upscale hotel full of veterinarians from all over the globe, should be a helluva story, and nobody's saying anything."

"You've got to talk to the police," I said. "That's how it works."

"Yeah, I never would've thought of that all by myself," he said. "Look, they held

130

their bullshit press conference. Said exactly nothing beyond the obvious. I want to talk to your client."

"You can't," I said. "No way."

"You, then," he said. "You'll do."

"Ha."

"Just answer a couple questions for me. Then I'll leave you alone. How'd that be?"

"Can't do it," I said. "You know that."

"You don't want this great opportunity to get your slant on it out there, massage public opinion, counteract the stories the police will produce, create sympathy for your pretty client?"

"No, thanks."

"Come on," he said. "Give me your side of it. I'll print it just the way you say it."

"No comment," I said.

He laughed. "Listen. Here's what I want to know. You can tell me in your own careful lawyer's way, or even better, Mrs. Nichols can tell me. I want to know why she was there on Saturday night, how it happened that the pretty ex-wife was the one who found her ex-husband's body in his hotel room. There's a story there. You know there is. Plus, I want to know about their kids, where they are, what they're doing, how they got along with the dead guy and with each other. Of course, I want to know who they think did it." He hesitated. "Unless one of them wants to confess to me."

"None of that's any of your business," I said. "That's private, personal stuff."

"It's gonna come out one way or the other," Josh Neuman said. "You know that. I either talk directly to them, get it straight from their mouths, or else I talk to neighbors and business acquaintances, cousins, uncles, fathers-in-law, and get fragments of the story and put it together as well as I can, and what I can't write straight, I can write innuendo, which I am very good at. This is a juicy story, Mr. Coyne. Sexy woman, secret rendezvous in ex-husband's hotel room, dead guy in a bathrobe, stabbed to death with a steak knife. Who's gonna be your prime suspect every time, huh?"

"You go making up irresponsible stories," I said, "and there will be a giant lawsuit, I promise you."

He laughed. "Can I quote you on that?"

"Good-bye, Mr. Neuman," I said, and I hung up.

A few minutes later there came a scratch on my office door.

"Come in," I said.

Julie poked her head in. "What's this I hear in your voice?"

"It's that damn reporter," I said.

"Looking for a story," she said. "Acting like a reporter. What do you expect?"

"I know," I said. "He almost made me lose my cool."

"The sign of a good reporter, I'd say." Julie sat in one of the client chairs by my desk, opened her stenography notebook on her knee, and said, "Now, you better bring me up to date on this new client of ours."

ELEVEN

I'd been home from the office for about an hour. I'd hung up my necktie and lawyer pinstripe and pulled on my jeans and a T-shirt, and I'd fetched myself a bottle of Samuel Adams lager, and now I was sitting out in my backyard sipping my Sam and watching the finches and nuthatches and chickadees peck sunflower seeds at my feeders.

Then my cell phone, which I'd left on the picnic table, began buzzing and jumping around.

I picked it up and looked at the screen. It was Horowitz. I flipped open the phone and said, "Roger. Hey."

"I'm parked in front of your house," he said. "Where are you?"

"I'm here. Out back. You want a beer?"

"That's exactly what I want. I just went off duty. Let me in."

"Okay." I snapped the phone shut, put it

back on the table, and went through the house to the front door. When I opened it, Horowitz was standing on the stoop. He was wearing his rumpled brown suit, and his red necktie was pulled loose at his throat. His Columbo outfit.

I held the door for him, and he pushed past me into the house.

We went out to the kitchen, where I grabbed a beer for Horowitz and a fresh one for me, and then on out into the back-yard.

We each sat in an Adirondack chair.

Henry came over and sniffed Horowitz's cuffs. When Horowitz ignored him, he sauntered over to where I was sitting and sprawled on the bricks beside my chair.

I reached down and scratched the scruff of his neck, which was all he wanted.

Horowitz tilted up his beer, took a long swig, and then put his bottle on the arm of his chair. "Ahh," he said. "That's good. And this" — he waved his hand around my little walled-in patio garden — "this is nice. Flowers, birds, brick walls. Privacy. It's so quiet you'd hardly know you were in the middle of the damn city. The air even smells clean up here."

"Yep." I nodded. "I like it."

"Must get a little lonely, though, huh?"

135

"I don't mind," I said.

"Looks like you've been working on your flower gardens," he said.

"Just cleaning out last fall's leaves."

"Evie used to take care of the gardens, didn't she?"

"She did," I said.

"So now what're you gonna do?"

I shook my head. "You enjoy this, don't you?"

He turned and looked at me. "What?"

"Reminding me that Evie's gone. Rubbing it in."

"Hey," he said. "You're the one who always screws up your relationships, not me. I feel sorry for you, that's all."

"Just what I need," I said. "Your pity. I bet that's not why you're here."

"Naw. That just occurred to me." He took another swig of beer. "Benetti would kill me if she knew I was here."

"You didn't tell your partner you were coming?"

He shook his head. "Consorting with the enemy, she'd call it."

"I'm not your enemy."

"In this screwy adversarial system of ours, I guess you are." He flicked that consideration away with a backhanded wave. "Fuck it. Benetti thinks your client there is good for the Nichols thing. She thinks her story about going to his hotel room to have sex with him is bullshit." He arched his eyebrows at me.

"What do you think, Roger?" I asked.

He shook his head. "I got some doubts about it. Anybody would. Plus, we haven't come up with any better suspects. So Mrs. Nichols there, she's pretty much our default suspect."

"Default," I said.

"We can't eliminate her," he said. "Means, motive, opportunity. She's got 'em all."

"You're pretty shaky on all three," I said. "Last I heard, you had no murder weapon. So much for means. Ken and Sharon Nichols had been talking about resuming their relationship, which hardly amounts to a motive for murder. Opportunity I might stipulate. She was there, though the times aren't right."

"No sense in arguing about those things now," he said. "I wanted to ask you about when you were with our victim the night before."

"I told you everything," I said. "About the bearded guy he called Clem who pointed his finger at him. The fact that Ken seemed kind of nervous. That his phone rang several times. I don't know what else you want."

"He didn't mention what he was nervous about?"

"No. He kind of hinted he was having some problems, but no specifics."

"Money? Love? Health?"

I shook my head. "No idea. You get a line on the guy with the beard?"

"Nope."

"What about the kid in the hoodie?"

"Not yet," he said. "Not that I need to share with you." He blinked at me. "Our victim had a cell phone with him, you said."

"Yes. You could probably get some useful numbers off of it."

"We can get his phone records," Horowitz said, "but it takes a while. Big pain in the ass. Privacy, all that shit. Helluva lot easier if we had his phone. Which we don't."

"You didn't find his phone in his room?" I asked.

"Nope." He took a swig of beer. "Funny, don't you think?"

"The bad guy took the phone and left that satchel of ketamine there?"

"No phone," Horowitz said, "no murder weapon. No laptop, no briefcase, no personal papers, no BlackBerry. Nothing like that — but, yeah, a gym bag full of illegal drugs."

"The killer must've taken all that stuff," I

said. "I know Ken had a phone, at least. Makes you wonder if the drugs had anything to do with the murder."

He shrugged and lifted his beer bottle and took a long pull. His throat muscles clenched and flexed like a biceps. When he put the bottle down, it was empty. He wiped his mouth with his sleeve and said, "Ahh."

"You want another one?" I asked.

He shook his head. "State cops in Maryland have had their eye on him."

"What for? Ketamine?"

He nodded. "Other stuff, too, that a vet would have access to." He squeezed the bridge of his nose.

"He said nothing to me about it," I said.

Horowitz looked at me for a minute. "There was one little piece of evidence at the crime scene that you might find interesting."

"You going to share it with me?"

"Benetti wouldn't like it, but, hey. Disclosure, right? Gotta disclose sooner or later. Anyway, I wondered if you might have a take on it."

"What is it?" I asked.

"A hotel matchbook," he said. "One of the techs found it, photographed it, tagged it, and bagged it. It was lying on the floor just outside of the door to the murder room.

It had indentations on it that exactly matched the shape of the latch on the door."

"As if it had been wedged in there so the door wouldn't lock," I said. "So somebody could get in from the outside without a key."

He nodded. "When your client pushed on the door, it opened and the matchbook fell out."

"She was telling the truth about that," I said.

"As far as it goes, yeah, looks that way," Horowitz said. "Maybe, but that doesn't exactly exonerate her. Her lover there, our vic, he could've jammed the latch with that matchbook so he could wait for her in his bathtub, or in his bed or something, and she could just waltz right in there with her steak knife."

"You really think that's what happened?" I asked.

"Benetti does," he said. "Me, I'm trying to think about some other scenarios. The null hypothesis. Suppose the lady did *not* stab our vic with a steak knife in that hotel room. Suppose her story *is* the truth. How else could it have gone down?"

"Who put the matchbook in the latch, for example," I said, "if you assume it wasn't Ken?"

Horowitz looked at me and nodded. "The

killer, for example."

"Could be, huh?" I asked.

"Why would the killer do that?"

"Because he planned to come back," I said. "Or he was leaving the room open for somebody else."

"Somebody who was gonna pick up that bag of Special K, for example."

"Sure," I said, "or if he somehow knew that Sharon was expected, he could've left the door that way so she'd walk in and become a suspect."

Horowitz grinned. "Which she did."

"That guy in the hoodie," I said. "He was heading for Ken's room. Looking to score that ketamine, maybe. The killer left the door unlatched for him. When he saw Sharon and me, he ran."

Horowitz shrugged. "Could be. Makes as much sense as your client doing it. Doesn't mean she didn't. Benetti might be right. Hell, for all I know you might be sitting there knowing how stupid this sounds, knowing what she did." He cocked his head and looked at me.

I smiled. "What do you want me to say?"

He shook his head. "Nothing."

"You know I can't —"

"Christ, Coyne. What do you think? I just wanted to relax, drink a beer, enjoy your little garden after a hard day at work, your nice little oasis of peace and calm here in the middle of the big bad city, have a little low-key conversation, share an interesting tidbit of information with you, that's all."

"Sounds good to me," I said.

"No more shop talk," he said. "Okay?"

"Sure," I said. "Okay."

"You won't tell Marcia I was here, right?"

I shrugged.

"Come on, Coyne. She'd kill me."

"Looks like you owe me one," I said.

"I told you about the damn matchbook," he said. "What do you want?"

I nodded. "You're right. Call it even. I promise I won't tell Marcia that you were here."

He grinned. "So," he said, "how about them Red Sox, huh?"

Horowitz stayed around for one more beer, and we talked baseball, with a little city politics and stock market thrown in. The subject of Ken Nichols's murder did not come up again.

After he left, Henry and I had dinner — a bowl of Alpo for him, a ham-and-cheese sandwich for me.

After dinner we went into my downstairs home office, where I called Billy's cell phone. It rang just once before he said, "Hey, Pop."

"Hey yourself," I said. "I'm calling to make a date."

"You name it," he said.

We decided that Billy and Gwen would come to my place for a cookout the next evening. He and Gwen would bring rib eyes and potatoes and salad fixin's. I'd provide beer for us guys and a good Shiraz for Gwen. If our mild late-April weather persisted, we'd cook on the gas grill on my back deck and eat outside at the picnic table, and Billy and Gwen would tell me whatever it was that they came east to tell me.

When I hung up with my son, I realized I was smiling. I liked having him nearby, for a change. I looked forward to hanging out with him.

Julie had insisted I bring home the remainder of the paperwork that I hadn't finished during the day, and I figured I better get on top of it, because she'd have more for me tomorrow.

I was making good headway on it when my phone rang. I glanced at my watch. It was a few minutes after nine o'clock.

It was Sharon Nichols. "I hope I'm not bothering you," she said.

"Au contraire," I said. "You're giving me a

reprieve from a pile of boring deskwork. How are you doing?"

"I'm okay, I guess," she said. "I don't know how I'm supposed to be. How is one supposed to feel when her ex-husband gets murdered?"

"I assume that's a rhetorical question."

"Sure," she said, "but if you've got an answer, I'd love to hear it."

"I guess you should just feel whatever you feel," I said.

"Well, that's what I've been doing. And I'm okay. I went to work today."

"Where do you work?"

"I manage a leather shop in Concord center."

"A leather shop."

She laughed quickly. "It's not how it sounds. Nothing kinky. Women's apparel. Jackets, belts, vests, skirts, sandals. Lots of boots. Hand-tooled stuff."

"Sounds classy," I said.

"It's nice," she said, "and I like it. Different from being a vet's assistant. I miss the animals, but I like the people. So, yes, I worked all day, and it was fine, and I guess I'm fine, and I'll be even finer if you can tell me they're not going to arrest me."

"I don't know that for sure," I said, "but every day that goes by, the odds get better.

You should just try not to think about it."

"Easier said than done." She was silent for a moment. Then she said, "You met Ellen today, I understand?"

"She dropped by my office. We had a good chat. She seems like a mature young woman."

"Can I ask you what she wanted to talk about?"

"She'll probably tell you if you ask."

"Oh," she said. "I get it. It's a lawyer confidentiality thing."

"Not really," I said. "It's just a human being confidentiality thing. Ellen's not my client, so I don't have a professional obligation to her. I wouldn't tell her things you said to me, either, whether or not you were my client."

"Okay," she said after a minute. "That's okay. That's good. I just . . ." She blew out a breath.

"What?" I asked.

"It's nothing," she said. "I just wondered if Ellen was blaming me. For what happened to Ken, I mean. I've always felt she blamed me for the divorce. She was always Daddy's little girl."

"Talk to her," I said. "If you want, I can set you up with a good counselor. That might not be a bad idea in any case. I know a homicide counselor. She specializes in helping the relatives and friends of people who are murdered. Her name is Tally Whyte. She works out of the medical examiner's office here in the city. If you and Ellen saw her together, you might . . ."

"Yes, hmm, maybe," she said. "Interesting. I'll think about it." She hesitated. "The other thing is, I haven't been able to get hold of Wayne. I don't quite know what to do."

"You've tried calling him?"

"A dozen times," she said. "He doesn't answer."

"His phone's turned on?"

"It rings five or six times, and then this recorded voice answers and invites me to leave a message. Which I have done."

"Is it Wayne's voice?"

"The recording, you mean? No. It's the phone company. A woman's voice. She just says, 'The person you are trying to reach is not available at this time. At the tone, please leave a message.' Or something like that."

"Is this unusual?"

"What do you mean?"

"Not being able to get hold of Wayne?"

"Truthfully," she said, "I don't try to get in touch with him very often anymore. He never answers his phone, never returns a call when you leave a message. Wayne's kind of off on his own. He has been for a while. We've been shaky ever since the divorce. Lately, the past few years, we've just drifted apart." She hesitated. "I haven't talked to him for a long time."

"Ellen gave me his number," I said. "I'll try."

"That would be great," Sharon said, "though I don't know what you can do that I can't do. He'll either answer or he won't."

"Maybe he's screening his calls."

"Because he doesn't want to talk to his mother?" she asked. "I suppose that's possible. Well, I hope you can catch up with him. He needs to know what happened."

"I'll see what I can do."

"Thanks, Brady. For everything. You put my mind at ease."

"Shall I make an appointment with Tally Whyte for you?" I asked.

"Let me think about it," she said.

After I hung up with Sharon, I tried Wayne's cell phone number. Just as Sharon had reported, a recorded voice answered after about six rings, informing me that the person I was calling was not available and inviting me to leave a message. I declined that invitation.

I would persist.

■ ■ ■ ■

I finished my paperwork a little after eleven. Henry and I went out back so he could pee and I could look at the stars. Alex loved the night sky. When she and her brother, Gus, were kids, they'd identified their own private set of constellations up there — Elvis and Snoopy and Marilyn Monroe. There were several others. When I was with Alex right after Gus was killed, she tried to teach them to me, and when she pointed them out, I could see them — Elvis's guitar, Snoopy's ears, Marilyn's bosom.

I could see nothing but a sky full of random, disconnected stars. She liked to say that it was one of the big differences between us — she saw order where I saw chaos. She said that I needed her to bring some coherence into my life, and I thought maybe she was right, although I doubted she'd ever convince me that life was orderly.

Standing out on my back deck looking at the starry sky made me feel closer to Alex. I knew that she always stepped out back behind her house up there in Garrison, Maine, before bedtime to check out her constellations. She said it was almost like being kids with Gus again. I knew that she missed him all the time. She said that it helped, knowing I was looking at the same sky she was, even if I was in Boston and she was in Maine, and even if I could see only randomness.

An hour later I was lying in my bed. Henry was curled up on the rug beside me. I picked up the telephone from my bedside table, rested it on my chest, and dialed Alex's number in Maine.

It rang four or five times before she picked up. "Hello?" she said. She sounded a little breathless.

"You're wide-awake, aren't you," I said.

"I was in the bathroom, brushing my teeth. I dashed for the phone. Wanted to grab it before you hung up on me. Wait a minute."

I heard what I guessed was the rustle of sheets and blankets, and then Alex said, "There. I'm all tucked in. Are you?"

"Yes. All tucked in."

"I miss you."

"Me, too. I wouldn't have hung up."

"Umm," she said. "I know. Why don't I come down to you this weekend."

"You know how much I like to get away from the city," I said, "and Henry loves your woods. But, yes, I think it would be better if you came here."

"Something's going on, isn't it?"

"I've got a new case that might require some attention," I said. "Plus, Billy's in town with his friend Gwen."

"His girlfriend?"

"He insists on calling her his friend. Says she's not his girlfriend. Anyway, you and Billy haven't seen each other in years."

"Not since our, um, first relationship," Alex said. "He was a kid back then. He must be a man now."

"He is."

"I like this one," she said softly.

"This what?"

"This relationship. Our second one. Maybe we'll get it right this time."

"I hope so," I said. "I bet we will."

"Do you really hope so?"

"Yes," I said.

"Even if you still miss Evie."

"I am still aware of Evie's absence," I said. "Which isn't quite the same thing."

"You shared a house with her for all those years."

"Those years after you," I said. "After you dumped me."

Alex chuckled quietly. "I'm not going to rise to that bait again."

"I shared a life with Evie," I said. "Not just a house. But I'm not doing that anymore. Sometimes, like when I see the daffodils blooming out back, the bulbs she planted, I'm reminded of her, and sometimes that makes me a little sad. Then I look up at the night sky and try to find Snoopy and Elvis, and even when I can't see them, I'm reminded of you. I know you can show them to me, and that makes me happy."

"That's nice," she said.

"Shall I expect you at suppertime on Friday?"

"I'll bring supper," she said. "Your job is to be sure there's plenty of beer in the fridge."

"Beer. You got it."

She was quiet for a minute. Then I heard her yawn. "I'm pretty sleepy. Gonna shut my eyes now. G'night, honey. Sleep tight, 'kay?"

"You, too, babe."

"I didn't dump you."

"It was my fault," I said.

"Mmm-hmmm," she mumbled. "My own sweetie." Then she disconnected.

I hung up the phone and put it back on the table beside my bed. Henry was snuffling in his sleep. I lay there for a few minutes, looking up into the darkness, and I felt happy. Then I closed my eyes and went to sleep.

TWELVE

I tried calling Wayne Nichols about half a dozen times on Tuesday. I called from my landline at home while I was eating breakfast. I called from my cell phone as I walked to the office. The first time I tried him from my office phone, I accepted the recorded message's invitation. "Wayne," I said, "my name is Brady Coyne. I'm an old friend of both of your parents. They used to take care of my pets when I lived in Wellesley. Maybe you remember my boys, Billy and Joey. They're about your age. Anyway, I have some news for you about your mother and father. It's very important. Please give me a call, the sooner the better." I left him my home, cell, and office numbers.

When he didn't call me back after an hour or so, I tried him again, and as the day passed I called his number several more times from my office, and then again from my cell phone as I walked home. Each time, the same recorded greeting answered after five or six rings and invited me to leave a message, which I didn't. If he wasn't going to answer my first message, I saw no point in repeating myself.

I didn't know how to interpret the fact that Wayne did not respond to his mother's or his sister's messages and did not answer mine. His phone was charged up and turned on, which seemed to mean that he was using it. I assumed that he heard it when it rang and had been collecting his messages.

I decided that on Wednesday I'd drive up to Websterville, New Hampshire, and try to track down Wayne Nichols. He needed to know that his father had been murdered.

On my way home from the office that afternoon, I stopped at the spirits store on Newbury Street, where I bought two six-packs of Long Trail Double Bag Ale, a tasty microbrew from Vermont, and a bottle of a Napa Valley Shiraz recommended by the clerk. Then at DeLuca's on Charles Street I picked up a wedge of brie, a hunk of extra-sharp cheddar, and two boxes of crackers.

By six o'clock, when Billy and Gwen, each bearing a big paper grocery bag, banged on my front door, I had the ale on ice and the wine decanted and the cheese and crackers on plates on my kitchen table.

Billy was wearing his usual outfit — jeans, flannel shirt, and sandals. His long dark-blond hair was pulled back into a ponytail and tied with a length of rawhide. Gwen wore snug-fitting jeans and a scoop-neck peasant blouse. Her hair was short and straight and black. She wore it combed back, with long dangly silver earrings. With her big dark eyes and olive skin, she looked like a gypsy.

They both gave me a one-armed hug, set their bags on the floor, and scootched down to rub Henry's belly. He'd rolled onto his back to make it easy for them. Then I led them through the house to the kitchen, where they stowed their provisions in the refrigerator.

Billy and I grabbed a bottle of ale, and Gwen poured herself a glass of wine, and we took the crackers and cheese and our drinks out back and sat in the Adirondack chairs.

I held up my bottle. "Cheers," I said. "Welcome to Beacon Hill."

Billy clicked his bottle on mine. Gwen held up her wineglass.

"This is nice," I said. "I like having you guys around."

"Won't be for long," Billy said. "We've got

to head out in a few days. We've got jobs to get back to."

"When're you leaving?"

"Sunday," he said. "I've got to help get the boats and stuff ready to go for the fishing season, and I've got a float trip scheduled for next Friday."

"Alex will be down from Maine this weekend," I said. "She's my, um, my new girlfriend. You met her several years ago when she was my old girlfriend. She was hoping she'd get to see you."

"Sure," said Billy. "I remember Alex. We'll make it happen."

I turned to Gwen. "What about you? What are you going back to?"

"My publishing house in Berkeley," she said. "I'm second in command in the subrights department. This week has been my vacation. It's my first time ever in New England."

"So what do you think?"

She smiled. "It's beautiful. So much variety. So different from what I'm used to. I mean, weather, climate, topography, flora, fauna, history. Everything. And it's all so . . . old. Everywhere you go, there's all this history. I'd never been east of the Mississippi in my life before now. Billy took me to Plum Island yesterday, and the other day we climbed Mount Monadnock. He showed me around Boston and Lexington and Concord, and he's gonna take me down to Cape Cod tomorrow." She turned to him and punched his arm. "Am I right, big fella?"

"Right, kiddo," Billy said. He gave her arm a gentle punch back, and it struck me again, as it had the other night at the North End restaurant, that these two treated each other more like buddies than lovers.

We were on our second bottles when Billy said, "The other night at the restaurant? When you had to leave? Was that Dr. Nichols, the vet?"

"It was his wife who called me," I said.

"You said he was murdered?"

I nodded.

"Murdered," said Gwen.

"Yes," I said. "That's right."

"Wow," she whispered.

"Dr. Nichols was the one who put down Bucky," Billy said. "I'll always remember that."

"You don't forget something like that," I said.

He looked up at the sky. "They had a kid about my age." He frowned. "Can't think of his name."

"Wayne," I said.

"Right," he said. "Wayne. He was a strange dude."

"How so?"

"Well, for starters, kids used to say that he tortured animals . . . and his old man a vet?"

"That's beyond strange," Gwen said. "That's totally sick."

Billy looked at her and nodded. "If it was true." He shrugged. "I wouldn't doubt it. I used to play with him sometimes. I guess we were ten or eleven, not much older than that. I remember this one time we were fooling around near some pond and Wayne caught a frog. He set it on top of a rock and stuck a firecracker in its mouth, and the dumb frog just sat there with this firecracker hanging out of the corner of its mouth like a cigar or something, and Wayne lit it, and . . ." Billy shook his head. "It was pretty horrible."

"Oh, gross," Gwen said. "That's evil."

"I always felt guilty," he said, "that I didn't take that firecracker out of the frog's mouth, or tell Wayne not to do it. Or something. I didn't do anything. I knew what he was gonna do, and I just watched."

Gwen reached over and held Billy's hand. "You were just a kid," she said.

"I was old enough to know better." He shrugged. "I wonder what ever became of

Wayne Nichols. They moved out of town when we were still kids."

I didn't say anything more about Wayne. His mother was my client, and that, by extension, gave me a certain responsibility to him, too.

So we drank wine and ale and nibbled cheese and crackers, and our conversation slid over to fishing and baseball and books, and after a while Billy and Gwen went inside to put our dinner together.

Henry and I, following their orders, stayed out back. A bright day of April sunshine had warmed the brick patio, and my little walled-in garden area had captured and retained the late-spring warmth. Now, even as the sun descended below the city horizon, it remained comfortable outdoors.

Billy grilled inch-thick rib eyes and roasted foil-wrapped potatoes and onions on the gas grill on my back deck. Gwen tossed a big green salad and sliced a loaf of fresh-baked rosemary bread.

By the time our dinner was ready to be eaten, darkness had seeped into my back-yard, and the chill of the evening had begun to displace the warmth of the day, so we decided to eat in the kitchen.

Henry stationed himself under the table, a smart strategic move, as each of us accidentally dropped a few fatty scraps of medium-rare rib eye and crusts of rosemary bread onto the floor.

It wasn't until we'd moved into the living room with our mugs of after-dinner coffee that Billy looked at me and said, "Well, we told you we had something we wanted to share with you." He glanced at Gwen, who gave him a quick smile. "I don't know if you've figured it out. Mom did, sort of."

I shrugged. "I've thought about it, got a hypothesis or two, but I don't want to play guessing games. Unless you want me to."

He grinned and shook his head. "Nope. Here it is. You're gonna be a grandfather."

This was more or less what I'd expected. "Well," I said, "congratulations. Both of you. Or all three of us, I guess. When . . . ?"

"October," said Gwen. "October fourth, says the doctor."

"I'm not old enough to be a grandfather," I said.

"Meaning," said Billy, "that I'm not old enough to be a father, huh?" He looked hard at me. No sign of a smile.

"You'll always be my little boy," I said, "but I didn't say that. Really, I was just kidding. I'm happy for you. For me, too. A lot of my friends are grandfathers. They tell me having grandkids is great fun." I looked from Billy to Gwen, then back at Billy. "So when are you two . . . ?"

He shook his head. "We're not getting married."

"We don't love each other," said Gwen. "Not husband-and-wife love, I mean." She glanced at Billy. "We kinda slipped last winter when I was out skiing with him. But that's not what we're about."

"We're good friends," said Billy. "Best buddies. We don't want to wreck a nice friendship. That's what marriage does."

I shrugged. "Not necessarily."

He shook his head. "Look at you and Mom. Hell, look at all the divorces you handle. You make a living off of marriages that don't work. Anyway, we've made up our minds, so don't try talking us out of it."

"Don't worry about that," I said. "It's your problem. Yours and Gwen's." I turned and gave her a smile.

"Actually," said Billy, "we don't have a problem."

"Problem was a bad choice of words," I said.

"We've both got lives," Gwen said. "Billy's is in Idaho. Mine's in California. My parents are nearby. They'll help with the baby."

I arched my eyebrows at Billy. He grinned and nodded. "We got it all worked out."

"I'm going to raise the baby," Gwen said. "Billy is the father. He can visit anytime he wants. He can teach him how to fly-fish and ski and shoot shotguns. You, too, Mr. Coyne. I want our baby to know his grandparents. You and Gloria can visit him. Maybe when he's older, he can come east and spend time with you."

"Him?" I asked.

She smiled. "It's a boy."

"You should call me Brady," I said.

"Okay. Sure."

"So that's it," said Billy. "We wanted you and Mom to know what was going on."

"So you're going to keep living in Idaho," I said, "teaching skiing and guiding fly-fishermen?"

"It's what I do," he said. "It's who I am."

"Even though you're going to be a father."

He nodded. "Gwen's with me on that."

"You're going to, um, support the child?"

He shrugged. "I don't make a shitload of money, you know — but, sure, as much as I can."

"My job pays well," Gwen said. "Plus, my parents have tons of money. That's not an issue."

"Not now it's not," I said.

Billy looked at me. "What're you saying?"

I shrugged. "Just that things change.

Gwen could lose her job, or she could get sick. You might decide you wanted to see more of your son. Or Gwen might get married, and her husband might want to adopt the child. Or —"

"Wait a minute," Billy said. "We got this all figured out, you know? I mean, we've talked a lot about it, and we know what we want to do."

"You want me to mind my own business, you're saying."

"Well, yeah."

I shrugged. "I'm just thinking of the future. You never know what's going to happen. You should plan for the unexpected."

"Why do you feel like you always have to complicate everything?" Billy asked.

I spread out my hands. "I'm sorry. I'm not trying to complicate anything. It's just how I think, I guess."

"Like a lawyer," he said.

I smiled. "You say *'lawyer'* as if it's a dirty word."

He shrugged.

"Well," I said, "in fact, it wouldn't do you any harm to talk to a lawyer. Both of you. A lawyer could help you think it through, anticipate issues that might come up in the future. A simple written agreement now could save you both a lot of problems and heartaches later."

"Christ," said Billy. "Gwen and I trust each other. We both want the same thing. We've got it all worked out. We don't need some fucking lawyer to come along and screw it up."

"Fucking lawyer," I said.

He narrowed his eyes at me. "That's what I said."

I looked at Gwen. "What will you do if five years from now Billy decides he wants fifty-fifty custody of your child?"

She shrugged. "He won't. He says he won't, and I believe him."

"What if you get married?"

"Whoever I marry will know about our child," she said. "If he doesn't accept the situation, I won't marry him."

"What if you run out of money, or the baby gets sick, or you do?"

"Look, Mr. Coyne," she said. "Brady, I mean. Billy and I have thought a lot about this, and we're cool with it. It's going to be okay. Really. You shouldn't worry about it."

"I was only —"

"Fuck this." Billy stood up. "Come on, babe." He held down both hands to Gwen. "Let's get the hell out of here. I thought he'd be happy to know about our baby. I didn't think he was going to play lawyer with us."

Gwen allowed Billy to pull her to her feet. She looked at me. "Everything's going to be all right, Mr. Coyne," she said. "Please don't worry."

"He wasn't worrying," Billy said to her. "He was just trying to ruin everything. He's always picking at things, making problems where there aren't any. You were wondering why a nice couple like him and my mom got divorced? That's why, right there. Come on. Let's go."

Gwen allowed Billy to tug her to the front door. He yanked it open, and as they walked out, she looked at me over her shoulder and mouthed the words, "I'm sorry."

I got up and hurried over to them. "Wait a minute," I said. "Don't —"

"We're outta here," Billy said. He slammed the door behind him, and they were gone.

I stood there for a minute. Then I went back to the sofa and sat down. I picked up my coffee mug and took a sip. It was cold.

"Did you see that?" I asked Henry. "Did you see how I screwed that up?"

Henry, who'd followed Billy and Gwen to the door and was sitting there as if he expected them to come right back, got up and came over and put his chin on my leg.

I patted his head. "If I talked to you like a lawyer, butted into your personal business, questioned your judgment, would you still love me?"

Henry rolled his eyes up at me, gave his stubby little tail a couple of wags, and licked my hand.

"So why can't people be more like dogs?" I asked.

Henry shrugged.

After a few minutes, I got up, went to the kitchen, cleared off the table, and loaded up the dishwasher. Then I wandered through the house straightening out the furniture and in general banging around, cursing myself for my stupidity.

Not that I didn't think I was right. If Billy and Gwen did what they planned to do with no written agreement, they'd be awfully lucky not to run into problems at some point.

Billy was right about one thing. It's one of the jobs of lawyers to anticipate problems and to plan for them. That's why I almost always suggest prenuptial agreements. It's one of the reasons people don't like lawyers. We raise subjects that they don't want to think about.

Billy's reaction to my suggestions was predictable. Not many couples like to talk about potential or hypothetical problems. They believe in love forever and ever — in Billy's and Gwen's case, friendship forever — and they can't imagine anything ever changing.

When it does, as it does more often than not, it's usually too late.

Henry and I caught the last three innings of the Red Sox game, and then I let him out back. While I was standing there on the deck looking up at the stars, searching idly for Alex's constellations, the phone in the kitchen rang.

Billy, was my first thought. Calling to apologize.

Nope. Not likely. Billy didn't cool off that quickly. Who else? Alex? It was a little early for her to call. Maybe it was Wayne Nichols, returning my call after all.

I hurried inside, picked up the phone, and said, "Brady Coyne."

I heard a soft chuckle on the other end. "Gloria Coyne," she said.

Gloria. My ex-wife. Billy's mother. I couldn't remember the last time she'd called me.

"Hey," I said. "Hi."

"You're all out of breath," she said.

I sat on a kitchen chair. "I was out back pondering my sins."

166

"Like pissing off your number-one son?"

"He went running to Mommy?"

"He and Gwen are staying here," Gloria said. "William came banging in like a thunderstorm a few minutes ago. I asked him what was the matter, and he said you went all lawyer on him."

"I offered advice to those two kids," I said. "It was stupid of me."

"Yes, no doubt," she said. "I imagine you had good advice, but you know how he can be."

"I guess I'd forgotten," I said. "I just talked to them as if they were sensible adults. I did have good advice. They're headed for trouble."

"Well," Gloria said, "there's your mistake right there. I think they both realize deep down that they're flying without a parachute. They're scared and insecure and full of doubts and questions. The last thing they need is to be reminded of it. Especially by a parent."

"You trying to make me feel better?"

"Why would I ever want to do that?" She chuckled. "You screwed up, no doubt about it, and if you were more tuned in to people's feelings, you wouldn't have done what you did. Who knows? Maybe William would've come to you for advice."

"That'd be a first."

Gloria laughed softly.

"Anyway," I said, "that's certainly not going to happen now."

"Probably not," she said, "but maybe they'll go to somebody else. Unless I'm mistaken, you put some doubts into their heads. If you hadn't, William wouldn't be so upset now."

"Small consolation," I said. "I'd much rather we'd just had a pleasant evening and talked about nothing significant whatsoever. I should've just said, 'That's grand. You're having a baby. Congratulations. I hope the three of you have a swell life.' But no. Not bigmouth Coyne. Now my son's not talking to me."

"He'll get over it," Gloria said. "I think Gwen's a pretty down-to-earth girl. She'll straighten him out."

"Well, thanks for the optimism."

"I know how you are. You've been beating yourself up, right?"

"Kinda. I deserve it."

"You were just being you," she said, "and you really aren't such a terrible person."

"Not that bad, huh?"

"William probably wouldn't agree with me right now," Gloria said, "but he'll come around. You've just got to be patient."

"Okay."

"Everything else all right?"

"Sure," I said. "Everything's good."

"Evie's gone, though, huh?"

"Long gone and hard to find," I said. "That's an old story."

"Well, Brady," Gloria said, "be happy, okay?"

"Sure," I said. "You, too."

"Oh," she said, "don't worry about me. I've been working on it for a long time."

THIRTEEN

I called my office phone on Wednesday morning while I was sipping the day's first mug of coffee out in the backyard. It was early enough that Julie wouldn't be there to answer, which was the whole point. That way, I could leave her a message without having to listen to her disapproval. "I know I have no appointments today," I said. "Don't make any. I'm taking the day to attend to some business connected to the Nichols case. I'll try to check in sometime in the afternoon, and I'll definitely be there tomorrow. Take a long lunch and close up early, why don't you."

I disconnected, put the phone on the picnic table, and blew out a breath. That wasn't so bad. Julie *would* disapprove, of course. A day without billable hours was a lost day, as far as she was concerned, and my mumbo-jumbo about the Nichols case wouldn't fool her. I had no intention of billing Sharon for the hours it would take me to drive to and from Webster State College in southwestern New Hampshire in search of her son.

I debated slipping into a comfortable pair of blue jeans and a flannel shirt and sneakers, but my better judgment told me that wearing one of my lawyer pinstripes might help with the day's quest. I didn't know how hard it would be to track down Wayne or, assuming that I succeeded with that, how cooperative he would be when I asked him some challenging questions, as I intended to do. Sometimes the gravitas of my being an attorney — and looking the part — helped convince people that they ought to cooperate with me.

Sometimes, of course, it had the opposite effect.

Henry and I had a discussion about whether he could come along with me. I'm not sure I entirely convinced him that he'd be happier lounging around the backyard than spending the day cooped up in the car. He did love road trips. I gave him a bully stick to gnaw on, though, and when I patted his head and said good-bye to him a little after nine that morning, he was lying on the back deck with the stick propped up between his front paws, and he barely glanced at me.

Dogs love you, no doubt about it, but they love food best of all.

Websterville, New Hampshire, was tucked into the southwestern corner of New Hampshire near the Vermont and Massachusetts borders. The little town had just one claim to fame. It was the home of Webster State College, formerly Webster State Teachers College, and before that Webster Normal School. I'd driven through the town many times. It straddled the two-lane east-west state highway through southern New Hampshire that was the most direct route from Boston to a lot of good trout fishing in southern Vermont. I didn't remember ever actually stopping in Websterville or having any kind of business to transact there, but I did remember the classic nineteenth-century brick buildings and the lovely Victorian houses that lined the street, along with the college's sterile brick-and-glass dormitories and classroom buildings and its manicured playing fields.

It took a little over two hours to drive from my parking garage on Charles Street in Boston to Main Street in Websterville, where I stopped at a coffee shop. It was the fish-shaped wooden sign over the door reading DANIEL WEBSTER'S TROUT that caught my eye. Daniel Webster, for whom, I assumed, Websterville was named, had no interest in dictionaries. That was another Webster. Daniel was a famous and influential New England politician in the first half of the nineteenth century, a native of New Hampshire who served as a United States congressman, a senator, and a secretary of state, and who probably deserved to be president.

He was once offered the position of vice president, which he turned down, saying, "I do not propose to be buried until I am dead."

Webster was even more famous in some circles for the fourteen-and-a-half-pound brook trout he caught on a fly rod from the Carman River on Long Island one Sunday morning in the spring of 1827 when he skipped out of church in the middle of the sermon.

Some spoilsports dispute the story of Daniel Webster's monster trout. They call it apocryphal or, even worse, just a damn fish story. Whether it's true or not doesn't interest me. If it's a damn fish story, it's a damn good one.

I could hardly resist a place called Daniel Webster's Trout, and I was overdue for a caffeine fix, so I slipped into a parking slot directly in front. The narrow coffee shop was wedged between a women's clothing boutique and an art gallery. Across the street were a Cambodian restaurant, a movie house with a marquee advertising a Bergman festival, and a sporting-goods store that, judging from the window display, specialized in mountain biking, cross-country skiing, and whitewater kayaking.

Websterville, in other words, appeared to be a typical New England college town.

Inside Daniel Webster's Trout I sat at a round metal table against the wall, and when the waitress, a slender young blonde who I guessed was a student at the college, came over, I asked for a mug of the "house blend," which she said was "just sort of your basic coffee" and which I figured was my best chance of avoiding something that tasted more like candy than coffee.

When she came back a few minutes later, I asked her if she could tell me how to find Chesterfield Road.

"Sure," she said. "Easy." She pointed out the window. "You go that way maybe a hundred yards to the blinking light. Turn right there. You'll go past the field house and the soccer field, and when you come to the stop sign, that's Chesterfield Road. If you turn left, it takes you to some freshman dorms and the physics and chem labs and the administration building. On the right, it's off campus. Mostly student apartments and some faculty housing."

I thanked her, and when I finished my coffee, I left an extra-generous tip.

I followed the waitress's directions to Chesterfield Road. The address I had for Wayne was number 188. I guessed he didn't live in a freshman dorm, since he hadn't been a freshman for a couple of years, and I was fairly confident that he wasn't living in a science lab or the administration building, so I turned right onto Chesterfield Road.

Number 188 turned out to be what would've been called a triple-decker if it had been located in South Boston instead of Websterville. It was a square three-story wood-frame building with porches spanning the front of each level. The only thing missing was underwear and diapers flapping from clotheslines.

Triple-deckers flanked number 188, and up and down this stretch of Chesterfield Road were what appeared to be other apartment buildings. There were duplexes, more triple-deckers, and some big rambling farmhouses and old Victorians that had been converted into apartments.

Both sides of the street were lined with

vehicles, and more cars were parked in the driveways that separated the buildings. They were mostly aging Hondas and Toyotas, along with some battered old pickup trucks and Jeeps, but there were also a few new-looking BMWs and Porsches and Audis and Lexuses, too. Webster State evidently boasted a heterogeneous mixture of student demographics.

I tucked my car into an empty space on the side of the road, turned off the ignition, and took out my cell phone. I tried Wayne Nichols's number. It rang half a dozen times, and then the now-familiar recorded greeting came on.

I closed my phone without leaving a message, got out of my car, and climbed the half-dozen steps onto the front porch of 188 Chesterfield Road.

On the outside door frame there were three doorbells, and taped over each bell was a list of two or three names written in ink. None of the names belonged to Wayne Nichols.

I looked through the glass on the front door into a small, dark foyer. There was a bank of locked mailboxes and two inside doors. Some magazines and envelopes had spilled onto the tiled floor.

I pressed the bell for apartment 1 and

waited, and when no one came to the door, I tried apartment 2. After a minute or two, I heard the echo of feet clomping down some inside stairs, and then one of the inside doors opened.

A young woman with tangly brown hair blinked at me through the window of the front door. She was wearing a wrinkled blue T-shirt and gray sweatpants.

I smiled at her through the glass and said, "I'm looking for Wayne Nichols."

She frowned and cupped her ear with her hand.

"Does Wayne Nichols live here?" I asked more loudly.

She shrugged and opened the door. "Who're you?" she asked.

"I'm a lawyer from Boston," I said. "My name is Brady Coyne. I have business with Wayne Nichols. I believe he lives at this address." I fished my card out of my pocket and handed it to her.

She was standing in the half-opened doorway. She squinted at my card, then at me. "I'm Judith," she said.

I smiled. "Nice to meet you."

"You're a lawyer?"

"Yes, that's right."

"You got business with Wayne Nichols, huh?"

177

I nodded.

"I bet," she said.

I smiled at her. "What do you mean?"

"I mean old Wayne probably could use a lawyer."

"You know him?"

"Sure," she said. "Webster State's a small school. Everybody pretty much knows everybody. Wayne Nichols doesn't live here anymore."

"Can you tell me where he does live?"

She shook her head. "Nope. He used to have the first floor with a couple other degenerates. I wasn't what you'd call close with any of them. They all moved out at the end of last term, for which I thank God, and I don't know where they went, though I do see one or the other of them around campus once in a while."

"Do you have roommates who might help me find Wayne?"

"I have roommates," she said, "but I doubt they could help you. We kind of avoided Wayne and his buddies when they were living here. We travel in different circles, you might say."

"What circles does Wayne travel in?"

"Just not mine," she said. "Let's leave it at that. I can't tell you how happy I was when he moved out of this building."

"No idea how I could find him, huh?" I asked.

"Nope. Sorry." She glanced meaningfully at her wristwatch. "I gotta go get ready for classes now," she said. "Sorry I couldn't help you."

I smiled at her. "I appreciate your talking with me."

She waved her hand at me, flashed a quick, shy smile, and stepped back into the foyer. The front-door latch clicked loudly behind her, and then she turned and opened the inside door and climbed back up the stairs to her apartment.

I went out to my car, turned around, and headed back the way I'd come on Chesterfield Road. On the other side of the intersection I passed a couple of brick dormitories, and then I came to a large square building with a sign out front that read WEBSTER STATE COLLEGE ADMINISTRATION.

I left my car in a section marked VISITORS in the side parking lot and went into the building. In the lobby a sign indicated that the registrar's office was in suite 206, so I climbed a flight of stairs, found the door with 206 painted on it, and went in.

I was faced with a room-length waist-high counter with four or five people standing on the other side, not unlike bank tellers. There

179

was a line of two or three people — students, I guessed — in front of each of the tellers. I stood at the end of one of the lines, feeling profoundly out of place in my lawyer pinstripe amid these young people in their ripped jeans, baseball caps, and rock-band T-shirts.

After about ten minutes, it was my turn. A young man who appeared to be a student himself faced me on the other side of the counter. "How can I help you, sir?" he asked. A nameplate on the counter indicated that his name was Matthew Trowbridge and he was an admissions intern.

"I'm trying to catch up with one of the students," I said. "The address I have for him appears to be out of date."

Matthew Trowbridge said, "Are you on the faculty or staff here?"

"No. I'm a lawyer. I drove up from Boston today."

"I'm not allowed to divulge personal information about our students," he said. "I'm sorry."

"How personal is an address?"

He shrugged.

"So who is?"

He frowned. "Excuse me?"

"Who is allowed to divulge information such as where a student is presently living?"

"I can talk to Mrs. Allen, if you want," he said. "She's the assistant registrar."

"Thank you," I said.

"Who is it you're looking for?"

"His name is Wayne Nichols," I said. "I'm Brady Coyne." I gave him one of my business cards.

He glanced at the card, then said, "Hang on. I'll see if Mrs. Allen's available." He turned, walked down to the end of the room, opened a door, and went into another room.

Matthew Trowbridge was back about five minutes later. "Mrs. Allen can talk with you," he said. "Just go down there." He pointed. "It's the second door on the left."

I followed his directions and came to a room with a plaque on the door that read CHARLOTTE ALLEN, ASSISTANT REGISTRAR.

I rapped on the door, and it opened a moment later. Standing there was a woman — early, maybe middle thirties — wearing what I guessed, judging by how perfectly they fit her slender body, were expensive designer jeans. Several of the top buttons on her bone white silk blouse were opened.

She had pale blue eyes and straw-colored hair and a generous mouth, and she was smiling at me as though I were just the person she'd been hoping to see.

"Mr. Coyne," she said. "Come on in. Let's sit."

Her office walls were lined with bookshelves full of books. A window that spanned the back wall looked out over a baseball diamond. On one side of the room sat a big oak desk with nothing on it except a telephone and a computer, and the other side served as a cozy sitting area, with four comfortable-looking chairs arranged around a square glass-topped coffee table.

Charlotte Allen pointed to one of those chairs and then sat in one herself. I saw that she had my business card in her hand. "Matthew said you were interested in Wayne Nichols," she said.

"I need to talk with him," I said. "I'm hoping you can tell me where he's presently living."

She smiled and touched her hair with her fingertips. "I'm afraid it's not that simple, Mr. Coyne."

"You can't tell me where he's living?"

Charlotte Allen was shaking her head. "Our regulations are very clear. It's all about protecting our students' privacy. I'm really sorry. I wish I could help you out."

"Since you can't," I said, "who can?"

"Nobody will," she said. "Or at least

nobody's supposed to."

"Look," I said. "Wayne's father was brutally murdered last Saturday night. His mother has been unable to contact her son to tell him what happened. She's asked me, as the family's lawyer, to see what I can do. I've tried calling Wayne, but he doesn't answer his cell phone, which is the only number I have for him. So I drove up here to Websterville in hopes of tracking him down. I just came from the last address his mother has for him, and he doesn't live there anymore. So now what am I supposed to do? What would *you* do, Mrs. Allen, if you were in my shoes?"

"Did you say *murdered?*" she asked.

I nodded.

"Oh, dear."

"Yes."

"Do they know . . . ?"

"The police have made no arrests," I said.

"Oh, dear," she said again.

"So you can see why I need to talk to Wayne," I said.

"He doesn't know?"

"No. We don't want him seeing it first on the news or hearing it as a rumor."

"Of course. Understandable." Charlotte Allen cleared her throat. "You drove all the way up here from Boston to deliver this horrible news to Wayne Nichols?"

"The victim's son," I said. "Yes."

"Let me check on something, okay?"

"Sure," I said. "Of course."

"Just wait here," she said. "I'll be back in a minute."

She got up and walked out of her office, trailing the faint scent of lilacs behind her.

She was actually gone for about ten minutes. When she came back, she sat down across from me and said, "I'm sorry, Mr. Coyne."

"What?"

"Under the circumstances," she said, "I was prepared to, um, bend our regulations and find a way to get that information for you. When I checked our records, though, I found that Wayne Nichols withdrew from school just before the end of the fall term. We have no more information about him since then. I can tell you where he was living, but that's student housing, and he'd've had to move somewhere else when he dropped out."

"I know where he was living then," I said. "He's not there anymore."

"Well, then," said Charlotte Allen.

"Well, then," I said.

She stood up. "Now what will you do?"

"I don't know," I said. "I'll think of something."

She held up my business card. "If I hear anything, I'll call you. How would that be?"

"That would be excellent," I said. I held out my hand to her. "I appreciate your time."

Her hand was soft, but her grip was firm. "I wish I could've been more helpful."

"Me, too," I said.

I walked out of Charlotte Allen's office and past the counter where I'd talked with Matthew Trowbridge, and I was halfway down the stairs when a woman's voice from somewhere behind me said, "Hey, mister. You in the suit."

I stopped and turned around, and a young woman came skipping down the steps toward me.

"You talking to me?" I asked her.

"You're the only one in a suit," she said. She was short and a little pudgy, with big dark eyes and a nice smile. "Did I hear you say you were looking for Wayne Nichols?"

"Yes," I said. "Do you know him?"

"I overheard you up there." She jerked her chin up to where I'd talked with Matthew Trowbridge and Charlotte Allen. "I bet nobody answered your questions. Am I right?"

"You're right," I said. "They're very conscientious about protecting their students' privacy."

"I'm Lila, by the way," she said. She held out her hand.

I took her hand and smiled. "I'm Brady."

We resumed walking down the stairs. "Lots of people know where Wayne Nichols lives," Lila said. "It's hardly a big secret."

"I'd appreciate it if you'd tell me." We came to the bottom of the stairs. I opened the front door and held it for her, and we both stepped outside.

She cocked her head and frowned at me. "You're not gonna, like, get him in trouble or something? You're not a cop or something, are you?"

"No," I said. "I'm just a lawyer. His family's lawyer. I need to talk with him is all."

She looked at me for a moment, then nodded. "He's on Blaine Street. That's over that way." She waved her hand off to the left.

"Can you tell me how to get there?" I said.

"Sure. You go back down that way for maybe two miles?" She pointed down Chesterfield Road in the direction of Wayne's old apartment building. "You'll come to an intersection with a white church on the corner on the left and a big cornfield on the right. Go left there by the church, and then Blaine Street is your, um . . . second or third right. There's street signs. Wayne's place is way down the end. There's all woods after that. It's like this old neighborhood, a bunch of shitty little ranch houses, excuse my language, where mostly married students live. Wayne's house is yellow with one of those carports on the side? Except there's all trash barrels and crap in the carport instead of a car."

"Do you know what number his house is?" I asked.

She smiled. "Sorry. Way down at the end where it turns around in one of those whatchamacallits is the best I can do for you."

"Cul-de-sac," I said.

She cocked her head at me. "Excuse me?"

"Cul-de-sac," I said. "The whatchamacallit. Where the road turns around."

She smiled. "Right. I couldn't think of it."

"You must be a friend of his," I said.

"Friend? Wayne?" Lila shook her head. "I been to a couple parties at his house is all. My boyfriend knows him." She looked at me. "Look, though, seriously. I hope you're not gonna get Wayne in trouble. My boyfriend would kill me if he knew I was telling you this."

"No trouble," I said. "Just some lawyer

business." I held my hand out to Lila. "I really appreciate your help. I didn't know what I was going to do."

She gave my hand a quick shake. "They can be awfully bureaucratic," she said. "I figured you were gonna end up frustrated."

"I surely would have if you hadn't rescued me." I gave Lila a wave and headed for my car, repeating her directions to Wayne Nichols's house in my head so that I wouldn't forget them.

FOURTEEN

Lila's directions were excellent, and fifteen minutes or so after I waved good-bye to her on the steps of the Webster State College administration building, I pulled up in front of Wayne Nichols's house in the cul-de-sac at the end of Blaine Street on the outskirts of Websterville, New Hampshire.

The place was even dumpier than I'd imagined from Lila's description. The little square of lawn in front was overgrown with last year's brown matted-down mixture of grass and weeds. It looked as if it had never seen a lawn mower. Dandelions grew from the cracks in the short blacktopped drive-way, where an aged blue-and-rust Ford Taurus sedan was parked. The carport, with its sagging roof, was stuffed with overflow-ing trash barrels, soggy cardboard boxes, and scraps of lumber. The house itself, a small boxy ranch, featured flaking yellow paint and a rickety television antenna and a

189

couple of missing window shutters.

A second-growth forest, a mixture of pine and oak trees with a thick understory of briars and brush, crowded close to the back of the house. There was a vacant lot on one side and an identical ranch-style structure, this one with blistering gray paint, on the other side.

I sat there in my car, looking at Wayne's house, trying to detect a sign of life inside. The place just sat there, too, still and forlorn.

After a few minutes, I slid out of my car and went up to the front door. I pressed the doorbell and heard the hollow *ding-dong* echo from inside.

When nobody answered after a couple of minutes, I hit the bell again and waited again. Still nobody came to the door.

I went around to the side door under the carport. This one appeared to open into a small foyer — what we New Englanders call a mudroom. There was no bell beside the door. I rapped on the window, waited, rapped again.

Maybe nobody was home, although there was that old Taurus crouching in the driveway. I walked around to the back of the house, where there was another outside door. I climbed the three steps onto a little concrete porch under a plastic awning, cupped my hands around my eyes, and looked in through the storm door and the window of the back door, which opened directly into the kitchen. Pots and pans were piled high in the sink. On a small table sat a Wheaties box, a cardboard orange juice carton, a plastic one-gallon milk jug, an open newspaper, and some glasses and bowls. The kitchen light was on, and I could hear the deep bass-line *thump-thump* of recorded rock music coming from somewhere inside.

I pressed the doorbell, and when that brought no response, I banged on the frame of the storm door.

That's when I heard a car door slam from the other side of the house, and then an engine sputtered, and it roared to life, and then came the screech of rubber on pavement.

I jumped off the back porch and ran around to the side of Wayne Nichols's house in time to see the rusty old Taurus sedan that had been in the driveway peel around the cul-de-sac and zoom down Blaine Street in a cloud of blue exhaust.

I stood there until the whine of the Taurus's engine faded into the distance. I looked at my watch. It was a little after one in the afternoon.

I considered my options. I could hop into my car, and if I drove fast and guessed right at the turns, maybe I'd catch up with the old Taurus.

Then what? Move up beside him and wave for him to pull over to the side of the road? Sideswipe him? Ram into him? Or maybe hang back and follow him until he stopped and got out, and then leap from my car and accost him?

Well, now it didn't matter. Hamlet Coyne had once again hesitated too long and given the whole situation too much analysis and too little action. By now Wayne was probably several miles away, and who knew which direction he'd taken.

Having screwed up this situation pretty thoroughly, and with nothing better to do, I went over and sat on the front steps. I figured I'd blown my chance to talk with Wayne Nichols. I'd spooked him, and he was gone. But, hey, it was a balmy April afternoon, and the sun was warm on my face, and the air smelled of fresh earth and lilac blossoms. There were worse things to do — such as shuffling papers in a law office or playing adversary with some other attorney in a courtroom — than sitting in the sun for a few minutes on such an April day.

Wayne Nichols, just a year or two older than my son Billy, was living here in this crappy little house on the slummy outskirts of Websterville, New Hampshire. I wondered how he made the rent. Monthly support checks from Sharon, I guessed. She probably thought she was giving her dropout son tuition and room-and-board money. I'd have to ask her.

Billy grew up in the same town and went to the same public schools as Wayne, and like Wayne, and at about the same age as Wayne, had lived through his parents' divorce. Both young men dropped out of college. Billy became a summer fishing guide and winter ski instructor.

I wondered about Wayne.

It was interesting, I thought as I sat there with the sun warm on my face, how parallel life paths sometimes converged, and sometimes they diverged.

Thinking about Billy reminded me of how he'd gone banging out of my house last night, angry and hurt, and how he was heading back to Idaho in a few days.

We'd had our rifts before. Billy was a prideful guy, unlikely to make the first move, but I knew that he'd come around if

I met him halfway. I could be pretty stubborn, too, but this wasn't worth it. I'd call him. I'd apologize, and then he'd apologize. We'd get together, and we'd touch fists and give each other a hug, and we'd be good again. When I got home —

I sensed motion behind me, a sudden prickly feeling on the back of my neck. Before I could react to it, a growly voice said, "Who the fuck are you?"

I jerked my head around and found myself looking into the bore of a square automatic pistol.

Behind the pistol was a young man's face. He had black hair, cut short, with the scruff of a beard and dark glowering eyes. Wayne Nichols, I assumed. He had evidently cut through the woods and sneaked around the side of the house.

"My name is Brady Coyne," I said, "and I don't like having guns poking at me."

"What do you want?" he asked.

"If you're Wayne Nichols," I said, "I need to talk to you. I have news for you. Put that damn gun down, will you?"

"What kind of news?" The pistol continued to point at my forehead.

"Please aim your gun somewhere else," I said, "before we have an accident."

He lowered the arm that was holding the

gun. "You left me a message the other day, right? Was that you? The lawyer?"

I nodded. "That's right. I'm your mother's lawyer."

I moved over to the side of the step I was sitting on. "Why don't you sit down."

He continued standing there beside me with the gun dangling from his hand. He was wearing blue jeans and a zip-up sweatshirt, with a Red Sox cap and expensive-looking sneakers. "I'm good right here," he said. "You drove up from Boston to talk to me?"

"Yes," I said. "Because you wouldn't talk to me on the phone."

"Your news is that important?"

I shrugged. "That's for you to judge, I guess."

"So go ahead," he said.

I turned to face him. "Do you recognize me?"

He shook his head. "No, I don't think so. Should I?"

"I used to live in Wellesley. You were friends with my son."

Wayne Nichols frowned for a moment. Then he nodded. "Coyne. Billy, right? He's your son?"

"That's right."

"Billy was a cool dude. Not sure I remember you, though."

"Look at me," I said. "Have you seen me recently?"

He frowned at me. "Like when?"

"Like last Saturday night?"

"No. Where do you think I saw you last Saturday night?"

"In the Beverly Suites Hotel in Natick. In the corridor on the third floor."

He shook his head. "I was nowhere near Natick. I've never been to that hotel. I never even heard of it before. You're playing games with me. What is this all about, the Beverly Suites Hotel in Natick?"

"That's where your father was."

Wayne frowned. "My father? What about him?"

"That's where he was last Saturday night when he got killed."

I watched Wayne Nichols's face. He stared at me. I couldn't read his expression.

After what seemed like a long minute, he blinked, and then he shook his head. "Killed," he said in a soft voice, making it a statement, not a question.

I nodded. "Murdered. He was stabbed in the abdomen and in the heart. He was there for a convention of veterinarians. He was in his hotel room. Your mother found him. His body."

Wayne looked down at his hand, as if he were surprised to see a gun in it. He stuck the handgun in the pocket of his sweatshirt, then came around and sat on the step beside me. "Who killed my father?" he asked.

"They don't know yet."

"You think I did it?"

"Me?" I shook my head. "Wouldn't matter what I thought."

"Yeah, but do you?"

"I'm your mother's lawyer."

His mouth opened, then closed. "So she did it, huh? She finally did it."

"You think so?" I asked.

"The way he treated her all those years?" Wayne nodded. "About time."

"How did he treat her?"

He shrugged. "You know. He was always putting her down. Insulting her. Making her feel like shit. I used to think, *How can she put up with that? Why doesn't she leave him? Why doesn't she kill the son of a bitch?*"

"He made you angry, then? How he treated your mother?"

"Sure. Me and my sister, we used to talk about how we wished he'd just go away and leave her alone." He smiled quickly. "Then they got divorced, and I thought after that everything would be better. But it wasn't.

That sucked, too."

"Did you talk about murdering him?" I asked. "You and Ellen?"

Wayne blurted out a quick laugh. "Murder? Christ. We were kids. Who knows what we talked about. Maybe we did. The way kids do, you know. We hated him, I can tell you that. And we didn't think so much of her, either, the way she just put up with all the shit he gave her, never stood up for herself."

I wondered if abuse had actually been a factor in the Nichols divorce. It wouldn't be part of the court record, because Massachusetts had been a no-fault divorce state for many years. Of course, Sharon would know . . . if she wanted to tell me.

If Ken had abused her — emotionally or physically or both — it could be construed as a motive for murder.

On the other hand, this was the perception of a boy, now the memory of a young man. Sharon — and Ellen, too — seemed to remember things differently. Each of them had fabricated a story to make sense of their experiences, and who knew where the truth lay?

"What about you?" I asked. "How did he treat you? You and your sister?"

Wayne shrugged. "Okay. Nothing bad. He

worked a lot. They both did. Me and Ellen both helped out at the clinic, feeding the animals, cleaning the kennels, and he paid us. That's how we earned our allowances. We didn't do a lot as a family. But it was all right. It was just the way he treated her. My mother. That's what I remember."

"So where were you last Saturday night?" I asked.

"Huh?" He looked at me for a second, then nodded. "Oh. You mean do I have an alibi."

"Yes."

"I was here. At my house. I —" Right then his head jerked up, and he looked out at the street.

I looked where he was looking. A large black SUV was coming around the cul-de-sac.

"I had some people over Saturday night," Wayne said. "There were twenty-five or thirty people here at one time or another. Of course, none of them would ever admit it." He stood up. "I'll be right back."

He walked to the curb in front of his house. He had his hand in the pocket of his sweatshirt where he'd tucked his gun.

The passenger-side window of the SUV slid down, and Wayne leaned his forearm on it and bent to talk with the driver. He kept his other hand, the one holding the gun, in his pocket. I got just a glimpse of the other man's face as it moved toward the window before it was hidden behind Wayne's body, enough only to give me the impression that he was young — maybe a few years older than Wayne — with dark hair. He appeared to be wearing a dress shirt and a necktie.

I noticed that the vehicle had Massachusetts license plates and tinted windows. It was a Lincoln Navigator, and it looked like a new model.

I took out a pen and one of my business cards from the inside pocket of my jacket and copied down the license number of the Navigator. Detective Horowitz might be interested.

After a few minutes, Wayne stepped away from the car, the tinted window slid up, and the Navigator pulled away from the curb and disappeared around the corner. Wayne stood there watching it go. Then he came back and sat on the step beside me. "So where were we?" he asked.

"You were telling me that you didn't have an alibi," I said.

"No," he said, "I told you I *did* have an alibi. It's just that I'm not sure anybody will confirm it."

"Why wouldn't they?"

He looked at me and smiled. "Do you have any idea who the guy in that Lincoln was?"

I shook my head.

"Let me put it this way," he said. "That kid's about my age, and he wears a suit and a necktie to work every day, carries a briefcase, drives the company car."

I shrugged.

"He was looking to do business with me."

"Business," I said.

"You're a lawyer," he said. "I can tell you anything. You've got to keep it private."

"You know your way around lawyers, do you?"

He shrugged.

"I'm your mother's lawyer," I said. "Not yours."

"Doesn't matter. This whole conversation is just between us. Like you were a priest. You can't tell anybody what I say. I know that. Anyway, I didn't say anything about what that guy wanted, and I don't want to talk about it anymore." Wayne looked at me with narrowed eyes.

"Sure," I said. "This conversation is privileged."

"So, okay," he said, "I was here Saturday night, like I am most Saturday nights, and there was a bunch of people over, and they probably wouldn't ever admit it, and they'd be totally pissed if I ever gave out their names."

"Why is that?" I asked.

"It was a college party, that's all. Use your imagination." He shrugged. "All I'm saying is, I'm just explaining to you that I was here, not there, and I did not murder my father, and I guess if you put somebody under oath they'd admit they were here and tell you that I was, too."

"What do you know about ketamine?" I asked.

Wayne cocked his head at me. "Where'd that come from? Ketamine?"

"I'm inferring that there might've been drugs at your party," I said. "Special K is a popular drug."

He grinned. "You got the terminology down pat, huh?"

"It's an anesthetic commonly used in animal surgery," I said.

"Shit," he said, "everybody knows that. And my father was a vet. So what? Look. I don't know anything about illegal drugs, okay? I feel bad my old man got murdered, but I didn't do it, and I don't know who did."

"Why won't you talk to your mother?" I

asked. "She left you several messages."

"Tell her I'm sorry," he said. "I'm sorry I don't want to talk to her. I'm sorry about what happened to my father, and I'm sorry that she's always been so unhappy, and I'm sorry about our totally dysfunctional family, and I'm sorry about my whole screwed-up life and all the misery I've caused everybody, okay?" He stood up and faced me. "I don't want to talk about this shit anymore. Just go home and leave me alone, will you?"

"I'll make a deal with you," I said.

"What?"

"I'll go," I said, "and I won't keep bugging you — but I want you to agree that if I call you, you'll either answer the phone or you'll listen to my message, and if I ask you to call me back, you'll do it."

"Why should I?"

I spread my hands. "Because I don't want to have to drive for two and a half hours every time I want to talk to you."

"So what do I get out of it?"

"Me not being pissed at you, for one thing," I said. "Maybe information you need to hear."

Wayne shrugged. "Yeah," he said, "that's fair, I guess. Okay. It's a deal." He held out his hand.

I shook his hand. "Any message for your

mother you'd like me to deliver?"

He looked at me for a minute, then shook his head. "No, nothing. Probably best if you don't tell her you were here, huh?"

I shrugged. "I'd like to tell her I saw you and that you're okay."

"Really?" He smiled. "Am I?"

FIFTEEN

It was about four in the afternoon, and I'd crossed the border back into Massachusetts, heading south toward Boston on Route 3, when my cell phone vibrated in my shirt pocket.

It was Roger Horowitz. "You're playing hooky today," he said.

"Sometimes my business takes me out of the office," I said. I sounded a little defensive, even to my own ears.

"Julie seemed annoyed," he said.

"You called my office looking for me, huh?"

"Yes," he said. "Talked to your poor secretary. Don't know how she puts up with you. She said she didn't know where you were or what you were doing, implying that you failed to consult properly with her and that you were behaving as if you were the boss, which, of course, you're not."

"She hates it when I'm not accruing billable hours," I said. "I imagine she was looking for sympathy."

"Sympathy from me?"

"I know," I said. "Ridiculous."

"So where are you now?" he said.

"On the road. Maybe a half hour from home. Why?"

"I need you to come to my office," he said, "look at something."

"When? Is it urgent?"

"Important, yeah. Urgent? Just, the sooner the better. Today, okay?"

"I can be there in an hour, maybe an hour and a half."

"Good." He hung up. No "Good-bye," no "Thank you," no "Have a nice day." That was Horowitz. Mr. Charm.

I drove straight to my parking garage at the Cambridge Street end of Charles Street, where I left my car in the reserved slot that I rented by the month. Then I walked down Charles toward the Beacon Street end and turned up the hill on Mt. Vernon to my townhouse.

Henry was pretty happy to see me. He whined and wagged his little stub of a tail and bumped his forehead against my leg. I scootched down for a minute to rub his ears and tell him how much I'd missed him, and then I let him out back.

I checked the kitchen phone for messages, found none, and went upstairs to change out of my suit. I pulled on a pair of jeans and sneakers, went back downstairs, snagged a bottle of Samuel Adams Cherry Wheat Ale from the refrigerator and a Milk-Bone from the box on the table, and joined Henry out back.

He was busy peeing on the shrubbery, marking his territory. I sat in one of my Adirondack chairs and took a swig of ale. I wanted to relax for a few minutes before I trudged over to Horowitz's office.

After a while, Henry came over and plopped his chin on my leg. I scratched the secret spot on his forehead and gave him his Milk-Bone. He lay down on the brick patio beside me to chomp on his treat.

I fished out my cell phone and tried Billy's number.

He answered on the second ring. "Hey, Pop," he said.

I said, "You're speaking to me, huh?"

He laughed quickly. "You know I love you, man," he said, "but sometimes you can be a pain in the ass."

"I apologize for that. That's why I'm calling. To apologize. I was out of line the other night, trying to cram my advice down your throat."

"Ah, your heart was probably in the right place," he said. "It's just, sometimes you treat me like a little kid, you know?"

"I do know," I said, "and sometimes the lawyer in me kicks in when I should just be the father, or the friend, and then I'm likely to treat anybody like a kid. Anyway, I just wanted you both to know, you and Gwen, that I trust your judgment. It sounds like you've worked this thing out in a way that makes sense for both of you, and I wish you the best of luck and much happiness. That's why I'm calling. To say what I should've said the other night. Good luck and happiness. And to apologize."

"I'm the one who should apologize," Billy said. "I said things I shouldn't've said. Things I didn't mean. I'm sorry. You know I respect the hell out of you. I hope you know."

"Sure," I said. "Don't worry about it."

"Gwen's been on my ass to call you," he said. "She says I acted like a baby. She said I was so immature that I obviously did need my father's advice, and I think she's right. So, sorry, man."

"So why didn't you call me?" I asked.

"I was gonna." He hesitated. "Shit. Don't start, okay?"

"Right," I said. "Sorry. Look, I think I told

you that Alex is coming down this weekend. She'd love to see you again, and meet Gwen. Can you guys come over on Saturday? We can have pizzas delivered. I'll provide the beer."

"Sounds good," he said. "Hang on. Lemme check with Gwen."

I sipped my Sam, and a minute later Billy came back on the phone. "She says good. She says she'd love to spend some time with you when I'm not acting like an asshole. We're heading out on Sunday, you know. Her to California, me to Idaho. Back to our lives. I'd like to see you again before we go. Alex, too. It's been a few years since you guys were together, right?"

"Seven years," I said.

"The Evie Banyon years," Billy said.

"Yeah, well," I said. "Evie's gone now."

"And Alex is back. Cool, the way it worked out for you."

"It's not that simple," I said.

"I didn't mean anything," he said. "I liked Alex, and I liked Evie. Whatever makes you happy, man."

"Seeing you and Gwen again will make me happy."

After I hung up with Billy, Henry and I went inside. I gave him fresh water, then told him I had to go meet with Roger Horowitz and assured him I'd be back for his dinnertime.

Then I left the house and walked over the hill, up Mt. Vernon Street and down Joy Street, to Horowitz's office. Horowitz was with the Suffolk County State Police Detective Unit. Their headquarters were located in the district attorney's office at One Bullfinch Place in Government Center on the other side of Beacon Hill, which used to be Scollay Square before the old bars and burlesque houses and by-the-hour hotels were razed in the early sixties. The old-timers still referred to the area as Scollay Square and told stories about the aging strippers and tired comics who used to work at the Old Howard. It was just a fifteen-minute walk from my townhouse.

I emptied my pockets, endured the mistrustful scrutiny of the big female guard as I passed through the metal detector, and took the elevator to the third floor.

I poked my head into Horowitz's office. He was leaning back in his chair at his desk with his jacket hung over the chair back and his necktie pulled loose and his fingers laced behind his neck. He was talking with Marcia Benetti, his partner, who was sitting across from him.

I waited for a minute, and when neither

of them seemed to notice me standing there, I rapped my knuckle on the door frame.

Horowitz turned his head and looked at me. "Oh," he said. "You're here. About time."

Benetti lifted her chin and smiled.

"We were just talking about you," Horowitz said.

"I can only imagine," I said.

"The case," he said. "Your client."

I said nothing.

"We ain't solved it yet," he said. "In case you were wondering."

"Disappointing," I said.

He jerked his head at the empty chair next to the one Marcia Benetti was sitting in.

I went into the office and sat down. "So what do you know?" I asked.

"What do *you* know?" he asked.

"Me?" I asked. "Not much. Nothing I can share with you."

"Too bad." He looked at Benetti. "In the spirit of cooperation," he said, "and because eventually we've gotta disclose what we got anyway, why don't you go ahead and fill him in."

"You told him about that matchbook, right?" she asked Horowitz.

He nodded.

She opened the manila folder that was on

her lap, glanced at the papers in it, and then turned to me. "The ME didn't come up with anything new and exciting," she said. "TOD is between seven and nine that night, just as we figured. Two stab wounds, one to the heart and one to the abdomen. The one to the heart killed him almost instantly. He'd eaten roast beef, green beans, baked potato with sour cream, and green salad, drunk one, possibly two martinis, including olives, within an hour or two of his death, consistent with attending a banquet, which several witnesses confirmed that he did. Forensics found dozens of random fingerprints, including those of your client, human hairs, fabric traces, other minutiae, all the stuff you'd expect from a hotel room, some of which matched up with the victim and some with your client, and a lot of which they couldn't match up with anybody. Hotel staff, previous guests, repairmen. Who knows? We get some suspects, we can maybe make some matches. They sent some stuff out for DNA testing, which'll take a few days to get back." She closed the folder and looked up at me. "Nothing to exonerate your client, in other words."

"Nothing to implicate her, either," I said.

Benetti smiled. "Right. Nothing new to implicate her. Not yet. We're trying."

I smiled. "Of course you are. What about the murder weapon?"

"It wasn't recovered," she said. "The ME said it was serrated, thin blade, five inches long, consistent with the hotel steak knives."

"Of which there was an abundant supply on the room-service trays up and down the corridors," I said. "Killer could've grabbed one, used it on Ken Nichols, rinsed it off, and put it back on one of those trays."

"Forensics took all the knives that were still there on the trays in the hallway for evidence, tested all of them." She shrugged. "None was the murder weapon. At this point, that's a dead end." She closed the folder on her lap. "That's about it for the forensics."

"What about drugs?"

Benetti shook her head. "They found nothing in his system except the alcohol."

"Did they test for ketamine?"

She nodded. "Yes. Negative."

I looked at Horowitz. "You said you had something to show me?"

"Yeah, I do." He took a manila folder off the top of a pile of papers on his desk, opened it, and slid out some six-by-eight photographs. He spread them out on the desk, facing me. "Whaddaya think?" he asked.

There were eleven photos in all. Some were overexposed, some underexposed, some sharply focused, some fuzzy. Each of them showed a bearded man. Some head-and-shoulder shots, some taken from a greater distance. The subjects ranged in age, I estimated, from midthirties to about seventy. Some had dark beards, some gray, some white. Some neatly trimmed, some bushy. Some of the men were bald; some had thick heads of hair.

None of them was the guy who'd shot Ken Nichols with his index finger the night I'd been there.

I looked up at Horowitz and shook my head. "The guy I saw was about fifty. Dark beard with gray in it, receding hairline. Ken called him Clem. None of these guys looks anything like him. This is all you've got?"

"What we pulled off the hotel surveillance cameras, Friday, Saturday, and Sunday. When the animal doctors were there. All the bearded guys we could find. I think I already told you there was nobody named Clem registered there."

"Clem could've been a nickname," I said.

"If so," said Horowitz, "no help whatso-ever."

"Well," I said, "the guy I saw was there Friday night, but he's not here in your photos."

"Well, damn," he said.

"He managed to avoid the cameras," I said. "Maybe he did that on purpose."

"Not hard to avoid those cameras if you were aware of them," said Horowitz. "Plus, half of 'em weren't even operating."

"Take another look at the photos, Mr. Coyne," said Benetti.

I shrugged, took another look, and shook my head. "Nothing even close," I said. "I asked my client if she knew of somebody named Clem, but she came up empty. Sorry."

"Me, too," said Horowitz. "I'd've liked to talk to that guy." He glanced at Benetti, then pulled open one of his desk drawers, reached in, and took out a DVD in a plain paper sleeve. "We got something else for you." He pushed himself out of his chair. "Come on. Follow me."

"What's this?" I asked.

"You'll see."

I followed Horowitz and Benetti down the hall to a small conference room. It was furnished with a rectangular wooden table, half a dozen wooden chairs, and four television sets lined up side by side on a long shelf against one wall.

"Sit down," Horowitz said.

I sat.

Benetti remained standing. She leaned against the wall behind my right shoulder, as if she wanted to keep an eye on me.

Horowitz slipped the disc into one of the television sets, picked up a remote control, and came over and sat beside me. "We got some stuff from two different security cameras at the Beverly Suites Hotel," he said. "For your viewing pleasure, but mainly in the hope that you can help us out, we copied the relevant parts onto this disc. Ready?"

"Fire away," I said.

He pressed a button on the remote, and a fuzzy black-and-white picture appeared on the screen. I recognized the area in the lobby of the hotel by the front desk. In the lower right corner of the screen was the date — the Saturday night four days earlier when Ken Nichols was killed. The time ticked along by the second. It showed 10:32:17 P.M., and counting.

People were moving jerkily in and out of the picture. After a minute or so, Horowitz said, "There." He paused the picture. "See? There, in the hoodie."

I saw what he saw. It was a figure wearing a dark sweatshirt with the hood covering his head. He looked like he was headed for the front entrance. From the angle of the camera, his face was hidden.

I recognized him by his hoodie and his baggy jeans and his white sneakers, and by the way he moved, and by his general body shape. He was young and slender and not very tall. His movements were quick and alert, like some wild prey species that thought he was being stalked by a big predator.

He could have been Wayne Nichols.

He could have been a million people.

"Yes," I said. "That looks like him. The guy I chased down the corridor. Same size, same clothes. Not sure what good that's going to do you. Did you get a shot of his face?"

"Hang on," said Horowitz. He fast-forwarded the disc, and when he stopped it, the picture came from a different camera. It was fixed on the entrance area in front of the hotel where taxis and limos and shuttle buses and private vehicles were picking up and dropping off guests. The time at the bottom of the screen was 10:36:44 P.M. — immediately after the previous sequence.

"There," Horowitz said after a minute or two. "There he is."

The hooded figure stepped into the picture from the bottom left corner. He stood there on the sidewalk with his back to the camera, pulled a cell phone from his pants pocket, pecked out a number on it, and put it to his ear. His conversation lasted less than a minute. Then he snapped the phone shut and stuck it back into his pocket.

A few minutes later — the digital time on the screen read 10:42:14 P.M. — a black SUV pulled up to the curb, and the guy in the hoodie went over, opened the door, and started to slide in.

Horowitz paused it there, with the SUV's passenger door open and our subject just bending to get in. His hood had slipped to the side, and half of his face was visible.

"See that?" asked Horowitz.

"I see part of his face," I said. "It's pretty fuzzy. Can't you enhance it or blow it up or something?"

"Who, Roger?" asked Benetti. "You kidding? He can barely work the remote."

"Ha," said Horowitz. "I can fast-forward this sucker like a pro."

"Somebody should be able to sharpen that image," I said. "On TV they do it all the time."

"This ain't *CSI*," Horowitz growled. "Just take a look at the guy's face for me and tell me if you recognize him, if he's somebody you can identify."

It wasn't Wayne, I could see that. This face was rounder than Wayne's, and unlike Wayne's, this one had no black scruffy beard growing on it.

I tried to conjure up the image of the face I'd seen in the black SUV in front of Wayne's house, but that had been just a quick glimpse, and it hadn't stuck in my memory.

I shook my head. "I don't think I ever saw this guy before. I don't recognize him."

"Well, shit," said Horowitz.

"What about the driver?" I asked. "Did the camera get a glimpse of him?"

"Don't think so," he said. "Keep looking."

He hit the play button, and on the screen the guy in the hoodie slipped into the car, which then began to pull away from the curb. At no time did the face of the driver show itself.

"Wait," I said. "Pause it."

He hit the pause button.

"Isn't that a Lincoln Navigator?"

"Yep," said Horowitz. "Black or dark blue, I'd say. This year's or last year's model."

"Can you read the plates on it?"

"We tried," he said. "Just too blurry. They got mud on them, and the light's bad. We've got our techs working on it. We should maybe be able to get a partial read on it, at least."

I took out my wallet and found the business card where I'd jotted down the plate numbers from the Lincoln Navigator that stopped in front of Wayne's house when I was there. I handed it to Horowitz. "See if these match those."

He took the card and frowned at it. "What's this?"

"The plate numbers from a Navigator I saw today, looks like that one on your tape."

"Where was this?" he asked. "Who does the vehicle belong to?"

"Where I saw it," I said, "I'm not prepared to say. Who it's registered to, you can look that up, I know that."

"Well, at least you could — ?"

"Look," I said. "I don't want to get ahead of myself here. If this plate doesn't match that one there at the hotel, then it's irrelevant."

"You withholding evidence, Coyne?" asked Horowitz.

"I think this would actually be called sharing evidence," I said. "Consistent with protecting my client's privileged status, of course."

"Sure," he grumbled. "Privileged. Of course."

"The Beverly Suites don't have security cameras in the corridors?" I asked.

He shook his head. "They got 'em in the elevators, but not the corridors."

"This guy," I said, "when I chased him, he went down the stairs."

"He probably came up the stairs, too," he said, "because we looked at the elevator tapes and couldn't find him. The way he kept that hood over his face, I'd guess he was aware of the cameras, avoiding them when he could, covering his face the rest of the time. Those shots you just saw are all we got."

"Trying to avoid cameras," I said, "would suggest that he was up to no good."

"Ha," said Horowitz. "No good, as in stabbing a veterinarian in the heart in his hotel room, you mean."

"That would qualify as no good," I said.

SIXTEEN

When I got back from Horowitz's office, I made myself two fried-egg sandwiches, with mayo on Cuban bread, and ate them at the kitchen table with a glass of orange juice. Under the table, Henry's tags clanged against his metal dish as he gobbled his Alpo. The Red Sox were playing the Blue Jays on my little kitchen TV. There was no score in the fourth inning, and nothing was happening. Mostly easy grounders and routine fly balls.

After I rinsed my plate and glass and stowed them in the dishwasher, Henry and I went into my downstairs office. He curled up on his dog bed for his after-supper nap, and I called Sharon Nichols at her condo in Acton.

When she answered, I said, "How are you?"

She hesitated, then said, "Oh, I'm all right, I guess."

"Tell me the truth," I said.

"The truth, huh."

"I'm your lawyer," I said. "You must always tell me the truth."

"Well, okay. The truth? Lousy, is how I am." She blew out a quick, cynical laugh. "I'm not sleeping. I lie awake. I toss and turn. My mind whirls around. Weird images, dark thoughts. Terrifying, sometimes. When I finally do drift off, I dream about violence and death. I wake up in the darkness and can't go back to sleep. I can't control my bad thoughts. It's like suddenly I can't take anything for granted. I doubt everything. The world is undependable. Out of control. Bad things can happen to anyone anytime, and I lie there thinking of all the possible bad things, and how I can't prevent them. Do you know what I mean?"

"Yes, I understand," I said.

"When I'm up and around," she said, "during the day, it's like this cloud of gloom surrounds me. I'm jumpy and irritable. Today a customer dropped her car keys on the floor, and I screamed and just about hit the ceiling." She hesitated. "This is to be expected, right? I mean, aren't these feelings pretty much normal for somebody who a few days ago discovered the bloody corpse of the man she was married to for many years, the man she was maybe falling in love with all over again? Not even to mention, someone who the police think did it?"

"What you're feeling might be expected," I said, "but it's not healthy, and it's not normal. You need to deal with it. Do you remember I mentioned my friend the homicide counselor to you?"

"A shrink, right?" asked Sharon.

"She's a psychologist," I said. "She specializes in helping the friends and relatives of homicide victims deal with their feelings. She says people like you are also the victims of homicide, just as much as the person who got murdered. Her name is Tally Whyte, and I'd like to arrange an appointment for you with her. Okay?"

"I don't feel like having to explain myself to anybody," Sharon said.

"You wouldn't have to explain anything to Tally," I said. "She understands all about it. Her own father was murdered. She has people who keep going back to her, years after the murder occurred."

Sharon was silent for a minute. Then she said, "I don't know. It seems too hard. What I really want is not to have to think about it."

"It's not going to go away," I said.

"I know," she said. "Yeah. Okay. I'll give it

a try. I've got to do something."

"I'll call Tally now," I said. "I'll get right back to you. Okay?"

"Sure," she said. "Okay. Thank you."

"Before you hang up," I said. "I left you a voice mail message yesterday asking about a man named Clem. Somebody Ken knew."

"You asked me that before," she said. "It still doesn't ring any bells. I'd've called you if I thought of anything."

"Could be a nickname or something."

"I'm sorry, Brady."

"He might be the one who killed Ken."

"I understand," she said. "I'm drawing a blank. I'll keep thinking about it, okay?"

"Sure," I said, "that's fine."

The instant Sharon and I disconnected, I realized I'd neglected to tell her about seeing Wayne. One of my shrink friends would find some kind of vast significance in that, no doubt.

Well, I'd tell her about it when I called her back.

Over the past few years I had introduced several of my clients, people who'd brushed up against murder, to Tally Whyte, and they all told me that she'd helped them deal with, and in some cases get rid of, their fears and guilt, their dark, oppressive thoughts and feelings.

225

Tally had given me her home and cell numbers. I'd written them down in my old-fashioned little black address book. I tried her at home.

She picked up the phone on the fourth ring. "Friend or foe?" she asked.

"Friend, definitely," I said. "It's Brady Coyne."

"Yep," she said. "Friend. My favorite lawyer. If I ever get divorced, you're my man. Of course, I'll have to get married first. How have you been?"

"Oh, I've been fine," I said, "but —"

"You've got a client, huh? Friend, relative of a homicide victim?"

"Right," I said. "She needs you."

Tally was quiet for a moment. Then she said, "The veterinarian in the hotel?"

"That's the one," I said. "His ex-wife."

"I've heard about this case," Tally said. "She's a suspect, isn't she?"

"Sharon is her name," I said. "Sharon Nichols. She found the body. Two stab wounds, abdomen and heart. They haven't eliminated her from their list of suspects."

"Did she agree to see me?"

"Yes," I said. "She's not doing very well. She knows she needs help. I was thinking, if she's willing to talk to you . . ."

She hesitated, then said, "What do you

226

think? If she's willing to see me, it means she's innocent?"

"That occurred to me, yes."

"It doesn't work that way, Brady," she said. "You're really not that confident about her innocence, are you?"

"I don't know, Tal. I don't think she did it, but I guess I've still got some doubts. Anyway, it doesn't matter. I'm her lawyer."

"I can't help you there," she said. "My clients have the same confidentiality protection as yours, you know. Anyhow, sure, I'd be happy to see her. We should do it soon. With these things, time is of the essence. How's tomorrow morning? Say around eleven?"

"Let's make it a date," I said. "I'll call Sharon right now, and if tomorrow at eleven won't work for her, I'll get back to you. Otherwise, I'll bring her to your office."

"I'll be waiting in the lobby for you," she said. "It'll be nice to see you again."

When I called Sharon back and told her that I'd set up an appointment for her at eleven the next morning, she said, "Boy, you did that fast. Before I could change my mind and chicken out, right?"

"I think it's important," I said. "Can you come to my office? I'll take you over there, introduce you."

"I'm a big girl," Sharon said. "You don't need to hold my hand."

"I'd like to," I said.

She laughed. "A woman would be a fool to refuse an offer like that. I'll take the morning off and be at your office — when? Ten?"

"Ten or ten thirty," I said. "Tally's office is on Albany Street, a five-minute cab ride from Copley Square."

"This is all way above the call of duty, Brady," she said. "I do appreciate it."

I cleared my throat. "I saw Wayne today."

Sharon blew out a quick breath. It hissed in the phone. "Really," she finally said. "Why didn't you tell me this when we talked before?"

"I'm sorry," I said. "I was focused on getting you together with Tally."

"Is he all right?"

"Yes, he's okay. I told him what happened to Ken."

She said nothing.

"He's dropped out of school," I said. "He's living in a little house on the outskirts of Websterville. He seems to be . . . he's okay." I wasn't going to tell her that Wayne fled in his car when I knocked on his door, or that when he came back, he pointed a pistol at me.

"So what's he doing?"

"For work, you mean? I don't know."

"Back to the drugs, huh?"

"What about drugs?"

I heard Sharon blow out a breath. "He got busted for selling drugs when he was in high school. He was on probation for eighteen months. This was a few years after Ken and I split. We blamed ourselves."

I remembered the shiny Navigator that pulled up in front of Wayne's house, and the parties at Wayne's house, and the ketamine in Ken's hotel room. Obvious connections. "I don't know if he's into drugs or not" was what I said to Sharon.

"Did you tell him I've been trying to reach him?"

"Yes. He got your messages. He doesn't want to talk to you. I'm sorry."

"No," she said. "I knew that. I just don't understand why."

"I think Wayne has a lot of complicated feelings about both of you," I said. "You and Ken, I mean, and your divorce, and the reasons for it, or what he imagines the reasons were."

"What reasons?" she asked.

"He thinks Ken was abusive to you."

"Abusive?"

"Mentally," I said. "Emotionally."

Sharon chuckled. "Aren't we all? I mean, isn't that one of the usual dynamics in a marriage? A certain degree of — I don't know what to call it — psychological abuse, I suppose, going in both directions? Both partners sometimes wanting to hurt each other?"

I thought of my marriage with Gloria. It was the only marriage I'd experienced. All the others I had just observed.

I didn't think abusiveness was a factor in our marriage, or in our divorce. Maybe I was remembering it selectively.

"I guess it's not uncommon," I said. "In failed marriages, anyway."

"Kids misinterpret what they see and hear," said Sharon. "Ken and I had our problems, obviously. There was a lot of conflict and tension, no doubt about it. I mean, we did get divorced. I can see how Wayne would think that Ken was abusive to me." She paused. "I suppose, in a way, he was. And I was probably abusive to him, too. I mean, one of the reasons I wanted to get divorced was to separate that stuff from the kids' lives before it scarred them." She blew out a breath. "Sounds like we were too late. Something else to feel guilty about, huh?"

"It's something else you can talk about

with Tally," I said.

"That's not really connected to Ken's murder."

"In your head," I said, "everything's connected."

"You're right about that," she said. "I can't tell you how it feels, having a child who refuses to speak to me."

"I can imagine," I said. I was thinking of Billy. "Anyway, you've got Ellen."

"Yes," she said. "Thank God for Ellen. She keeps me almost sane. Well, Brady Coyne. Thank you for all of this. I'll see you in the morning."

"Get some sleep."

"Ha," she said.

I was in bed with my shoulders propped up against my pillows and my tattered copy of my bedtime book, *Moby-Dick,* resting on my lap. Melville, digressing again, had devoted an entire chapter to the subject of the tail of the sperm whale. He had a great deal to say about the power and size and functions of this part of the whale's anatomy, some of it marginally interesting, and after several thousands of words, he wrote, "The more I consider this mighty tail, the more do I deplore my inability to express it."

That's how I feel about it, too, I thought.

Then the phone on my bedside table rang.

I shut the book, picked up the phone, and said, "Hey."

"Hey, yourself," said Alex. "Reading *Moby-Dick*?"

"It's scary," I said, "how you know things like that."

"I do know a lot," she said.

"You know way too much."

"Do I threaten you?"

"Only in the most interesting ways."

"Ho, ho," she said.

"Did you have a good day?"

"I spent all day trying to write," said Alex.

"That's what writers do, isn't it?"

"Some writers actually do write."

"You saying you had a bad day at the keyboard?"

"I'm saying I had a typical day," she said. "Maybe something salvageable came out of it. I'll have a better idea when I look at it tomorrow. Right now, it feels like I wrote nothing but crap. How about you? What'd you do today?"

"I had some minor adventures," I said.

"Your cases."

"Yes."

"Which you can't talk about."

"Right," I said. "Sorry."

"That's all right," she said. "I'm used to

it. Probably boring anyway."

"Oh, definitely boring. Billy and Gwen are coming for supper on Saturday, by the way. I hope that's okay."

"It's great," she said. "It'll be nice to see your Billy again. He was just a kid last time I saw him. So what do you think? *Is* Gwen his girlfriend?"

"You'll see for yourself. Then you can tell me. We'll have pizza and beer."

"I love pizza and beer. Sausage. Mushrooms." I heard her yawn. "Sleepy Alex," she murmured. "I just called to say good night to my honey."

"Good night, babe."

"Sleep tight, swee'ie."

"See you Friday, huh?" I asked.

"Before you know it, darlin'. Mmm. Hug and kiss, 'kay?"

"Back atcha," I said.

SEVENTEEN

Julie buzzed me on my office console a little before ten thirty on Thursday morning. "Your appointment is here," she said.

"Sharon Nichols?"

"Correct."

I hired Julie when I opened my law practice. She was my first and only secretary. Much of the communication that passed between us was unspoken. We read each other closely and accurately — tone, inflection, body language. No words needed.

"Why don't you like her?" I asked into the phone. "Or can't you talk?"

"That's right," she said. "She just arrived, and she's standing right here."

"She's my client, for God's sake," I said. "I'm not dating her."

"I've heard that before."

I found myself smiling. "Just bring her in, will you?"

"Certainly, sir."

Oh-oh. When Julie called me sir, it meant she was upset — and when Julie was upset, I had learned, it was a sound policy to try to figure out why and then do something about it.

When she opened my office door and held it for Sharon, I understood. Sharon was wearing a narrow black skirt that stopped just above her pretty knees, with an off-white linen jacket over a tight-fitting red sweater that left little about her upper body to the imagination. Some tricky makeup emphasized her big eyes and good cheekbones and expressive mouth.

Julie, I guessed, thought Sharon looked slutty and dangerous, but that was Julie. I thought Sharon looked classy, in fact, and quite beautiful, although behind her eyes and around the corners of her mouth I saw tension and sadness and fatigue.

Julie, ever protective of my current relationship, in the present case with Alex, assumed that Sharon had dressed for my benefit.

I stood up, came around from behind my desk, and held out my hand to Sharon, who gave me a quick, knowing little smile and a hearty, formal handshake.

"Would you like coffee?" Julie asked.

"No, thank you," I said. "We'll be leaving

in a minute."

"As you wish," said Julie.

After Julie closed the door, Sharon sat in one of my client chairs, and I resumed my seat behind my desk.

"She doesn't like me," Sharon said.

"She thinks you've got designs on me," I said.

"Oh, dear."

"Don't worry about Julie," I said. "She thinks every attractive woman is a threat to my virtue. Take it as a compliment." I looked at my watch. "It's a fifteen-minute walk or a five-minute cab ride to Tally's office over on Albany Street. Your pick."

"Oh, let's walk," she said. "It's a gorgeous day out there."

"We can have lunch after you're finished with Tally."

She smiled. "That would be nice, but I told my partner I'd be at the shop by two. Now I wish I'd taken the whole day."

"Another time," I said. I stood up. "We better get going."

It was an April-in-Paris spring morning in Boston. In the vacant lots and in the little side gardens and in the patches of yard in front of the buildings along Mass Ave, the forsythia and honeysuckle were blooming aromatically. The new leaves on the maple trees were lime green, the size of mouse ears. The easterly breeze that came wafting in from the harbor smelled like freshly turned earth and spring rain. The sun was warm on our faces, and puffy white clouds drifted harmlessly across the high blue sky. It was the sort of morning that made you want to grab the hand of the first pretty girl you saw and go skipping down the sidewalk.

I managed to resist the impulse.

Tally Whyte, as promised, was waiting for us in the lobby of the square brick building at 720 Albany Street that housed the OCME, the Office of the Chief Medical Examiner for the Commonwealth of Massachusetts.

Tally was a tall, lanky gal somewhere in her thirties. She reminded me of the actress Laura Dern. She was quite pretty in an angular, interesting way, with big expressive eyes and high cheekbones and a tangle of blondish hair.

When Sharon and I walked through the front door, Tally flashed her great warm smile, came over, gave me a hug, then held out her hand to Sharon. "I'm Tally," she said.

Sharon took her hand. "I'm Sharon. Sharon Nichols."

Tally kept hold of Sharon's hand. "Let's

talk. Come on. My office is this way. You'll have to meet Penny. She's my dog. Nice to see you again, Brady. Thanks for bringing her over." She tugged Sharon toward a door off the lobby in a cloud of happy chatter.

"I'll wait for you here," I called to Sharon.

"You don't need to," she said over her shoulder. "I left my car at Alewife and took the T in. I'll just hop back on the subway when we're done."

"No, I'll be here," I said.

I found a comfortable sofa and a stack of magazines on a side table, and in the pleasant sitting area off the lobby, it was easy to forget that this building was the place where the Commonwealth's medical examiner and his assistants performed postmortem examinations on homicide victims and, in fact, on anybody whose death was suspicious or unexplained or unattended. Somewhere behind the doors that opened into the lobby was the refrigerated room where dead bodies lay in their body bags on stainless-steel tables.

I found the *Sports Illustrated* special springtime issue with the annual Major League Baseball forecast, and I was halfway through the section on the American League before I realized that the magazine I was reading was over a year old. The winners and losers and final standings these articles were predicting were history.

I read the forecasts anyway, and compared the *SI* experts' prophecies with how I remembered the baseball season had actually played out. Thankfully, there had been many surprises that the prognosticators failed to anticipate. What fun would it be if all the teams performed as expected?

Sharon and Tally came back into the lobby a little over an hour later. Penny, Tally's three-legged German shepherd, hobbled along beside them. The two women were walking slowly, their shoulders almost touching. Tally was tilting her head toward Sharon, talking softly to her, and Sharon was looking down at the floor, nodding at what Tally was saying to her.

When they came over to where I was sitting, I looked up at them as if I hadn't expected them and said, "Hey. You're back." I reached out and gave Penny's muzzle a scratch.

Sharon smiled. "You waited." Her eyes were puffy, and I guessed she'd been crying.

"I didn't want to walk back alone," I said.

Tally touched Sharon's arm. "Next week, then?"

"Same time, same place," Sharon said.

"I'll be here."

"You've got my numbers if you ever . . ."

"Yes," Sharon said. "I can't tell you how much I appreciate it."

"It's going to be fine," Tally said. "Really."

Sharon nodded and smiled. "I'm beginning to believe you." She turned to me. "She's amazing."

"I know," I said.

Sharon gave Tally a hug and Penny a pat, and then we walked outside.

"I can't talk you into lunch?" I asked.

"I'd love to," Sharon said, "but I really must get back. Another time, I hope."

"You have an appointment next week?"

"Yes," she said. "Maybe we can have lunch then."

"Let's plan on it," I said. "So it went well with Tally?"

"You know," she said, "I understood that I was sad and frightened and depressed, but I didn't realize how guilty I was feeling. I was being smothered by my guilt. About what happened to Ken, I mean. Tally helped me understand that I was blaming myself, beating myself up, as if I was the one who killed him. She got me talking, and the next thing I knew, I was telling her how it was my fault, and then we talked about that, and then I cried for a while, and pretty soon it was like I was standing up and straightening my spine and shrugging some giant weight off of my shoulders. She didn't really explain anything to me. She just asked me a few questions, and I explained it to her. I mean, I knew it all the time, but I was blocking it out. That's how guilt works, Tally said."

"I'm glad you're feeling better," I said.

"Tally says I should expect those awful feelings to keep coming back for a while," she said. "Lying awake at night, the dreams, the glooms, all that. Now I've got some ways to deal with them. She gave me some tools. They give me power. Now I believe I can control those feelings. Plus, I'm going to keep seeing her. She's quite wonderful." Sharon put her arm through mine and held it tight against her side. "For the first time since it happened, I actually feel as if I might become normal again. I can't tell you how good that feels."

Provided, I thought, *you don't end up going to trial for Ken's murder. That might tend to slow down your recovery.*

We were shutting down our office computers, closing the blinds, cleaning out the coffee urn, all the things we do at the end of a workday, when Roger Horowitz came blustering into the office.

Julie smiled at him. "You're too late," she said. "We just threw out the dregs of today's coffee."

"Well, damn," he said. "Everyone knows Coyne's office is the place to go for coffee dregs."

"How about a Coke?" asked Julie. "Bottle of water?"

"I only got a minute," he said. "Benetti's double-parked in front of the library." He looked at me and jerked his head at my office.

I nodded, and he followed me in.

He sat on the sofa. I took the upholstered chair across from him. "What?" I asked.

"Your client," he said. "We gotta talk to her."

"Interrogate her, you mean?"

He shrugged. "Call it whatever you want. Ask her a few questions, sure. Benetti was all for sending the troops to her house with handcuffs, sirens screaming, and hauling her in. My idea is this. Why don't we meet here in your office, your home field, you might say, tomorrow morning?"

"That's very considerate of you," I said. "Surprising."

"Yeah," he said. "I surprise myself sometimes. Benetti and I don't see this case the same way, which isn't such a bad thing, but it causes some disagreement on tactics. Anyway, I'm senior in the partnership, so we're doing it my way. Can you have Mrs. Nichols here at ten tomorrow morning, do you think?"

"Sure I can," I said. "You want to tell me what it's all about?"

"I absolutely do not," he said.

"You come up with something you think is new evidence on this case?"

"Don't push me, Coyne, or I'll defer to Benetti. She's ready to dust off the water-board. I think there's some girl thing going on between her and your client. A pair of nice-looking women like the two of them, you know what I'm saying?"

"I have no idea what you're talking about," I said, "but you better keep your partner in line. Whisper the word 'harassment' into her ear."

Horowitz grinned and pushed himself to his feet. "We'll be here at ten. We'll bring the recorders, you take care of the coffee."

I stood up and held out my hand to him. "Seriously," I said. "I appreciate it. Whatever people are saying about you, don't listen to them. You're not such a bad person."

"For God's sake," he said, "don't tell anybody."

EIGHTEEN

Sharon showed up in my office a little after nine thirty on Friday morning. We went into one of my conference rooms, sat side by side at the rectangular table, and sipped coffee.

She wore tailored slacks and a blouse that was buttoned to her throat. She looked tired and edgy. "Your secretary was actually pleasant to me," she said. "Smiled, asked how I was doing, Mrs. Nichols, if I wanted coffee. I asked her to call me Sharon."

"She probably won't," I said. "She likes to keep the distinction between client and friend clearer than I do."

She nodded and took a sip of her coffee. "So when you called last night, you said you didn't know what was up. Can you tell me now?"

"I still don't know," I said. "I told you last night not to worry about it. Did you obey me?"

She rolled her eyes. "Oh, sure. You know, the things Tally and I talked about yesterday, in her office, with her there, her calm, warm self, Penny snoozing peacefully at our feet, sunshine coming in through the window, it all made sense, and I really thought I was suddenly and magically okay again. But last night? I'm here to tell you, Tally was right. It's not going to be that easy. I stared up at the ceiling for a long time, wondering what the detectives wanted to ask me." She shook her head. "I came up with some pretty wild possibilities."

"Like what?" I asked.

She shook her head. "Now, in the daylight, I can see that they were all stupid. Things look different in the middle of the night."

"Nothing plausible, then?"

"Well," she said, "if the murder weapon showing up in my kitchen dishwasher or under my bed is plausible, okay, then. Or if somebody said they heard me and Ken talking or yelling or something in his hotel room that night, then, yes, my craziness was plausible."

"Ken was dead when you got there, right?"

Sharon frowned. "Are you questioning that?"

"If somebody could've heard you and him . . ."

"That's my point," she said. "They couldn't have, because he was already dead. So it's stupid of me to invent the idea that somebody heard something, or thought they did, and then to obsess on it — but it's what I did instead of sleeping."

"Maybe you should see your doctor," I said, "get a prescription for sleeping pills."

"I'll run that idea past Tally," she said. "I want to get better so I can sleep. I don't think it works the other way around. I'm not sure if sleeping pills would help the process."

There came a discreet tap on the door, and then it opened, and Julie stepped inside. Marcia Benetti and Roger Horowitz came in right behind her. Benetti had a big leather bag slung over her shoulder. Horowitz was carrying an attaché case.

I stood up and shook hands with both of them.

They both nodded at Sharon, who remained seated.

"I'll bring coffee," Julie said, and she walked out of the room.

Horowitz and Benetti sat across from me and Sharon at the conference table. Benetti took her digital recorder out of her bag and put it on the table. Then she reached back into the bag and came out with a stenographer's notebook, which she flipped open and put on the table beside her.

Horowitz slid a manila folder out of his attaché case, put it on the table in front of him, and placed his clasped hands on top of it.

We looked across the table at each other.

Benetti cleared her throat and glanced at Horowitz, and that's when Julie shouldered open the door and came in carrying a silver tray with a carafe of coffee, two bone china cups with matching saucers, and milk and sugar in little silver pitchers. Our very best tea service.

She put the tray on a side table, poured coffee into the two cups, and raised her eyebrows at Horowitz and Benetti.

Horowitz said, "Black," and Benetti said, "Just one sugar, thank you."

Julie served each of them, then refilled Sharon's mug and mine. Then she slipped out of the room and shut the door behind her.

Horowitz sipped his coffee. "Okay," he said. "Let's get started."

Marcia Benetti hit a button on the recorder, said, "Testing," set it in the middle of the table, and said, "Say something, please, each of you."

I said, "Here we are again," and Sharon

said, "I wonder why."

Benetti replayed what we'd said. It sounded fine to me. "Okay," she said. "That's loud and clear. We can get started." She cleared her throat and fixed her gaze on Sharon. "Just so you understand, Mrs. Nichols, anything you say here today can be used against you in a court of law. You have the right to refuse to answer any question. You have the right to have your attorney present." Benetti smiled at me. "Which, of course, you do. Do you have any questions about this?"

"No," said Sharon. "I understand."

"Attorney Coyne?"

"Are you planning to take my client into custody?" I asked.

Horowtiz shook his head. "Not at this time."

"So why are you Mirandizing her?"

"We are being scrupulous about protecting her rights," he said. "We thought you'd appreciate it."

"We do," I said.

"Means she better tell the truth, though," he said.

"We get that," I said.

Horowitz said, "Okay, for the record, I'm Homicide Detective Roger Horowitz, Massachusetts State Police. My colleague Sergeant Marcia Benetti is here with me. We're in the law office of attorney Brady L. Coyne with him and his client, ah, Sharon Nichols. It's Friday morning, ten oh six, April the twenty-seventh." He slipped some papers out of the manila folder. "What I got here," he said, looking at Sharon but speaking for the benefit of the recorder, "is a copy of Mrs. Nichols's divorce agreement. I made copies for all of us. You want to take a look at them?"

"We certainly do," I said.

Horowitz pushed two paper-clipped stacks of paper across the table to us. Sharon pulled one stack in front of her. I took the other one and flipped through it. There were fourteen pages altogether. They included the four articles that specified, defined, and enumerated the "Parties," the "Recitals," the "Covenants of the husband and wife," and the "Interpretation and execution," followed by six exhibits, A through F: "Custody and parenting," "Alimony, child support, and college costs," "Taxes," "Division of personal and real property," "Insurance," and Exhibit F, "Miscellaneous." Standard stuff.

I turned to Sharon. "Okay?"

She shrugged. "I guess so. It's a copy of my divorce agreement, all right."

I looked across the table at Horowitz. "Okay," I said.

"Mrs. Nichols," he said, "that's your signature there on the bottom of page five?"

"It is," she said. "On the next page you can see where two notary publics signed it, authenticating that it's my signature and the other one is my husband's."

I smiled at her mild sarcasm. I was glad to see it. It meant that Horowitz hadn't intimidated her.

"Thank you for pointing that out," Horowitz said. He turned to Benetti. "You want to take it from here?"

"I do," she said. She thumbed through a few pages of the divorce agreement. "Let's look at Exhibit B, paragraph one, where it says, 'The husband shall pay child support to the wife.' " She looked up at us. "Got it?"

I nodded, and then Sharon said, "Yes."

Benetti said, "It goes on to say that the child support ends when the children are emancipated, and it defines that as when they've finished college or reached the age of twenty-two, whichever comes first. Is that right?" She cocked her head and looked at Sharon.

Sharon turned to me. Before Horowitz and Benetti arrived, I'd told Sharon that she should answer no questions without my assent.

"That's right," I said to Benetti. "It's right there in plain English, or as plain as English can be in a legal document."

Benetti looked at me, gave me a quick smile, then turned back to Sharon. "How old are your children, Mrs. Nichols?"

Sharon looked at me.

"Go ahead," I said.

"Wayne's twenty-two, and Ellen is twenty-five."

"They're both in school?"

"Ellen's in graduate school," Sharon said. "Getting her master's at BU. Wayne was, up until . . ." She looked at me.

"Last fall," I said. "He dropped out."

"So you've been getting child support checks every month from your ex-husband since your divorce, is that right?"

"That's right," Sharon said.

"In the amount specified in this agreement?"

"We renegotiated the numbers when Ellen entered college," Sharon said. "To reflect the realities of college costs, which had changed a lot since we first signed our agreement. After she graduated, we negotiated them again."

"You're paying Wayne's college bills?"

251

"Yes," said Sharon.

"With the child support money your ex-husband sends you."

"That's right."

"Your checks come regularly?"

Sharon shrugged. "Pretty much. Ken missed a few payments here and there. I called him and reminded him, and they started coming again."

"Reminded him?" asked Benetti.

Sharon smiled. "I told him I'd turn it over to my lawyer, and the checks started coming again."

" 'Threatened' would be the word for it, then, right?"

Sharon shrugged. "Sure. I guess so."

"Did the checks stop when Wayne dropped out?"

"No," Sharon said.

"Did you and your husband talk about it?"

I touched Sharon's arm and spoke softly into her ear. "Tell me."

"No," she whispered to me. "I didn't know he'd dropped out, and I don't think Ken did, either. If he did, we never talked about it."

"The answer is no," I said to Benetti. "They did not talk about it. They didn't know their son had dropped out."

"Now, about Ellen," said Benetti, "she's on her own?"

"That's right," said Sharon. "She's taken out student loans, worked part-time. Ken and I haven't helped her financially since she graduated."

"Okay, Mrs. Nichols," Benetti said. "Now I'm looking at paragraph four, same exhibit. Alimony. Your husband — your ex-husband, I should say — has been paying you alimony all these years, is that right?"

"That's right," Sharon said.

"Has this number been renegotiated?"

"No."

"So every month since this agreement was approved, you've gotten monthly checks for alimony and child support."

"One check, actually," said Sharon. "He lumped the child support and the alimony together."

"You've been financially dependent on him. Your ex-husband."

"I wouldn't —"

"Don't answer that," I said. To Benetti I said, "The numbers are right there. You can judge them."

"Let me put it this way," Benetti said. "Did what your husband pay you in alimony and child support adequately cover your children's college expenses and your own

253

living expenses?"

Sharon looked at me, and I nodded.

"Not really," she said. "I've always had to work."

"Did you ever ask him to increase his payments?"

"We already stipulated that the child support was renegotiated," I said.

"How about since then?" said Benetti. "That was quite a few years ago. Alimony or child support?"

"No," said Sharon. "Well, yes. The child support. When Ellen graduated from college."

"Other than that?"

"No," Sharon said. "It stayed the same. We didn't talk about changing it."

"The subject was never even mentioned? You never complained to him about how hard it was to make ends meet? You never told him that you and the kids were struggling, or that college costs were skyrocketing, or how hard you were working just to keep your head above water?"

"You're being argumentative," I said.

"You can't object," said Benetti. "This isn't a courtroom. There's no judge."

"Well," I said, "I'm telling you, I do object." To Sharon I said, "Don't answer those questions."

"I don't mind," she said.

"No," I said. "Please don't." I looked at Benetti. "My client answered your question. She and her ex-husband did not discuss or argue about finances, and I object to your browbeating her."

"I'll remind you again, Mr. Coyne," she said, "this isn't a courtroom, and you can't object to something just because you don't want to hear it."

"Okay," I said, "but we don't have to sit here and pretend that this wild stuff you're throwing around should be taken seriously, either."

Benetti shrugged.

"You have nothing except some supposition, then," I said. I set my forearms on the table and leaned forward. I looked at Horowitz, then at Benetti. "If this is all you've got," I said, "this unsubstantiated implication that my client and her ex-husband might have discussed family finances, might even have had a disagreement about money, which, if it did happen, which my client says it didn't, would only make them just like everybody else — if that's what you've got, then we're done here."

Horowitz grinned. He was leaning back in his chair with his arms folded across his chest. He was enjoying the show.

Benetti smiled across the table at me. "We're not quite done yet," she said. She looked at Sharon. "Do you know who the beneficiary of your ex-husband's will is?"

I touched Sharon's elbow. "Don't answer," I said.

She looked at me. "But I don't —"

I held up my hand, and she stopped.

I looked at Benetti. "I bet you already know the answer to your question."

She smiled. "In fact, I do." She leafed through some papers and held up a thick document. "The Last Will and Testament of Kenneth Roland Nichols." She pushed it across the table to me.

It was nearly half an inch thick, held together by one of those big spring-loaded paper clips. I glanced through it. It was, of course, a photocopy, and it included not only Ken's Last Will and Testament but also his Declaration, his Durable Power of Attorney for Health Care, his General Power of Attorney, and his Trust Agreement. The boilerplate was similar to what my clients and I worked with all the time.

It had been properly signed, dated, and notarized. I didn't bother studying the details. I pushed it back. "It appears to be a copy of his will, all right," I said to Benetti. "What about it?"

"Mr. Nichols had it rewritten last October," she said. "You can see the date on it." She looked at Sharon. "Did you know about that?"

"Stop that," I said quickly, before Sharon could say anything. "Don't answer," I said to her. I turned back to Benetti. "This is relevant why?"

"Your ex-husband," Benetti said to Sharon, "didn't appear to have much of an estate. In fact, he owed quite a bit of money."

"That doesn't surprise me," Sharon said.

"Mr. Nichols's father is a different story," Benetti said. "The elder Nichols is in poor health, and he happens to be extremely wealthy. I'm talking several million dollars." She looked at me. "Up until last October, when Mrs. Nichols was the primary beneficiary of her former husband's will, she'd have been first in line for the elder Mr. Nichols's estate if her husband was deceased."

Sharon was frowning and shaking her head.

"Do you understand what I'm saying?" Benetti asked her.

"You're saying that Ken wrote me out of his will."

"That's right."

"So there'd be no money coming to me if he died."

"As far as it goes," said Benetti, "that's right. His children are his cobeneficiaries, and, in fact, they are also the contingent beneficiaries of the elder Mr. Nichols's will."

I cleared my throat. "This is interesting," I said, "and we appreciate your sharing this solid evidence that since she's no longer his heir, my client would have no motive to murder her ex-husband. Or was there some other point you thought you were making?"

Benetti looked at Sharon. "So how do you feel about being written out of your husband's will, Mrs. Nichols?"

"Stop that right now," I said. I turned to Horowitz, who'd been sitting there all this time with his arms folded across his chest and a bemused smile playing around his mouth and eyes. "Tell her to back off," I said to him, "or we're ending this right now."

"Back off." Horowitz grinned. "Or they'll end it right now."

Benetti returned his grin, then turned to me. "We haven't quite exhausted this subject," she said. She flipped through some documents. When she found the page she wanted, she frowned at it for a minute, then looked up. "Back to the divorce agreement.

Let's take a look at Exhibit E. Insurance. It's on page thirteen, paragraph four."

Sharon and I turned to page thirteen, paragraph four.

"Got it?" asked Benetti.

We nodded.

"Mrs. Nichols," said Benetti, "you want to read paragraph four out loud for us?"

"Mrs. Nichols absolutely does *not* want to read paragraph four out loud," I said. "As you have pointed out, this isn't a courtroom. We can all read paragraph four for ourselves."

Benetti grinned across the table at me. "For the record," she said, "I will read paragraph four out loud." She cleared her throat. "Here it is. It says, 'The husband shall maintain his current life insurance policies for the benefit of the wife and dependent children. The issue of the husband's obligation to maintain life insurance for the wife after the children's emancipation may be reviewed upon such emancipation.' " Benetti looked up at Sharon. "So did he?"

Sharon frowned. "Did who what?"

"Did your husband — your former husband — maintain his life insurance?"

Sharon turned to me.

I shrugged. It was a question of fact that

could easily be checked. "Go ahead," I said to her. "Answer the question."

Sharon looked at Marcia Benetti. "I don't know," she said.

"You don't know? Really?"

Sharon shrugged. "Really. I never asked Ken about his life insurance, and he never mentioned it. I assume he maintained it. If he didn't, he'd've been breaking the law, wouldn't he?"

"So you believed that he continued to invest in life insurance for which you and your children were the beneficiaries, even though he wrote you out of his will. Is that right?"

"I didn't know he'd written me out of his will," Sharon said, "but as far as keeping up the insurance goes, yes, I guess so. I really never thought much about it. It didn't seem, um, relevant to my life. I mean, that was in our agreement so that if something happened to Ken, the kids' education would still be covered." She turned to me. "Isn't that right, Brady?"

"It's standard in most divorce agreements," I said. "A way of guaranteeing that the husband's obligations to the dependent children are fulfilled even in the event of his death."

"So," Benetti said to Sharon, "as far as

you know, your husband was carrying up-to-date life insurance in your name at the time of his death, is that right?"

Sharon shrugged. "As far as I know. In my name and my kids' names, I assume. Like I said, I haven't really thought about it."

"Do you know how much coverage he had, in your name, payable to you upon his death? Money that, in fact, you are now entitled to?"

"No." Sharon shook her head. "I have no idea."

"Really?"

"She answered your question," I said.

Benetti gave me a quick smile, then shifted her gaze to Sharon. "In fact," she said, "your ex-husband's life insurance policies, of which there are three, are all payable to you. You are the primary beneficiary. Your children are contingent beneficiaries, meaning they'd get the money only if you were dead. Did you know that?"

"I might have," Sharon said. "I honestly don't remember. It's not something I've ever given much thought to."

Benetti said, "Does one-point-nine million dollars sound familiar, Mrs. Nichols?"

Sharon said nothing. I glanced sideways at her. She was looking down at the sheets of paper on the table in front of her, avoiding Benetti's hard look. I read tension — or maybe it was anger — in the set of her jaw.

I cleared my throat. "This has been a lot of fun," I said, "but now we really are done. On behalf of my client, I'd like to thank both of you for dropping by this morning and sharing your fascinating, and very creative, speculations about your murder investigation with us. Now, if you don't have anything new you'd like to talk about . . ."

"I'd just like a clarification," said Marcia Benetti.

"Of course you would," I said. "Go ahead."

"Mrs. Nichols maintains that she didn't know what Mr. Nichols's life insurance was worth, or that she was the sole beneficiary. Correct?"

"Your recording will confirm that she said that, I believe," I said.

"She has also told us that she and her ex-husband did not even discuss, never mind argue about, finances."

"She said that, too," I said.

"She further said she didn't know that Mr. Nichols had changed his will."

"That's right."

"And Mrs. Nichols," said Benetti, looking hard at Sharon, "you understand that what you've said to us here can be used in a court of law, and that if you lied to us today, it would be tantamount to perjury."

Sharon nodded. "I understand that, yes."

"I have just one more question for you, then," Benetti said.

Sharon looked at me. I nodded.

"Mrs. Nichols," said Benetti, "did you know that your husband — your ex-husband — had requested some documents from his insurance company that would enable him to cash out his life insurance policies, and that if he had not died, he would apparently have done so?"

Sharon shook her head. "Cash out?"

"Terminate them for their cash value."

"So he'd get the money," Sharon said, "and I would no longer be insured? Is that what you mean?"

Benetti nodded. "Luckily he was killed before he could complete the paperwork."

"Luckily?" I asked. I looked at Horowitz.

He grinned and shrugged.

"I didn't know anything about this," Sharon said.

"Please think carefully about your answer," Benetti said.

"She said no," I said.

"Could he do that?" Sharon asked me. "I mean, the divorce agreement says he's supposed to maintain his life insurance."

"The insurance company doesn't know about divorce agreements," I said. "They'd do it, unless your lawyer intervened."

"How could he if we didn't know?" she asked.

"Exactly," I said. "So he'd do it, and he'd get the cash, and then it would be too late." I looked at Benetti. "Your question's been answered. My client knew nothing about this. Is there anything else?"

Benetti glanced at Horowitz. He shrugged. "Okay, then," she said, "we're concluding this interview now. Thanks for your co-operation." She looked at her wristwatch. "It's, um, twelve minutes after eleven." She reached out to the recorder and snapped it off.

Horowitz slid his paper back into his manila folder, stuck the folder into his attaché case, and stood up. Marcia Benetti put the recorder into her bag, and she stood up, too.

Sharon and I also stood up, and we reached across the table and shook hands with the detectives. Then I opened my office door and held it for them. I followed them out into my reception area. Sharon remained in my office.

"You'll be hearing from us," Horowitz said.

"I hope you're pursuing some other avenues in your investigation besides this one," I said.

"Thanks for the reminder," he said. "We appreciate your guidance."

"You check out that license plate I gave you?"

"Was I supposed to submit a report to you?" he asked.

"I do have an interest in this case."

"You take care of your client," he said. "We'll take care of our investigation."

"Good deal," I said.

After they left, I went back into my office. Sharon was standing by the big window, looking down onto the courtyard outside the Copley Plaza Hotel. She looked up when I closed the door. "Are they gone?"

I nodded. "Are you okay?"

She rolled her eyes. "My head's spinning."

"It's a lot of pressure. You handled it well."

"So what was that all about?"

"What part of it?"

"Right there at the end," she said, "reminding me that what I said could be used against me, and cautioning me about lying, and smiling at Detective Horowitz as if she'd caught me red-handed."

"Nothing to worry about," I said. "Assuming you told the truth."

"Well, I did," she said.

"Okay, then. Good. So you're all right, huh?"

"I'm fine," she said. "It was easy. When you've got a clear conscience and you tell the truth, it's pretty unstressful."

"I'm glad," I said. "So tell me. If the detectives look into your finances, will they find unpaid bills, maxed-out credit cards, gambling debts, anything like that?"

Sharon shrugged. "I'm carrying a balance on two credit cards. That's about it. Why? Is that bad?"

"If you owed a lot of money," I said, "it would make murdering Ken for his insurance, and doing it now, before he could cash it in, a believable motive."

"I guess it would," she said, "but I don't owe that much. Six or seven thousand on one card, a couple thousand on the other. I pay every month. I'm not behind on anything. I'm getting by."

I nodded. "Okay. Good."

"So now what?" she asked.

"Now," I said, "we go back to living our lives. Assuming they can't come up with somebody who can testify that they heard you and Ken arguing about money, or somebody who says you were telling them about how you were going to spend his life insurance, then one of their theories was destroyed here this morning."

"That I killed Ken for money."

I nodded.

"I didn't, you know."

I nodded.

"I didn't kill him for money," she said. "I didn't kill him, period."

"I know," I said.

"I mean," she said, "how stupid would that be? To hang around the hotel where a hundred people could see me and testify I was there, and then go up to his room and kill him, and then hang around and call my lawyer, for God's sake, and wait there in his room for the police to show up? And do it for his life insurance? I mean, is that not the world's most obvious motive for murder? Do they think I'm completely clueless?"

"Most murderers are utterly clueless," I said. "In fact, the scenario you describe is quite plausible."

"Except for the fact that I didn't do it."

"Except for the fact," I said, "that you didn't confess to doing it."

"Most clueless people would just confess," she said.

I nodded. "Happens that way all the time."

"Well," she said, "I'm not clueless, but I do not have anything to confess." She started to stand up. Then she sat down again. "Oh. I remembered something."

"What's that?"

"Clem. You've been asking about some friend of Ken's named Clem, and I've been racking my brain, and I finally came up with something."

"You remember this Clem? Salt-and-pepper beard, receding hairline?"

"I have no idea what he looks like. Maybe it's not the man you're looking for. It was a long time ago. Ken had this old friend from college days named Sean Clements."

"Did Ken call him Clem?"

She shrugged. "I'm not sure. I just flashed on his last name last night. I don't think I met him more than a couple of times, and like I said, it was a long time ago."

"Any idea where Sean Clements is now?" I asked. "Is he a veterinarian?"

"Last I heard," Sharon said, "he was teaching at BU, I think it was. Or BC. I get them confused. History, I think."

"When was that?"

"Back when Ken and I were still married. Are you going to tell the police about him?"

"Probably ought to make sure it's the

right guy first," I said. "I'm glad you remembered."

"Me, too." She stood up. "I've really got to get going. I'm supposed to be at the shop this afternoon."

"Will you be all right?"

She shrugged. "I don't know. This — what we just did, the fact that those detectives really seem to think I did it, that they're trying to make a case against me — I don't think it's sunk in. Like the night I found Ken's body. I thought I was fine. I felt calm, in control, but pretty soon, wham, I was a basket case."

"Call Tally," I said.

"I already thought of that."

NINETEEN

I walked Sharon out through our reception area to the door, where we exchanged hugs. After she left, I went to Julie's desk. "I'd like to talk to a man named Sean Clements," I said. "He might be a history professor at BU or BC."

"Might?" Julie asked.

"That was a few years ago," I said. "Best I can do."

"BU or BC?"

"Maybe," I said.

I went into my office and fooled around with some paperwork, but my mind kept wandering back to Marcia Benetti's interrogation of Sharon, and Sharon's responses, and when I tried to be objective about it, it was hard not to take her seriously as a suspect. She had the means and the opportunity to murder Ken right from the beginning. She could easily have picked up a steak knife from one of the room-service trays in the corridor, and she was, of course, there in Ken's room around the time he was stabbed.

Now Horowitz and Benetti had come up with a motive. Ken's insurance money, nearly two million dollars, plus the fact that he was evidently planning to cash it in. That would make killing him a matter of both greed and urgency.

So instead of whacking away at my pile of paperwork, I sat there playing with scenarios and hypotheses, and after fifteen or twenty minutes, my console buzzed. I picked up the phone and said, "Yes?" and Julie said, "I've got Professor Sean Clements of the Emerson College history faculty on line two."

"Emerson, huh?"

"Tracked him down," said Julie.

"You're amazing," I said.

"And don't you forget it."

I hit the blinking button on the phone console and said, "Professor Clements?"

A deep voice with just the hint of a British accent said, "That's right. You're an attorney?"

"I am," I said. "Brady Coyne is my name."

"What does an attorney want with me?"

"I want to buy you a drink."

"Why should I have a drink with you?" he asked.

"I'd rather talk about it face-to-face," I said.

"Am I in some kind of trouble?"

"Nothing to worry about. Meet me at Remington's at three o'clock. You know Remington's, don't you?"

"I'm not meeting some random lawyer anywhere, no matter who's buying, if I don't know what his agenda is."

"I'm not that random," I said. "It's about Ken Nichols."

"Who?"

"Ken Nichols. The vet."

"I don't know any Ken Nichols."

While I was talking with Professor Sean Clements, I had googled Emerson College on my desktop computer and clicked my way to the faculty directory. I found Professor Sean Clements's name listed there, along with the courses he taught. Twentieth-Century American History Survey. The History of American Labor. The Utopians. The Great Awakening.

I clicked on his name, and his picture popped up on my screen. He had a broad forehead and a neatly trimmed beard, flecked with gray. He was the guy.

"You don't know Ken Nichols?" I asked him.

"Never heard of him."

"How about last Friday night. At the Beverly Suites Hotel in Natick."

"I don't like your tone, sir," he said. "I'm going to hang up now."

"Fine," I said. "You don't want to talk with me, I'll just give your name to Detective Horowitz. He's with the state police homicide division."

"Homicide," said Clements softly.

"Why are you lying to me?" I asked. "I saw you there. You saw me."

He blew a breath into the telephone. "Remington's at three, you said?"

"Know where it is?"

"I do," he said. "It's right around the corner. I'm supposed to be holding office hours until four, but I can slip out early. Okay. Three o'clock at Remington's, then." He paused. "You called me Clem."

"Isn't that what people call you?"

"Not since college," he said.

Friday turned out to be another glorious late-April day, and I was glad I'd walked to the office that morning, because now I could walk down Boylston Street from my office in Copley Square to Remington's, which was across from the Common almost to the corner of Tremont Street.

The afternoon sun was warm on the back of my neck, and the easterly breeze coming in off the ocean was soft and tasted of brine and seaweed. I was in no hurry, so I crossed over to Commonwealth Avenue, where robins were plucking worms from the squares of lawn in front of the brownstone apartment buildings. Daffodils and pansies blossomed in the sun, and beagles and terriers tugged old folks around on leashes, and kids wearing T-shirts and baggy shorts scooted along the sidewalks on their skateboards.

Ah, spring. Its arrival always erased the bleak leftovers of a grim winter. It was April, and the world was mud-luscious and puddle-wonderful, and when I listened hard, I imagined I could hear a goat-footed balloonman whistling far and wee.

I reminded myself again to call J. W. Jackson and Doc Adams and Charlie McDevitt and get some fishing plans etched in stone. Springtime in New England, the best time of year in the best part of the world to enjoy it, had a habit of slipping through my fingers before I'd had the chance to properly savor it. The best way to avoid that was to make plans with friends.

I cut diagonally across the Common and

walked into Remington's about ten after three. Professor Sean Clements — he was, indeed, the same fiftyish man with the dark, neatly trimmed beard and the high forehead whom Ken Nichols had called Clem that night in the Beverly Suites Hotel on Route 9 in Natick — was sitting at a table in the corner with a glass of draft beer in front of him.

I went over and sat down across from him.

He looked at me, frowned for a moment. "I remember you," he said. "You were with Ken at the hotel."

"So were you. Why did you lie to me?"

"I heard what happened. I didn't want to be involved."

"Why?"

He shrugged. "It had nothing to do with me."

At that moment, a waiter came to the table. "Can I get you something, sir?" he asked me.

I pointed at Clements's beer glass. "One of those."

"Michelob draft?"

I nodded. "Sure."

The waiter left. I looked at Clements. "So did you kill Ken Nichols?"

"No," he said. "Of course not."

"You were there. I saw you."

"I was there the night before it happened," he said. "I wasn't there on Saturday night. That's when it happened, according to the news reports."

"Where were you Saturday night?"

"I was at a faculty party at the home of my department chair in Wenham," he said. "Not that it's any of your business."

"Actually," I said, "it is my business. Sounds like you've got yourself a really neat alibi."

Professor Sean Clements shrugged. I wondered if his alibi would hold up.

"I'm going to have to give your name to the police," I said. "I'm sure they'll want to talk to you."

"Must you?"

"I'm an officer of the court," I said.

"Whatever the fuck that means."

The waiter came back and put a glass of beer on a coaster in front of me. I picked it up and took a sip.

I wiped the foam off my upper lip with the back of my wrist. "You and Ken seemed to be having some, um, conflict," I said to Clements. "You made a pistol with your hand and shot him with your forefinger."

"Yeah," said Clements. "Bang, bang. Sonofabitch owed me money."

"You shot him with your forefinger," I

said, "and next thing you know, somebody murders him."

"Stabbed, I heard," said Clements. "Not shot."

I smiled. "How much did he owe you?"

"Hundred thousand. That was about ten years ago. Add some interest to that. Not that I was ever going to see a penny of it."

"What was the loan for?"

"To start up an animal clinic in Maryland. This was around the time of his divorce. He tapped a lot of his friends, I understand."

"Who else?"

He shrugged. "I don't really know. It's what Ken said. When I told him he owed me money and I wanted it back, he said something like 'You and a lot of other people.'"

"A hundred grand is a significant amount of money," I said.

"To me it is," Clements said, "and I wanted it back. He was evasive. Said he was working on it."

"You didn't kill him, though, huh?"

"Felt like it," he said.

"Somebody beat you to it."

"You had to take numbers," he said, "get in line." He picked up his beer glass and drained it. "He claimed he was going to be coming into some money very soon, and he'd be able to clean up all his debts. His father was dying, he said. It could happen any day. His father was very rich, he said, and he, Ken, was his only heir." He looked at me. "Now that he's dead — Ken, I mean — will I be able to recoup my money from his father's estate, do you think?"

"You better get yourself a lawyer," I said.

Sean Clements and I shook hands on the sidewalk outside Remington's. He headed toward Tremont Street, and I walked across the Common. On the way, I called Roger Horowitz on my cell phone.

When his voice mail picked up, I said, "The guy named Clem that I saw at the hotel, middle-aged man with the beard and the big forehead? He's a history professor at Emerson College name of Sean Clements. Lied to me about being there at first. Admitted that Ken Nichols owed him money. Says he's got an alibi for Saturday night. Have a nice weekend."

I picked up two takeout orders each of pad Thai and tom kha goong, the soup with prawns that Alex liked, at my favorite little Thai restaurant on Charles Street, and two bottles of a nice pinot verde from the wine store next door. Then I climbed the hill to my house on Mt. Vernon Street. Alex's battered Subaru with its ski rack and Maine plates was parked in the RESIDENTS ONLY slot in front of my house. She had her own key. She'd be inside waiting for me. That made me smile.

I climbed the steps onto my front porch, put down my bags, unlocked the door, held it open with my hip, picked up the bags, and shouldered my way inside.

"I'm home, kids," I called. I waited a minute, then yelled, "Hello?"

Henry did not come bounding into the living room to lick my face, nor did Alex appear with her arms opened wide for a hug. My voice echoed in the emptiness of a house where nobody was home.

I lugged the take-out bags into the kitchen and set them on the table. When I looked out through the back window, I saw Alex sprawled in an Adirondack chair with her legs splayed out in front of her and her arms folded over her chest and her head slumped on her shoulder. She was wearing an orange dress of some kind of silky material. Its hem was hiked halfway up her thighs, as if she'd been sunning her legs. A pair of sandals lay on the brick patio where she'd apparently shucked them off. Her bare feet were small and elegant, with orange nail polish that matched her dress.

A beer bottle sat on the arm of her chair. Henry lay on his side on the patio beside her. Both of them appeared to be sound asleep.

I put our dinner and wine into the refrigerator, then went upstairs and changed into a pair of jeans and a flannel shirt.

Back downstairs, I snagged two bottles of Samuel Adams lager from the refrigerator and took them out back.

Henry lifted his head, blinked at me, and wagged his stubby tail a couple of times. I gave his belly a rub, and he kind of smiled, then laid his head back down, sighed, and closed his eyes.

I sat in a chair facing Alex. She hadn't stirred. I sipped my bottle of beer and watched her sleep. Her pink tongue licked her lips, and then her eyes opened and looked directly at me.

"Mm," she murmured. "You're home. Hi."

"Hi yourself," I said. "Sorry if I woke you up."

"Oh, I was sort of half awake," she said. She sat forward and held out her arms. "Gimme a hug."

I got out of my chair and hugged her, and I gave her a kiss on the mouth, too, which threatened to evolve into something more before she put her hand on my chest and pulled back. "Sweet," she said.

I sat down again. "How hungry are you?" I asked.

"You talkin' about food?"

I smiled. "Not necessarily."

Her glasses sat on the arm of the chair. She picked them up and fitted them onto her face and looked at me. "Ah, that's better," she said. "It's really you, isn't it?"

"None other."

"It's been a while."

"Three weeks," I said, "but who's counting."

"Three weeks is too long," she said. "It makes me feel . . . shy. You know what I mean?"

"It's like we need to get to know each other all over again," I said.

"You feel that way?"

"Sure I do," I said. "For me, the shy boy battles with the dirty old man. Hard to say which might win."

She smiled.

"Hey, we've got all weekend," I said. "No agenda, no obligations, no deadlines, no rush. Let's just relax, go with the flow."

"It's not that I don't want to . . ."

"I know," I said. "I brought you a fresh beer." I handed the bottle to her.

281

"Thank you, dear man," she said. She held up her bottle. "Here's to our flow."

I clicked her bottle with mine, and we both drank to our flow.

When I woke up on Saturday morning, Alex's side of the bed was unoccupied, and Henry was not curled up on his braided rug.

The salty damp smell of fresh spring rain seeped in through the open bedroom window. I looked outside. The leaves on the maples that lined the street glistened wetly. Gray clouds were skidding across the sky, and patches of blue appeared here and there. An April rainstorm had come and gone in the night, and it promised to turn into another nice day.

I had a quick shower, got dressed, and stumbled downstairs. Henry was waiting at the foot of the stairs. I bent down and rubbed his ears, and then he followed me to the front door, where the thin Saturday *Globe* was waiting on the porch.

In the kitchen, Alex was sitting at the table with her chin on her fists and a coffee mug by her elbow. She was frowning at her laptop computer, which was opened in front of her. "I fed Henry," she said without looking up. "Made coffee."

I poured myself a mugful, went over to

the table, lifted the hair away from the back of her neck, and gave her a nuzzle.

"Umm," she said. "Nice. Cut it out."

I sat across from her. "You're working?" I asked.

"Sorry. Yep. Gotta."

"Your novel?"

She mumbled something that sounded like "Doo-wah-diddy-doo."

"Excuse me?" I asked.

"Don't wanna talk about it now," she said.

"How long?"

She blew out a breath, turned, and looked at me. Her glasses were perched down at the tip of her nose, where she wore them when she was working at her computer. Behind them, her eyes were magnified and looked quite fierce. "I'll be at it a long time if you don't leave me alone," she said. "Okay?"

"You got it," I said. "So why don't you take your computer into my office, or up to the bedroom, where you can have some privacy?"

"Humph," she said. She poked at her glasses with her forefinger. Otherwise, she did not move. I assumed that she hadn't registered what I said. Sometimes her powers of concentration were inhuman.

I toasted an English muffin, spread peanut

butter on it, poured myself a glass of orange juice, clicked my tongue at Henry, and took muffin, juice, coffee, and newspaper out back.

I sat at the picnic table, ate my breakfast, and read the *Globe,* beginning, as I always did, with the sports section, where good news was quite common and the worst possible news was a loss for the home team or an injury to one of the players or a salary dispute, which was the kind of bad news that wouldn't cost me any sleep. The political and economic and international news was invariably bad, and since there wasn't much I could do about it, it always felt a little masochistic to read about it, which I nevertheless always did.

After a while, Alex came out. She had her mug and the coffeepot with her. She refilled my mug, put the pot on the table, and sat across from me.

"You done?" I asked.

"Not done, exactly," she said. "I'm never done. I can't get away from my story. My brain whirls and bounces day and night. Anyway, I've shut down the writing machine for the day."

"How's it going?"

She shook her head. "I have no idea. I'm trying not to judge it. That comes later. Now it's all about getting the story out." She took a sip of coffee and looked at me over the rim of her mug. "Sorry about last night," she said.

I shrugged. "You don't need to be sorry."

"I thought I wanted to . . ."

I waved my hand. "I doubt if talking about it will do any good."

"That's a funny thing for a lawyer to say."

"What do you mean?"

"Oh, you know," she said. "With lawyers, it's all about putting things into words, getting every nuance explained and itemized, making sure every semicolon is in place, leaving nothing unanalyzed, nothing overlooked, nothing unaccounted for. No tern unstoned."

I smiled. "You talking about seagulls?"

She smiled back. "Sorry," she said. "I've got this wordplay thing running around my brain. One of my characters says things like that. No tern unstoned. A doctor a day keeps the penny away. Inversions that seem like they should mean something."

"Fun," I said. "Like 'The fan hits the shit.' "

"What happens to a baseball player who refuses to sign an autograph, huh?" She smiled. "Like a head with its chicken cut off. These things my character says, like

285

'The early worm gets the bird.' They come out of her mouth as mistakes, like things Yogi Berra might say, and they're more than just nonsense. Like when Yogi says, 'When you come to a fork in the road, take it.' That's silly, but it makes sense, too. I mean, there's a kind of wisdom in that. You understand what I'm trying to say?"

"I really don't," I said. "You're the novelist. You're the creative one. Me, I'm just a lawyer. All literal. Reducing everything to words and semicolons and analysis. Right?"

She smiled. "Now I've hurt your feelings."

"Am I really like that?" I asked.

She gave her head a little shake, which could have meant *No,* or *I don't know,* or *Well, sure you are, but I don't want to upset you by saying so.* "You *are* a lawyer," she said.

"That's my job," I said, "but, geez, I'd like to think I'm a person before I'm a lawyer."

Alex smiled. "Of course you are. A person. You're a terrific person. I didn't mean anything."

"But you're still feeling shy, huh?"

"I thought you didn't want to talk about it."

"I don't know," I said. "Maybe we should."

She leaned back in her chair and looked

up at the sky. "I have trouble enough with intimacy," she said, as if she were talking to the clouds. "This way, the way we are, you and me, I just . . ." She shook her head.

I waited, but she didn't continue.

"We should spend more time together," I said.

"We've got this whole history," she said.

"A good history."

She smiled. "Mostly good. The thing about having a history is, you keep comparing the way things are with the way you remember they used to be."

"What you remember isn't always how things actually were," I said.

"That's true," she said. "We're not the same people we were, either."

"We hump our expectations around on our shoulders."

"Hump." She smiled.

"Burdens," I said.

"Expectations," she said. "The burden of memories. Hopes. Disappointments."

"Wow," I said. "Heavy shit."

"I'm sorry," said Alex.

"Hey," I said. "It's a beautiful day. *Carpe diem.* What do you say?"

She turned her head and looked at me. "I think you're right," she said. "Let's not talk about that stuff. It's my fault. I'm just preoccupied with my novel right now. Makes me feel all moody and sensitive and introspective. I'm going to go up and have a shower. When I'm done, I'll feel better." She took a sip of coffee, put her mug down, stood up, came around to my side of the table, and kissed me on the side of my neck.

"Need someone to wash your back?" I asked.

She straightened up and smiled at me. "I don't think so, thank you."

TWENTY

In the afternoon Alex and Henry and I crossed the pedestrian bridge at the foot of Charles Street and walked the entire length of the Esplanade, from the Museum of Science to the BU Bridge. The college kids from MIT and BU and Harvard swarmed the place, as they always did on a sunny Saturday afternoon in the spring. They were lying on blankets with their faces to the sun, the girls in their skirts and tiny bikini tops, the boys bare-chested. They were riding their bicycles and Roller-blades and skateboards over the paths that paralleled the river. They were feeding the ducks and throwing sticks in the water for their dogs to fetch. They were playing Frisbee and Hacky Sack; they were kicking soccer balls; they were tossing around baseballs and footballs. They were doing just about everything that college kids should be doing on a fine spring day except reading physics textbooks and medieval poetry anthologies and studying for final exams.

We got back to the house a little before five. Billy and Gwen would arrive in an hour or so. Henry sprawled on the floor and commenced to snore. Alex went upstairs to change her clothes.

I checked the voice mail on my telephone. I had one message. It was from Sharon Nichols. "I'm sorry to bother you on the weekend," she said, "but there's something I need to talk to you about. Can you call me?"

I took the phone out to the patio and dialed Sharon's number.

"Thanks for getting back to me," she said when she answered. "This has been really bothering me."

"That's what we lawyers are for," I said. "What's going on?"

"Ellen came over for a visit this afternoon," she said, "and she reminded me of something, and it made me think . . ." Her voice trailed off. "I'm sorry. I probably shouldn't say anything."

"It's up to you," I said, "but if it pertains to what happened to Ken, you should tell me."

"I don't know if it does," she said. "No, that's wrong. I think it might. That's why I wanted to talk to you."

I waited, and after a pause, Sharon said, "There was a time back when Ken and I had the kennels when some of our animals, the pets that were boarded with us, might've had something happen to them. People told us that when they brought their pets home, their personalities had changed. They were suddenly skittish around people, acting spooky or frightened."

"As if they'd been abused," I said.

"Yes, exactly. These people, they practically accused us of being abusive to their pets."

"Which you weren't."

"Of course not," she said.

"But . . . ?"

"Well," she said, "we never figured out what happened, or even if it was something that happened while the pets were with us. The people, of course, they didn't board their animals with us anymore. We had no other complaints, though, and the issue went away, and I hadn't thought about it for a long time."

"So what about it now?" I asked.

"Ellen and I were talking about it today," Sharon said. "I don't know how it came up. We were just reminiscing, talking about her childhood, her mostly happy memories of growing up with animals, and how awful it was to think that something bad could happen to the animals that we loved and cared for. Ellen said she always suspected that Wayne did something to those animals, and when she said that, I realized that somewhere inside me I had the same suspicion, but I guess I'd repressed it or something."

I remembered Billy's story about how Wayne Nichols had blown a frog's head off with a firecracker. "Suppose it *was* Wayne," I said. "That was a long time ago."

"If my son was capable of that . . . of some kind of cruelty to animals . . . do you see, Brady? Do you understand what I'm thinking?"

I hesitated. "You're thinking that Wayne killed Ken?"

"I guess I am, yes."

"Sharon," I said, "what do you want me to do with this idea? Why are you sharing it with me?"

I heard her blow out a breath. "I don't know," she said. "Nothing, I guess. I'm sorry. I just needed to get it off my chest. It's such a horrible thought. I couldn't keep it inside. Maybe I just wanted you to tell me it's stupid."

"If Wayne did it," I said, "it means you didn't. It would be good to know who did it. Even if it was your son."

"Well, I don't know if it was Wayne," she said, "but I know it wasn't me. So it was somebody else. I've been trying to figure out who that could be. So what if it was Wayne?"

"There's no evidence that Wayne was anywhere near that hotel on Saturday night," I said. "Nothing to connect him to what happened. Not to mention, no motive that we know of."

"I know. You're right. Thanks for saying it. I need to think that way. About evidence. Facts, not feelings. I don't like to think that my son could've killed his own father."

"You should talk to Tally about this," I said.

"I definitely will," she said.

At that moment, Henry came bounding down the back steps. I looked up. Alex was standing on the deck with her eyebrows arched at me.

"Sharon," I said, "I've got to go. We can talk more about this another time if you want."

"Sure," she said. "Thanks for listening. I guess I just need to get better control of my thoughts."

"Call Tally."

"Yes," she said. "I will. Thank you, Brady."

I put down the phone and smiled at Alex. She'd changed out of her walking clothes. Now she was wearing blue jeans and a long-sleeved striped jersey.

I gave her a wolf whistle, and she looked cross-eyed at me and put one hand behind her head and the other one on her hip and did a little pirouette on the deck.

I got up and went to her. She stood there watching me, and when I started to climb the three steps onto the deck, she lowered her head and let her arms hang by her sides.

I put my hands on her hips and said, "Hey."

She looked up at me. "Hey," she said.

I kissed her forehead, and she smiled and pressed the entire length of her body against me, and then she put her arms around my neck and went up on her tiptoes and lifted her face, and our mouths met, and our tongues touched, and Alex murmured, "Mmm."

After what seemed like a long time, our mouths slid away from each other. She put her arms around my waist, and she hugged me hard against her and pushed her face into my chest.

"Wanna go upstairs?" I asked.

That, of course, was when the front door-bell rang.

■ ■ ■ ■

Billy and Gwen had brought three pounds of ground sirloin and two packages of bratwurst, a tub of potato salad, and another of cole slaw. There were buns, jars of relish and mustard and dill pickles, two big tomatoes, and a Bermuda onion.

They banished me and Alex to the backyard with chilled bottles of beer. Billy hogged the grill, and Gwen usurped the kitchen, and Henry stuck close to Billy, where the food was.

We ate on the picnic table out back, and by the time we finished, darkness was beginning to seep into the patio, and the evening air had grown damp and chilly.

We carried the dirty dishes and leftover food into the kitchen, and Billy and I told Gwen and Alex to get out of our way so we could clean up. The women poured themselves glasses of wine and went into the living room without arguing.

"You wanna wash or dry?" I asked Billy after they'd left.

"You dry," he said. "You know where things go."

"Supper was great," I said. "I told you we could've just ordered pizza."

"I wanted to do a cookout," he said. "Like the good old days."

"Nothing's ever really as good as the good old days," I said.

"Yeah, no shit." He was up to his elbows in the soapy sink water. "Mostly the good old days weren't even that good."

"You got something on your mind?"

Billy shrugged. "What you were saying the other night?" he asked. "What got me all pissed at you?"

"I was hoping that was behind us," I said.

"It's not about you," he said. "I guess both me and Gwen had already been thinking things like what you were talking about. You know, what if this, what if that. We didn't bring it up because we didn't want to hurt each other's feelings." He turned and looked at me. "So now she says she's decided to get in touch with a lawyer when she gets home, and she says I should, too."

I didn't say anything.

"So," he said, "now it's a big frig with lawyers."

"Sorry," I said. "My fault."

"So what do you say?" he said. "You wanna be my lawyer?"

"Me?"

"Sure. You. You're a lawyer."

I shook my head. "No."

296

"Huh? You don't?"

"I don't want to be your lawyer, no. I want to be your father."

"Yeah, well . . ."

"If I was a doctor," I said, "I'd refuse to operate on your heart. Do you see?"

"Not really."

"It's a moot question anyway," I said. "You need a lawyer from Idaho, where you live."

"That how it works?"

"That's how it works," I said. "If you want, I can ask around, get some recommendations for good attorneys out there."

Billy was shaking his head. "I really thought . . ."

"Remember the year I coached your Little League team?"

He smiled. "That was fun."

"For you, maybe," I said. "For me it was gut-wrenching. I worried about showing favoritism, and I also worried about erring in the other direction, being too hard on you in order to avoid showing you favoritism. I worried that the other kids on the team would resent you. I worried that they'd think I wasn't being fair to them. Their parents, too. I worried about what they were thinking. You were by far that team's best pitcher, you know."

"Me?" he asked. "I never pitched. Not once. I played center field."

"You were our best hitter, too."

"So why was I sixth or seventh in the batting order all the time?"

I spread my hands. "You see?"

He looked at me and nodded. "Shit. You mean if you hadn't been the coach I could've been a pitcher and a cleanup hitter?"

"You probably would've been if you hadn't been my kid," I said.

"So you're saying it's the same thing with being my lawyer?"

"No, not exactly. A lawyer's supposed to show favoritism for his client. It's just not a good idea for a lawyer to be emotionally involved with his client. Personal things can distract a lawyer from legal things, and I happen to love you. Anyway, as I said —"

The phone on the kitchen wall rang. I made no move for it.

"You wanna get that?" Billy asked.

"Let it ring," I said. "If it's important, they'll leave a message."

When the phone stopped ringing, Billy said, "Look. Don't worry about the lawyer thing. I get it. There's a million lawyers. You're my only dad. And for the record, all the sports I played on all those different

298

teams? That year you coached Little League was the best."

I smiled. "It was a nightmare."

After Billy and Gwen left, Alex and I let Henry out back, and we stood there on the deck looking up at the stars.

"Thinking about Gus?" I asked her.

She put her arm around my waist and leaned her head against my shoulder. "I think about him all the time. When I see the stars, his constellations, it makes me feel like he's up there watching over me, my big brother, protecting me like he always did."

I hugged her against me and said nothing.

"Who called?" she asked after a minute.

"Huh?"

"When you guys were doing the dishes, I thought I heard the phone ring."

"Oh, right. It did. I didn't answer it. Billy and I were talking."

"What about?"

"He wanted me to be his lawyer."

"You refused, I bet."

"I did."

"Was he mad?"

"I think he understands." I kissed the top of her head. "I better see if I've got a phone message."

"I'm going to get ready for bed," Alex said.

We went inside. Henry got his bedtime Milk-Bone. Alex headed upstairs.

I picked up the phone and heard the *beep-beep* indicating I had a message.

I went to voice mail. "Mr. Coyne," came a male voice, "it's Wayne. Wayne Nichols." He paused, and I heard voices and music in the background. It was Saturday night, and it sounded like Wayne was hosting another party. "Look," he said. "I got something here I think you'll be interested in. So, um, you want to see it, come on up. You know where I live. Make it tomorrow. Sunday, that is. Tomorrow night, say around seven o'clock. Not before that. I'm busy until then. Anytime after seven, okay? No need to call me back. I'll be here either way."

TWENTY-ONE

When Sunday morning dawned sunny and sweet-smelling and rife with vernal promise, another in a string of delicious late-April days, Alex, Henry, and I piled into my car and drove out to Concord, where we rented a seventeen-foot double-ended aluminum canoe at the South Bridge Boathouse on the Sudbury River.

Alex wore cutoff shorts, a tank top, and one of my faded old Red Sox caps with her ponytail sticking out the back. From my seat in the stern, I enjoyed watching the clench and flex of her shoulder muscles as she paddled. Henry sat straight upright at the middle thwart, his ears cocked and his nostrils flared as we passed pairs of mallards paddling in the lily pads and a couple of great blue herons high-stepping along the riverbank with their necks bent like bows ready to release their arrows.

The river was wide and flat with no discernible current, and we glided along up-stream, paddling easily, all the way to Fairhaven Bay. There we beached the canoe, spread my ancient army blanket on the grassy bank, and had a picnic of the freshly baked and still-warm Anadama bread and extra-sharp Vermont cheddar that we'd picked up at a farmstand at Nine Acre Corner, washed down with cold bottles of root beer. We fed each other green grapes for dessert.

After we ate, Henry sprawled on his side in a patch of sunshine, and Alex and I lay back side by side on the blanket with our faces turned up to the sky and our eyes shut.

She found my hand with hers, interlaced our fingers, and held it tight against her hip. "What's going to become of us?" she asked.

"We're going to live happily ever after," I said.

"Ever after *what?*"

"After we slay the wicked stepmother," I said, "and escape from the castle and outwit the trolls at the bridge."

"All that, huh?"

"Nobody ever said that happily ever after was going to be easy."

She gave my hand a squeeze, then let it go. "Well, I don't see why it has to be so hard," she said.

We got back to my place on Beacon Hill a little after four in the afternoon. Alex went upstairs to pack. Henry and I went out back. I thought about Wayne Nichols. He said he had something to show me. As soon as Alex left, I would climb back into my car and drive up to Websterville, New Hampshire, to see what it was.

"And you can't come," I said to Henry.

He was lying on the bricks with his chin on his paws and his ears perked up, watching me. It was approaching his suppertime, so nothing would escape his notice. Henry lived with the chronic fear that I'd forget to feed him, or that he might sleep through dinner. It kept him alert and anxious.

Now, when he heard my voice, he lifted his head. Had I just uttered a *food* word?

"Sorry," I said to him.

He sighed, and his ears went flat on his head. He dropped his chin to his paws and closed his eyes. He knew that "sorry" was a bad word, an antonym of "cookie" for example, or "bone," or "dinner."

After a few minutes, Alex came out and sat in the chair beside me. She'd changed into khaki pants that stopped halfway up her calves and a dark green cotton shirt, which she wore untucked with the tails flapping.

"All packed?" I asked.

"Yep." She smiled. "All set to go."

"What about next weekend?" I asked. "My house or yours?"

"I don't know," she said.

"Let's make it yours," I said. "It's my turn to do the driving."

She shrugged. "I don't know, Brady."

"What do you mean?"

"I'm in a place where I don't like to interrupt my writing," she said. "I was in a pretty good groove for a while, and now I feel like I've lost it."

"Henry and I can stay out from underfoot. You know that. We've done it before."

"We can talk about it," she said. She was gazing up into the afternoon sky.

"What's going on, babe?"

She turned her head and looked at me. "Nothing, really. I don't mean to be grouchy. It's been a lovely weekend. I know as soon as I get into my car I'll start missing you terribly. You and dear Henry."

"But now . . . ?"

She pushed herself to her feet. "Now it's time to leave. I want to get home before dark. Gonna walk me out to my car?"

Her duffel and backpack were sitting on the floor by the front door. I picked them up, took them out to her Subaru at the curb, and loaded them in back.

Alex was leaning against the driver's door. I went to her, and she hooked her arms around my neck. "Thank you, sweet man," she said softly.

"For what?"

"For putting up with me," she said.

"Hey," I said. "I love you."

She smiled. "I know. Me, too."

"Call me when you get home?"

"Sure," she said. "Will you be here?"

"Actually," I said, "maybe not. Call my cell. I want to know you got home all right."

"I will." She tilted up her face and kissed me hard on the mouth. When she pulled back, I saw that her eyes were glittering.

"What's this?" I asked. I touched my fingertip to the dampness on her cheek.

She smiled. "It feels like I've been trying to get away from trolls all my life," she said. "I'm ready for the happily ever after part."

"You deserve that," I said. "Let's make it happen."

After Alex left, I gave Henry his supper and then let him out back. When he finished his business, we went inside, and I gave him a bully stick. He took it in his mouth and looked at me, and it wasn't hard to read his expression. *You give me these treats,* it said, *as a sop to your conscience because you're going somewhere and not bringing me. I like bully sticks, even if they are dried bull penises. But I'd rather be going with you.*

"Sorry, pal," I said. "Guard the house. I'll be back, I promise."

There were stretches of the two-lane east-west highway from Boston to Websterville, New Hampshire, where the descending April sun hung low in the sky, dead ahead, and the glare on my windshield almost blinded me, even though I was wearing sunglasses and had the window visor flipped down. I felt the beginnings of a headache blossom behind my eyes as I squinted and strained to focus on the lines on the middle of the road so I could stay on my side and avoid a headon.

I pulled up in front of Daniel Webster's Trout, the coffee shop on the main drag in Websterville, a few minutes after seven. I needed a shot of caffeine to banish my headache, and I wanted to get out and stretch my legs after the tension of driving half-blind into the setting sun.

Unfortunately for me, a sign hanging on the door read that Daniel Webster's Trout closed at four o'clock on Sunday afternoon. That was how they did business in New Hampshire college towns.

So I got back into my car, and ten minutes later I turned into the cul-de-sac where Wayne Nichols lived. Now the sun had sunk behind the wooded hills in back of Wayne's house. A dim light shone through the front window, and his rusty old Taurus sedan crouched in the cracked driveway.

I parked out front, went to the front door, and pressed the bell. It went *bong-bong* inside. When Wayne didn't come to the door, I hit the bell again, and still he didn't answer.

I went around to the carport and banged on the side door, and then I tried the back door, the one that opened into the kitchen.

Either Wayne wasn't home, or he'd decided he didn't want to talk with me after all.

There was another, more ominous explanation. I pulled open the storm door and tried the inside door. It was unlocked. I pushed it open, hesitated, then stepped inside.

I stood there in the doorway. No music was playing in some other room. No television droned. Somewhere a clock ticked hollowly. The refrigerator motor hummed.

It was gray and shadowy. Yellow light filtered in from the next room.

"Hey, Wayne," I called.

No answer.

I moved into the kitchen, and that's when the familiar harsh odor of burned gunpowder hit my nostrils.

"Oh, shit," I said.

I found Wayne in the living room. A floor lamp shone on him and made the rest of the room seem dark. He was slouched on the sofa with his chin on his chest, his arms at his sides, and his legs stretched out in front of him. A round brick-red splotch the diameter of a grapefruit stained the front of the gray sweatshirt he was wearing. The blood looked dark and sticky — not quite dry, but not wet, either.

I went over to him and pressed two fingers against the side of his neck. I didn't expect to find any pulse, and I didn't.

When I straightened up, something rubbed against my leg. I whirled around and clenched my fists and started to drop into a defensive crouch. Then I blew out a breath and smiled.

It was a black cat with white boots and a white blaze on her chest. She was sitting there on Wayne's living room floor twitching her tail and looking up at me with her greenish yellow eyes.

I picked her up and held her against my chest. I could feel the vibrations of her purring. "I wonder what you saw," I said.

She was wearing a collar with a tag. The tag read SPARKY and had a phone number.

I put Sparky on the floor, then reached into my pants pocket, took out my cell phone, and flipped it open. I hit the nine and the one. Then I stopped, snapped the phone shut, and put it back into my pocket. Another few minutes wouldn't do Wayne any harm.

Sparky came padding along behind me when I went to the wing on the left side of the one-story ranch house. In the early evening twilight, the shadows were growing dark inside the house, so I took my handkerchief from my pants pocket and held it over my finger as I flicked on some lights. There were two small bedrooms and one bathroom. Only one of the bedrooms appeared to be used for sleeping. A king-sized mattress with a tangle of blankets, pillows, and sheets on it took up most of the floor space. There was a bureau and a closet, and I prowled through them and found nothing but clothes.

The other bedroom was evidently Wayne's storage room. Some wooden chairs were stacked in a corner. There was an unmade twin-sized bed and a drop-leaf dining table with a couple of lamps and some boxes sitting on it. Half a dozen big cardboard boxes sealed with packing tape were piled against one wall. I wondered what they held but decided that it would be imprudent to cut them open. The closet had sliding mirrored doors that were half open. A couple of winter-weight coats hung inside. Otherwise it was empty.

In the bathroom, the medicine cabinet was empty except for a bottle of Tylenol, a tube of Crest, a container of Right Guard, and some hair gel. Towels and extra rolls of toilet paper were stacked on shelves in the shallow linen closet, and a kitty-litter box sat next to the toilet.

Sparky followed me back to the other side of the house, which included the living room, a dining room, and the kitchen. In the living room were the sofa, where Wayne hadn't moved, a couple of mismatched easy chairs, a faded braided rug, and a flat-screen television on the wall. A rectangular wooden table sat in the middle of the dining room with four matching chairs around it. Dishes and gravy boats and serving platters filled a glass-front built-in cupboard.

I found nothing of interest in the kitchen.

Milk and orange juice, eggs and bread, jelly and spaghetti sauce, and a few containers of leftovers in the refrigerator. A tub of ice cream and a tray of ice cubes in the freezer. Cans of soup and beans and Diet Coke in a little pantry in the mudroom.

The entire house, with its cheap, impersonal furnishings and black-and-white cat, seemed somehow incongruous for a young guy who'd recently dropped out of college. Except for the wide-screen TV and the mattress on the floor, his was a house that should have been inhabited by an old widow lady on food stamps.

Maybe the furniture came with the house. That would explain it. Still, there was nothing intimate in these rooms, nothing that revealed the person who lived here. There were no framed family photos sitting on the shelves, no paintings hanging on the walls, no music posters tacked to the backs of doors.

On second thought, I guessed that the house and its contents probably revealed a great deal about Wayne Nichols.

I clicked my tongue at Sparky, and she followed me down the stairs into the basement.

A washer and dryer sat against one cement wall, and a furnace and an oil tank stood next to another wall. An unfinished plywood partition sectioned off half of the basement, and behind the partition was a small office. When I flicked on the wall light, my finger covered with the handkerchief, I saw that it had been trashed. Papers and manila file folders littered the office floor. The desk drawers hung open. They'd been emptied, and so had the drawers of the head-high file cabinet.

On the corner of the desk sat a surge suppressor with six sockets and two empty cords plugged into it. A laptop hookup and a cell phone charger, I guessed. No computer or phone, though.

So much for whatever it was that Wayne had wanted to show me. It looked like whoever shot him had got there first.

I climbed back up the cellar stairs and took one last look around. Sparky jumped onto the sofa and lay on the cushion beside Wayne with her tail curled around her face, and the question occurred to me: How could somebody who'd tortured animals as a kid grow up to be a man who kept a pet?

I went outside and sat on the front steps, where I'd sat a few days earlier. I took out my cell phone, dialed 911, and told the dispatcher that I'd found a dead body at a house in the cul-de-sac at the end of Blaine Street.

She asked my name and told me to wait there, don't touch anything, and somebody would be along in a few minutes.

Then I called Roger Horowitz's cell phone.

"You again," he said when he answered. "What is it this time?"

"Ken Nichols's son, Wayne," I said. "His body. It's here, at his house in Websterville, New Hampshire. Shot in the chest."

"Websterville, huh?" he asked. "Christ, Coyne. How do you keep doing this?"

"Doing what?"

"Stumbling upon corpses. Finding trouble."

"It's a gift, I guess," I said.

"So whaddaya want me to do?"

"I don't know," I said. "I figured you should know. It's fairly unlikely that this isn't related to what happened to Ken, don't you think?"

"You call the locals?"

"They're on their way."

"Shot in the chest, you said?"

"That's right."

"Not stabbed, huh?"

"No."

"Murder weapon?"

"I didn't see one."

"And you're there why?"

"He called me," I said. "Said he had something to show me."

"What was it?"

"He didn't say. I don't know."

"Connected to our other murder," he mumbled, talking to himself, not me. "Might've been a God damn clue. Woulda been nice."

"I guess so," I said.

"Yeah, well," he said. "How it goes sometimes. It's never easy."

I heard the wail of sirens in the distance. They were growing louder.

"The cops are on their way," I said to Horowitz. "The place has been tossed. Desk and file cabinet drawers dumped on the floor. Laptop's missing, and maybe his cell phone, too. I don't know what else. I'm guessing they got whatever it was that Wayne was planning to show me."

"There's your motive right there," Horowitz said. "You find any drugs?"

"Tylenol."

"No ketamine, huh?"

"I didn't look that hard," I said. "So what do you want me to do?"

"Do what you're supposed to do," he said. "Cooperate with the authorities. Answer their questions. Tell the truth."

"Yeah, well, I'm a lawyer, and I've got a client who happens to be a suspect in another homicide."

"Do what you gotta do, Coyne. You don't need my guidance."

"What about you?" I asked.

"Me?" he asked. "I'll do what I'm supposed to do, too." Then he disconnected.

"You're welcome," I said into my dead phone. I snapped it shut and shoved it into my pocket, and that's when the two black-and-white cruisers, with their sirens screaming and their blue lights flashing bright in the gathering gloom of an April evening, came careening around the corner and slammed to a stop in front of Wayne Nichols's house.

TWENTY-TWO

WEBSTERVILLE POLICE was printed in big block letters on the sides of the cruisers. Two uniformed officers jumped out of each vehicle. One of them stayed there at the side of the road, one went around to the back of the house, and the other two approached me where I was sitting on the front steps.

They were both male, both, I guessed, somewhere in their forties, one black and one white. The white one stood in front of me and said, "You the one who called it in?"

"That's right," I said.

"Sir," he said, "if you'd come with me."

I stood up and followed him to his cruiser. He opened the back door. "We'd like you to wait here," he said.

"Wait for what?" I asked.

"The state detectives will be here pretty soon. They'll need to talk to you."

"Okay," I said. When I bent down to get in, he put his hand on top of my head.

He left the back door open and leaned against the side of the cruiser, guarding me, or making sure I didn't try to get away, or maybe both. After a few minutes, more vehicles appeared, and pretty soon the cul-de-sac at the end of Blaine Street looked like a multicar pileup on the Mass Pike during an ice storm, with ten or a dozen vehicles — cruisers and vans and unmarked sedans — parked at odd angles in the street and nosed up onto the front lawn, their doors hanging open, their red and blue lights flashing, and the static from their radios crackling in the twilight.

Uniforms and plainclothes people milled around the yard, talking with each other and moving in and out of Wayne's house. A woman led a German shepherd out of the back of a van and took him inside on his short leash. A pair of uniformed officers strung yellow crime-scene tape around the property.

At one point a white-haired guy in a brown suit came over and spoke to my personal guard. After they'd exchanged a few sentences, the white-haired guy turned and went back into the house without even looking at me.

When the cell phone in my pocket vibrated, I fished it out, opened it, and saw that it was Alex. "Hi, babe," I said.

"I'm home safe and sound," she said.

"Oh, good," I said. "Thanks for calling. Uneventful trip?"

"Totally uneventful. Thanks for a lovely weekend. I had fun. I know I was kind of moody. Please don't take it personally."

"It's okay," I said. "I understand. You're a writer. Goes with the territory."

"I'll make it up to you, I promise. Next weekend, right?"

"We'll be there. Me and Henry."

There was silence for a moment. Then Alex said, "Brady? Is everything all right?"

"Sure. Fine."

"Where are you? What's going on? Something's going on. I can hear it in your voice. There are background noises. What is it?"

"I can't talk about it right now," I said, "but don't worry. I'm fine. Really."

"Call me when you can talk, will you?"

"I will." I looked out of the open car door and saw the white-haired guy headed in my direction. "I gotta go now. I'll call you."

"Take good care of yourself," Alex said.

"Sure," I said. "You, too." I shut my phone and slipped it into my pants pocket.

Neither of us had said "I love you."

The white-haired guy walked up to the open cruiser door and spoke to the uniformed officer. Then he bent down, poked his head in, and said, "Shove over, Mr. Coyne."

I slid over, and he got in beside me. He held out his hand. "Wexler," he said. "Homicide, New Hampshire state cops."

I gripped his hand. "Coyne," I said. "Lawyer, Massachusetts bar."

He smiled quickly. "Who were you talking to?"

"On my phone? Just now?"

"Yes."

"My, um, just a friend."

"You tell him what's going on here?"

"It was a woman," I said, "and no. I know better than to do that."

"That's your vehicle?" He pointed at my green BMW, which I'd parked directly in front of the house. It was now surrounded by other vehicles.

"Yes, it's mine," I said.

"Just so you know," he said, "I've talked with your buddy Detective Horowitz. He filled me in. I understand that you're a lawyer with a client who's involved in a homicide case in Massachusetts and there are things you probably won't be able to talk about."

"I'm glad he told you that," I said.

Wexler took a leather-bound notebook

319

from the inside pocket of his jacket. He opened it on his leg. He had a ballpoint pen in his hand. "So tell me what you can tell me," he said. "Like, for example, how come you happened to be here to find Mr. Nichols's body."

"Wayne called me," I said, "asked me to come up. Said he had something he wanted to show me."

"Show you what?"

I shrugged. "He didn't say."

"You didn't ask?"

"I didn't actually talk with him," I said. "He left me a phone message."

"When was that?"

"Last night. On my home phone. That's in Boston. He just said he had something he thought I'd be interested in, and I should come up the next day, which was today, sometime after seven. I got here a little after seven."

"Not till seven? Did he say why then?"

"He just said he had things to do before that."

"You didn't call him back, ask what it was all about?"

"He said not to in his message," I said. "Wayne's not big on returning calls. I figured if I tried, he wouldn't pick up and it would just annoy him. So, no, I didn't."

"Is that message still in your voice mail?"

"No," I said. "I always erase voice mail messages after I listen to them."

"Why do you do that?"

"To keep things neat," I said. "I don't like junk piling up. When I lived in the suburbs, I loaded all of the week's trash in the family station wagon and went to the dump every Saturday morning. I took the dog, and afterward we went to a bagel place."

"Every Saturday?"

"Every single one."

"A ritual."

I shrugged. "I like getting rid of junk."

"Like old voice mails."

"Exactly."

Wexler smiled and glanced out the window. Then he turned back to me and said, "Any idea what our victim wanted to show you? You must've thought about what it was?"

"I did think about it," I said, "but nothing occurred to me."

"What time did you say you got here?"

I shrugged. "About a quarter, twenty past seven, I think. I didn't check the time."

"And before that?"

"Before I got here?"

Wexler nodded.

"I was on the road. It takes a little over

two hours to get here from my house, which is where I was before that."

"You were in Boston," he said.

"Right."

"Alone?"

"No. My, um, girlfriend was there. And my dog."

"Your girlfriend being the one you were just talking to on your cell phone?"

"That's right," I said. "She lives in Maine. She left a little before I did. She called to tell me she got home all right."

"This afternoon, before you were on the road? Where were you then?"

"Look," I said. "What time do you need my alibi for?"

He smiled. "Between one and five this afternoon ought to take care of it, according to the ME."

"Well, that's easy," I said. "We rented a canoe at the South Bridge Boathouse in Concord — Concord, Massachusetts, that is, not your state capital. That was around noontime. We turned it in around four. Paid with a credit card. Talk to them. They should have those times on their paperwork. They rent the canoes by the hour."

Wexler wrote something into his notebook, then looked up at me. "What's your girlfriend's name?"

At that moment my cell phone buzzed in my pants pocket. I decided to let it go. If it was important, they'd leave a message.

"My girlfriend's name is Alexandria Shaw," I said. "She lives in Garrison, Maine. She's a writer."

He wrote that into his notebook, too. "Okay, good," he said. "We'll check it out." He stuck his pen in his shirt pocket but kept the notebook open on his leg. "So when you got here, Mr. Coyne, you went right into the house?"

"I rang the bell and knocked on the doors. The back door was unlocked, so when nobody answered my knock, I went in."

"That's when you saw the body?"

"That's right."

"Then you called it in?"

"Not right away."

"No," Wexler said. "you didn't. You didn't make the call until seven fifty three. You were in there for about half an hour before you called it in."

"I looked around first," I said. "After I saw that Wayne was dead, I went through the whole house."

"What the hell were you thinking?" he asked. "You're a lawyer. You know time is of the essence. You should've called it in immediately."

"I was thinking," I said, "that another few minutes wouldn't make any difference to Wayne. I was thinking that he'd wanted to show me something that might've had a bearing on . . . on my case, not to mention on what happened to him, and I wondered what it was, and I thought I might know it if I saw it. So I decided to look around."

"A few minutes makes a difference to us."

"I know," I said. "I wasn't thinking about you."

He shrugged. "So did you?"

"Did I what?"

"Did you see it? What you were looking for? What Mr. Nichols wanted to show you?"

I shook my head. "I don't think so."

"What did you touch and move when you were in the house?"

"The only thing I touched was some light switches," I said. "I used a handkerchief. I didn't move anything. Oh, and Sparky."

"Huh?"

"Sparky the cat. I patted her."

He grunted a humorless laugh. "The cat. That's it?"

"I didn't disturb your crime scene," I said. "I know how to behave in a crime scene."

"Yeah," he said, "that's what Horowitz said." Detective Wexler blew out a breath.

"You went down to the cellar?"

I nodded. "I saw that the office down there had been tossed."

"I bet you figure that whoever shot Nichols was looking for whatever it was he wanted to show you."

"That occurred to me," I said.

"Looks like they took his laptop," said Wexler. "We didn't find a cell phone on his person or anywhere in the house, either. He didn't have a landline."

Wexler had been half turned on the backseat of the cruiser to face me while he talked with me. Now he leaned back against the seat and tilted up his face so that he was looking at the roof of the cruiser. "I doubt if this has got anything to do with your case, Mr. Coyne."

"You don't think so?" I asked.

He shrugged. "We're not discounting anything at this point, of course — but we've had our eye on Wayne Nichols for a long time, waiting for something like this to happen."

"Waiting for someone to shoot him?"

"Shoot, stab, strangle, club. Guys like him, sooner or later something happens to them."

"Guys like him," I said.

"Small-timers," he said. "Marginal players who think they can mix it up with the big-timers. You know what he was into, don't you?"

"Not really."

"Drugs," Wexler said. "He supplied the college kids. Wayne Nichols was crawling around down there at the very bottom of the food chain. He owned the little corner grocery, you might say. He worked the longest hours, took the most risks, had the thinnest profit margin, and reaped the fewest rewards."

"So you're saying that what happened to him, getting shot and killed, it was business."

"His business," he said. "Retailing drugs to college kids. Yes. That's what it looks like."

"What kind of drugs?"

"A little of this, a little of that. Whatever the kids wanted. Weed, coke, pills, acid."

"Ketamine?"

He turned his head and looked at me. "What do you know about ketamine?"

"Ask Horowitz," I said.

He smiled. "Sure. I will." He took his pen out of his pocket, clicked the button, and wrote something in his notebook.

"Whatever it was that Wayne wanted to show me," I said. "You think it was related to his, um, his business?"

"I don't know. What else could it be?"

"Something related to my case," I said. "That's what I assumed. It's the only thing that makes any sense."

"What, then?"

"I don't know."

"What if it *was* something else?" Wexler asked. "What if it was his, um, business?"

"Why would he want to bring me into that?"

"You tell me," he said.

"Because I'm a lawyer, I suppose." I hesitated. "Because his business was connected to my case. Is that what you're thinking?"

Wexler shrugged. "We're coordinating with Detective Horowitz. Which reminds me. You are not to talk to your client about this until after we have."

"That's harsh," I said. "You know who my client is?"

He nodded. "Our vic's mother. Getting it from the cops is a lousy way to hear your son is dead, I know, but it can't be helped."

"I should be with her when she hears about it, at least."

"She needs her lawyer for this?"

"She needs her friend," I said. "Anybody would."

Wexler glanced at his wristwatch. "Well," he said, "it's probably too late anyway. When

I talked to him, Horowitz said he and his partner were on their way, and that was, oh, an hour ago." He turned on the seat so that he was facing me. "Is there anything I should know that you haven't told me, Mr. Coyne?"

"I don't think so. Not that I can talk about, anyway."

"Your case."

"Yes. My case. My client. I'm not going to talk about it with you."

"Because it might be connected to this case?"

"Because I don't talk about my clients," I said.

"Horowitz can fill me in," he said. "He doesn't have client confidentiality to worry about."

I shrugged.

Wexler handed me a business card. "If you think of anything."

I stuck his card in my shirt pocket without looking at it.

"You got one for me?" he asked.

I took out my wallet and handed him one of my cards.

"Thanks," he said. "You're free to go."

"You're done with me?"

He smiled. "You sound disappointed."

"Not hardly," I said.

"You're not a suspect," Wexler said, "if that's what you were thinking. I assume your alibi will check out, and we've already got plenty of suspects. Horowitz said not to waste our time with you."

"Well," I said, "good. Guess I'll go home, hug my dog."

Twenty-Three

Detective Wexler got out of the cruiser, spoke to the officer who'd been babysitting me, ducked under the crime-scene tape, and headed across the brown lawn to Wayne's house. I got out, too. I nodded to the uniformed cop who was still leaning against the side of the cruiser, and he nodded to me. Then I climbed into my car, got it started, and eased around the vehicles that surrounded it. Once I'd driven out of Wayne's cul-de-sac, I remembered that my cell phone had buzzed while I was talking with Wexler, so I pulled over to the side of the road, fished out my phone, and saw that I had a message.

It was from Horowitz. "Mrs. Nichols ain't home," he said. "I need to talk with her. Any idea how I can get ahold of her? Call me."

I rang Horowitz's number. He didn't say, "Hello," like a normal person, when he answered. Not Horowitz. What he said was "Where the hell is your client, Coyne?"

"I don't know," I said, "but I can give you her cell phone number."

"Gimme," he said.

"You're going to tell her that her son got murdered this afternoon, huh?"

"Benetti's with me. I'm gonna make her do it."

"You planning on treating her like a suspect?"

"I don't know," he said. "Should I?"

"You better not," I said. "Not without her lawyer present."

"Thanks for telling me my job," he said. "What's her number?"

I recited Sharon's cell number to him.

He repeated it back to me, and when I said, "That's right," he disconnected. No "Thank you," no "Good-bye." Typical.

I pulled away from the curb, drove back to downtown Websterville, and turned onto the two-lane highway heading east.

I stopped at a convenience store cum gas station a few miles outside of town, where I filled my tank and got a foam cup of surprisingly good coffee, and I'd been driving through the Sunday evening darkness for about an hour and a half, and had just crossed the state line into Massachusetts, when my phone vibrated. It was Sharon.

"I don't think I can do this anymore," she said when I answered. I heard the tears in her voice.

"I'm sorry" was all I could think of to say.

"You know what happened," she said.

"Wayne?"

"Yes. My son."

"I do know," I said. "I'm so sorry."

"Marcia and Roger were terribly nice," she said. "They came to tell me personally. They just left a minute ago."

It's "Marcia and Roger" now, I thought. Telling a mother that her son had been murdered was a little different from interrogating her. The yin and the yang of the police officer's job.

"Are you at home?" I asked.

"I'm still here at the hospital," she said.

"Huh?" I said. "What hospital?"

"I'm sorry," Sharon said. "I don't know why I thought you knew. It's the Burbank Hospital in Fitchburg. Ellen and I have been here since, oh, around five o'clock. Charles — Ken's father — he was admitted to the ICU this afternoon. He's in a coma. They don't know whether he'll come out of it or not. They think it's his aneurysm. The facility where he's living called Ellen, and she called me, and I met her here. So we sat with Charles, and then the officers called, and they came here, and they told us about . . . about what happened to Wayne, and . . . oh, Brady. This is the worst thing. I'm a mess."

"Why did they call Ellen?"

Sharon hesitated. "Well, I guess, now that Ken's gone, Ellen would be Charles's next of kin. He has no brothers or sisters. She's his eldest grandchild."

"Are you going to be there for a while?" I asked.

"Here at the hospital, you mean?"

"Yes. When are you leaving?"

"I don't know," she said. "I guess we're going to stay here with Charles. It's — he's in pretty bad shape. He might not make it through the night."

"I'm sorry to hear that," I said.

I was heading southeast toward Boston on Route 3. I'd just passed a sign that said that Route 495 was two miles ahead of me. I pictured the map in my head — 495 south to Route 2, west to Fitchburg where I'd come to a capital *H* sign on the highway. "I can be there in about an hour," I said.

"You'll come here?"

"Sure. For a little while, anyway. Hold your hand, if you'd like."

"That would be lovely," she said. "I'm . . .

I'm touched, Brady."

"Ellen's there with you, you said?"

"She is," Sharon said. "I don't know what I'd do without her."

"She knows about Wayne, then."

"She was here when Roger and Marcia told us. We've been crying together."

"Where will I find you?"

"I guess we'll be in the ICU with Charles," she said. "You'll have to ring the bell."

"Okay," I said. "I'll find you. I'm on my way."

The visitors' parking area at the Burbank Hospital in Fitchburg was bathed in a weird bluish light from halogen lamps on tall metal poles. The lot was virtually empty, with just a few vehicles scattered here and there. It was after midnight on this Sunday night, and visiting hours had ended a long time ago.

I followed the sign to the main entrance and went in, half expecting somebody to stop me, but the white-haired woman who was sitting at the round desk in the lobby talking on the telephone didn't even look up when I pushed through the glass door. I went to the bank of elevators, where a directory indicated that the ICU was on the third floor.

When I stepped out of the elevator on the third floor, I found myself in an open square area with closed doors on the walls and a corridor heading east and west.

One of the doors had INTENSIVE CARE printed on it. Beside the door was a doorbell. RING FOR A NURSE, read a little sign above the bell.

I rang the bell, and after a while, the door opened, and a gray-haired woman in a white jacket looked out at me. "Yes?" she asked.

"You have Charles Nichols in there?"

"Yes," she said.

"His daughter-in-law and granddaughter are with him, I believe," I said. "Would you mind telling Mrs. Nichols that I'm here? My name is Brady Coyne."

"Coyne?"

"Yes. I'm a friend."

"All right," she said, breaking her streak of monosyllables. Then she pulled her face back, and the door shut and latched with a solid-sounding click.

A minute or two later the door opened again, and Sharon and Ellen came out. Both of them were red-eyed. Their faces looked swollen.

Sharon came over to me and put her arms around my waist and pressed her face against my chest. I patted her shoulder and mumbled something inane like "It's all right. It's okay."

Ellen stood there hugging herself and shaking her head. She looked bewildered.

After a minute, Sharon pulled back and looked up at me. "Thank you so much," she said.

"I haven't done anything," I said.

"You're here." She found my hand with hers and gripped it hard. "Come on. There's a waiting room over there. Let's go sit."

Sharon tugged me over to a closed door. It opened into a little room with two sofas, three or four soft chairs, and a coffee table with a dozen or so old magazines scattered over it.

Sharon sat on one of the sofas and pulled on my hand to signal to me to sit beside her.

Ellen stood awkwardly inside the doorway. "Why don't I go get us something to drink," she said. "Mr. Coyne? Coffee? A Coke?"

"A Coke would be good," I said.

"Mom?"

Sharon looked up at Ellen. "A Diet Coke, dear. Thank you."

After Ellen left, Sharon slouched back on the sofa and gazed up at the ceiling. "It's absolutely surreal," she said. "I thought nothing could be worse than what happened to Ken, finding his body, being accused of it — but now? Wayne? I don't know how to feel, Brady. I don't — I'm numb. That's how I feel. I mean, here we are in this hospital, and poor Charles should be getting our attention, our prayers. But my son is dead. Could anything be worse than that?"

"What did Horowitz tell you?"

"It was Marcia who did the talking," Sharon said. "She just said that somebody had shot Wayne in his house up there, and that you were the one who found him." She turned her head and frowned at me. "Why were you there, Brady?"

"Wayne called me," I said. "Said he had something he wanted to show me."

"What was it?"

I shrugged. "I don't know. He didn't say. I was going to ask you if you had any idea."

"Me?" She shook her head. "No. Not a clue. Who'd want to kill him?"

"According to the police up there," I said, "Wayne was dealing drugs. He'd make a lot of enemies doing that."

Sharon shook her head. "It's surreal. I haven't seen Wayne for a long time. I can't even picture him in my head. That's how long it's been. At least with Ken, we'd been talking, and I felt like I knew him. With Wayne, I didn't even have that. I love him just as much, you know?"

"I do know," I said. I put my arm around her shoulder, and she kind of snuggled against me.

A minute later Ellen pushed open the door and came in. She handed cans of Coke to each of us — Diet in a silver can to Sharon and regular red to me. Then she sat on the sofa across from us with her own can of Diet. She looked at me. "What happened to Wayne?"

"Somebody shot him. I don't know who or why."

"You found him?"

I nodded.

"You're the only one of us who's seen him or even talked to him in such a long time," Ellen said. She looked at Sharon. "It's been years."

Sharon nodded. "Since he went off to school."

Ellen turned back to me. "Do you think Wayne . . . ?"

"I only saw him once when he was . . . alive," I said. "It's not like I knew him."

"I was thinking about what happened to Daddy," she said.

"The New Hampshire police don't think there's necessarily any connection," I said.

"No connection?" asked Ellen. "They

think both of them being murdered is just a coincidence? I mean, first Daddy and then Wayne? Really?"

"Aside from the fact that they were father and son," I said, "there was nothing similar about their . . . about what happened."

"But," she said, "I mean, they *were* father and son."

"A father and a son," I said, "who had been out of touch with each other — and with the other members of their family — for a long time."

Ellen nodded. "Yeah, I guess." She looked up at the round clock on the wall. It was after one o'clock in the morning. "Mom," she said, "I've got classes tomorrow morning. I don't know —"

"Go, honey," said Sharon. "Go home, get some sleep. You can't do anything here."

"You're going to stay?"

Sharon shrugged. "I guess so."

"I can be with you."

Sharon smiled. "I'm okay, dear. Really. Go ahead. I'm so grateful you came here. If . . . when . . . your grandfather wakes up, I know he'll be pleased."

Ellen stood up. "You'll keep me posted on Grampa?"

"Of course." Sharon stood up, and the two women hugged each other.

When they stepped apart, I saw that both of them had wet eyes.

"I better get going, too." I turned to Ellen. "I'll walk down with you."

She smiled and nodded. "Thank you. That's nice."

Sharon came over to me, smiled, and gave me a hug. "You're a wonderful friend," she said. "I appreciate all that you do. This, tonight, was special."

"You have my numbers," I said. "Call anytime, for any reason."

She smiled. "I guess that's what I've been doing, isn't it?"

"It's fine. I'm glad." I patted her back. "I'm so sorry about all of this . . . what you've had to go through."

"Well," she said, "if it wasn't for you and Ellen, I don't know what I'd do. It's just horrible. My husband, and now my son. You can't imagine. I feel like I'm going to be all right, though, I really do."

"You're a tough lady," I said. I looked at Ellen. "Ready?"

Ellen and Sharon hugged again, and then all three of us left the waiting room. Sharon went over to the ICU door and rang the bell, and Ellen and I went to the elevator.

Outside the hospital entrance, I said to Ellen, "Where'd you park?"

She pointed to an area not far from where we were standing. There were three or four cars there. "Mine's the old beat-up Honda."

"I'll walk you over," I said.

She hooked her arm through mine. "Thank you. That's sweet."

"How are you holding up?" I asked. "This has to be pretty tough for you, too."

"I'm doing okay," she said. "I've been so focused on Mom that I guess I haven't thought much about me."

"It's going to hit you," I said.

She squeezed my arm. "When it does, can I call you?"

"I'm not sure what good I could do, but . . ."

"You're a kind man," she said. "I feel like I can talk to you."

"Well, sure," I said. "You can call me if you want. Of course."

We arrived at Ellen's car. It was an old sand-colored Honda Civic with missing hubcaps and a long scrape along its side. A graduate student's car. She leaned back against it. "I feel awful about Wayne," she said. "I was having bad thoughts about him. I even told Mom that I thought Wayne could've been the one who . . ." She shook her head.

"Who killed your father?"

"Yes. And now . . ."

"You feel guilty about what you were thinking?" I said. "Is that it?"

"Kind of. I mean, what it really is, I feel bad about saying those things to Mom, putting thoughts like that in her head."

"It's not like you knew what was going to happen," I said.

"I know," she said. "Still, having those thoughts, and then this happening . . ." She dug into her pocket and pulled out a bunch of keys. She turned, unlocked her car door, and slid in behind the wheel, leaving the door open. She looked up at me. "Are you okay? You look like you've got things on your mind."

"Actually," I said, "I was just thinking about Sparky."

"Wayne's cat, you mean?" she asked.

I nodded. "I don't know what they do with the pets of murder victims."

"They'll probably put her in a shelter." Ellen buckled her seat belt, turned the key in the ignition, and put on the headlights. Then she shut the car door and rolled down the window. "Well, Mr. Coyne, thanks for everything." She waggled her fingers at me.

I waved. "Drive carefully."

She rolled up her window, backed out of her parking slot, and pulled away.

I watched her turn at the hospital exit. Her brake lights flashed, and then she pulled out of the parking lot onto the street.

I went over to my car, slid in, and fished out my phone. I held it in my hand for several minutes, trying to figure out what the right thing was. Then I dialed Roger Horowitz's cell number.

It rang several times. Then he said, "Jesus Christ, Coyne. Do you know what time it is?"

"It's after one o'clock in the morning," I said. "I figured you'd be sleeping."

He sighed. "Not fuckin' hardly. Me and Benetti are here in my office conferring. We just got off a conference call with a New Hampshire detective named Wexler, who you met, and now we're putting our heads together, comparing notes, trying out hypotheses, and making up scenarios. What detectives do, even sometimes at one o'clock on a Monday morning. So whaddaya want?"

"I just wanted to leave you a message."

"Well," he said, "ain't this better? Now you get to talk to me."

"It would be easier to leave a message," I said. "I'm uncomfortable with the ethics of this."

"Christ," Horowitz said. "Spit it out, willya? Whaddaya want?"

I took a breath and blew it out. "I want to tell you who killed Ken Nichols and his son, Wayne."

"Really?"

"Yeah, really."

"You got it figured out, huh?"

"I think so."

"Us cops, we ain't smart enough — but Mr. Lawyer knows."

"Okay," I said. "Forget it."

"Take it easy," said Horowitz. "We can use all the help we can get, believe me. Who is it? Who's our killer?"

"Ellen Nichols," I said, "and that's all I'm gonna say."

TWENTY-FOUR

Horowitz was silent for a moment. Then he said, "The daughter, huh?"

"I think so," I said.

"He thinks it's the daughter," he said, and then I heard Marcia Benetti's voice in the background, though I couldn't tell what she said.

"Benetti wants to know what makes you think it's her?" Horowitz said to me.

"Means, motive, opportunity," I said.

"Thanks a lot. You think maybe you could be a little more specific?"

"That's all I want to say," I said. "You figure it out, see if I'm right."

"Bullshit," he said. "Come on, Coyne. Help us out here."

"Dumb me," I said. "I thought with a little guidance, like, say, giving you the name of the bad guy, you could figure out the rest of it."

"You're an officer of the court," he said.

"Look. Why don't you come on over, we can talk about it. Me and Marcia, we're here at my office, just around the corner from your house. You can drive over from that hospital and park right in front. We're only about an hour from Fitchburg. Marcia brewed up a nice pot of coffee, and we got a box of fresh doughnuts from the Dunkin' on Cambridge Street. They're still warm. We got plain, glazed, jelly, apple-and-cinnamon, and this place reeks of coffee and doughnuts. Ain't your mouth watering?"

"It sounds great." I hesitated. "Ellen knew about Wayne's cat."

"Huh?"

"Why I think it's her. Wayne Nichols had a cat named Sparky. She claims she hasn't seen or even talked to her brother since he went off to college, but she knew he had a cat named Sparky."

"So how'd she know that?"

"Bingo," I said, and with that, I snapped my phone shut. No "Good-bye," no "Nice talkin' to you." Just like Horowitz.

It felt great.

I found an FM station playing smoky wee-hours-of-the-morning jazz on my car radio, and my mind drifted on the music as I drove east through the darkness on Route 2. The music was sexy and moody, and it made me think about Alex. Sexy, moody Alex.

I wondered what would become of us.

Some wisps of fog materialized and dissipated in my headlights. The speed limit was fifty-five, and I kept the needle on sixty. The last thing I needed was to get snagged in a speed trap. Traffic was light on the highway — now and then a big twelve-wheeler rammed past, and a few automobiles came up fast from behind and then pulled around me. I stuck to the right lane, grooving on the radio music, and pretty soon I was turning off Storrow Drive onto Charles Street. I wasn't even tempted to hook onto Cambridge Street and go to Horowitz's office. Already I felt that I might've nudged my toe over the fuzzy ethical line by giving him Ellen's name.

Besides, it was way past my bedtime.

I pulled into my parking garage, nosed my car into its reserved pay-by-the-month slot, shut off the lights and the ignition, got out, locked up, and headed down the ramp for the door that opened onto Charles Street. The lights inside the garage were dim and yellow, and they cast spooky, distorted shadows against the dirty walls. My footsteps echoed, and somewhere in the depths of the big concrete structure water was dripping on the hood of a parked vehicle. It made a rhythmic *ping-ping* sound.

I was about to push open the door and step out onto the Charles Street sidewalk when a voice behind me said, "Hold it there, Mr. Coyne."

It was a woman's voice, at once soft and assertive.

"Ellen?" I asked. I stopped and started to turn to look at her.

"Don't turn around," she said. "I'm pointing a gun at you. Back away from the door."

"You've got a gun?" I asked. "Jesus, Ellen. What's going on? What are you doing?"

"Please don't play dumb," she said. "Don't insult my intelligence." I heard a soft mechanical click, the unmistakable sound of a pistol's hammer being cocked. "Step back from the door, please."

I did what she said. "You followed me here?"

"All the way from Fitchburg."

"Why? What do you want?"

"I want you to tell me how you figured it out."

"Figured what out?" I asked. "Look. We're both tired. It's been a hard night. I just want to go home and go to bed. I bet you do, too. You're upset. Hard to blame you. Your father getting murdered, and then your brother, not to mention your grandfather in the hospital. Let's just forget about this. A good night's sleep, and the world will look a lot different. Go on. Go home."

"I wish it was that easy," she said, and I thought she actually did sound regretful. "You should've just minded your own business."

I turned around to look at her. She really did have a gun. It was a revolver with a short barrel, and it was pointed at my midsection. I guessed it was the same weapon that had killed Wayne.

"I told you not to turn around," she said.

"You were planning on shooting me in the back?"

"It was the cat, huh?"

I shrugged.

"You had some kind of suspicion," she said, "or you wouldn't have tried to trap me like that."

"I was just fishing," I said. "If you'd said 'Who's that?' when I mentioned Sparky, that would've been the end of it."

"Now I've got to kill you, you know," she said.

"How do you feel about that?"

"What kind of a question is that?"

"You stabbed your father," I said. "You shot your brother in the chest. How did it make you feel, killing people like that?"

Ellen mumbled something so softly that I couldn't understand her.

"What did you say?" I asked.

"I said it didn't bother me," she said softly.

"It's like torturing those pets in the kennel, huh?"

She shook her head. "I'm not talking about this anymore." Ellen gestured at me with her gun. "Move away from the door. Over there. Do it now."

I figured she intended to shoot me. Why not? She'd already killed two men, and she admitted that she didn't mind doing it. As I eased away from the door that opened to the street, I tried to figure a way out. The hammer on Ellen's pistol was cocked. All she needed to do was touch the trigger to blow a hole in me. Her revolver looked like a .38. It would make a big hole, and even though snub-nosed revolvers are notoriously inaccurate, from where Ellen was standing, it would be hard to miss.

I could make a move on her. Fake left, go right. Or I could try to run away. Or I could drop, go into a roll, hit her at the knees. Or I could just make a bull rush at her and hope she panicked and forgot to shoot, or shot wildly, or, if she hit me, that it wasn't in some vital spot and wouldn't stop me.

Maybe twenty years ago a quick evasive flight — or a sudden attack — would've worked. Maybe not. Twenty years ago I was stronger and faster . . . and stupider.

I moved away from the door, keeping my eyes on the handgun she was holding. I figured as long as I could keep Ellen talking, she wouldn't be shooting.

"So after you left the hospital," I said, "you pulled over and waited for me to go by, and then you eased in behind me, huh?"

She nodded.

"Because you made a mistake about Wayne's cat."

"You tricked me," she said. "That won't happen again."

We were standing in the entryway to the parking garage. On the wall behind me was the big glass-fronted door that opened onto Charles Street, which was empty of traffic now at two o'clock on this Monday morning. On one side was the curving ramp that led up to the second floor. Directly behind Ellen was the opening to the dimly lit first floor of the garage, where rows of cars were parked.

I thought I saw the flicker of a shadow in the garage behind Ellen. It was quick, and then it was gone. Probably my imagination.

Maybe not.

Keep her talking.

"So," I said, "that wasn't Wayne who tortured the animals when you were growing up, right? It was you."

She was shaking her head. "I don't want to talk about that."

"You told your mother it was Wayne," I said. "You put those awful thoughts into her head."

"Stop that. I'm going to kill you. Nothing you say will change my mind."

"I already gave the police your name," I said. "If you kill me, it'll just be worse for you."

"There's no proof," she said. "You tricked me with the cat, that's all. I can explain that."

A shadow appeared behind her, and in the dim yellow light I saw the shadow materialize into Marcia Benetti. She wore a dark windbreaker over a black T-shirt, with blue jeans and white sneakers. She was holding her service revolver in both hands beside her face, pointing up at the ceiling, and she was easing along with her back against the wall, moving toward Ellen.

"Was it really just about the money?" I asked Ellen.

"Of course it was the money," she said. "He was going to keep it all. He said he needed it more than I did."

"Your grandfather's inheritance?"

"I've got a right to that money," she said. "My father didn't deserve it, and neither did my brother. You can understand that, can't you?"

That's when Benetti darted out of the parking garage shadows. Her scream echoed and rebounded off the concrete walls. It was a wild canine sound, a growl from deep in her chest, and then she slammed into Ellen, grabbing the arm that held the gun and sprawling her sideways. Ellen bounced off the wall, and when her shoulder slammed against the floor, her revolver came out of her hand and went skittering across the concrete, and Benetti was on top of her, rolling her onto her belly, pushing her face against the floor, and twisting her arms behind her.

Then the door to Charles Street flew open, and Roger Horowitz burst in from the sidewalk with his weapon in his hand. He looked at Marcia Benetti and Ellen Nichols on the floor, and then he looked at me. He smiled and gave me a little shrug, then put his gun back into his shoulder holster. "She's something, ain't she?" he asked.

"She just saved my life," I said, "if that's

what you mean."

Benetti had everything under control. Ellen was lying on her belly with her hands cuffed behind her. Her gun lay on the parking-garage floor near the wall, safely out of reach, and Marcia was kneeling beside her with her own handgun now in her hip holster.

Horowitz stood there inside the door. He looked at Marcia Benetti, smiled and nodded, then turned to me. "You okay?"

I nodded. "Thanks for showing up."

"Marcia's idea," he said. "She said we had to pick your brain. Said we shouldn't let you off the hook. She said, let's intercept the son of a bitch, bring him in whether he wants to or not. Woulda been easier all 'round if you'd come to the office voluntarily, had coffee and doughnuts with us." He cocked an eyebrow at me. "The offer still stands."

I shook my head. "The doughnuts are tempting, but you don't need my help anymore."

"Your *help?*" Horowitz asked. "Correct me if I'm wrong, but we just saved your sorry ass here. This pretty little girl was gonna blow a hole in you."

"I had everything under control," I said, "and now you've got yourselves a real live double murder suspect. That should keep you busy for a while. Have a nice night. I'm going home."

I had started to push open the heavy glass door to the sidewalk when Horowitz said, "Hold on a minute."

I stopped and turned to look at him. "What?"

"How'd you figure it out?"

"Ellen, you mean?"

He nodded.

"If it had been only Ken who got killed," I said, "or only Wayne, I probably wouldn't've. Each of them had plenty of enemies, just like most of us. Could've been anybody. Tonight, though, when I found Wayne murdered, I assumed it was the same killer, and that narrowed it way down. I just asked myself who was linked to both men, and of those people, who'd benefit from them both being dead." I jerked my head in the direction of Ellen, who was now sitting on the floor with her back against the concrete wall. "Ken Nichols stood to inherit several million from his father, Ellen's grandfather, who's old and in bad health, and, in fact, is comatose in the hospital as we speak. Ken had huge debts. With him out of the way, the two grandchildren, Ellen and Wayne, were next in line for it. With

Wayne gone, it'd all be Ellen's."

"If it ain't for love," Horowitz said, "it's for money."

"Just about every time," I said.

TWENTY-FIVE

My alarm went off at eight in the morning. I wasn't happy to hear it. I'd read *Moby-Dick* for a while after I finally got to bed, but my adrenaline had juiced me up so high that even Melville's usually reliable prose had failed to ease me to sleep. I'd lain there thinking about what must have gone wrong with Ellen Nichols, what wires got crossed so badly that as a child she could torture pets and then, as an adult, murder her father and her brother with malice aforethought — and tell me that it didn't bother her — never mind try to murder me.

I found no answers. Words like "sociopath" and "psychopath" were meaningless, except as descriptors. They didn't explain anything.

Nature or nurture. Whatever. It has usually seemed to me that anybody who had the capability of murdering another human being epitomized the definition of insane. Then again, there were times when I thought I understood how a sane person could decide that murder was a reasonable solution to a problem.

In that gray light just before sunrise, nothing made a lot of sense, and when I finally managed to drift into edgy sleep, I had nightmarish dreams about blood and explosions and hospitals.

I'd set my alarm so that I could catch Tally Whyte before she left for her office. Smart me, I'd also set my automatic coffeepot to begin brewing at seven thirty, so when I went downstairs a little after eight, the aroma in my kitchen was enough to perk me up.

I filled a mug, picked up my phone, and grabbed a Milk-Bone for Henry, and he and I went out back. I sat at the picnic table, and Henry flopped down underneath it with his treat propped up between his front paws.

I took a big swig of coffee, sighed at the miraculous infusion of energy and clarity, and called Tally's home number.

She answered with a cheerful "Tally Whyte. Good morning."

"Good morning yourself," I said. "It's Brady."

"Uh-oh," she said. "What's wrong?"

"Sharon Nichols," I said. "Events of the weekend. She's going to need you, but knowing her, she might not call you. I don't know if you —"

"I never hesitate to reach out to my clients," Tally said. "Talk to me."

I proceeded to tell her about Wayne's murder and Ellen's subsequent arrest. I left out the details of my own role in the drama.

"Ellen did it, then?" Tally asked when I finished. "She murdered her father and her brother?"

"It looks that way," I said.

"Wow," Tally said. "It's an old-fashioned Greek tragedy. It's going to be a tough one for Sharon. This means she's off the hook for her ex-husband's murder, though, huh?"

"I'm sure of it," I said.

"Well, that's something, anyway." She blew out a breath. "Okay. I'm glad you called me. I'm gonna say bye-bye now so I can call Sharon. I'll spend time with her today, you can count on it. If necessary I'll drive to her house. She's going to need a lot of help with this."

"Thanks, Tal. Keep me posted?"

"Not me, pal," she said. "You know better than that. I don't talk about my patients, any more than you talk about your clients. Don't worry, though. I've done this before. I'll take good care of her, and I'll encourage her to keep in touch with you. Thanks for calling. You did the right thing. You're a good man, Brady Coyne."

I spent the next few days catching up with my other clients and plowing through the never-ending reams of paperwork that Julie kept dumping into my in-box. Sharon called me at home on Tuesday evening, just to tell me that she'd been spending a lot of time with Tally and was doing as well as could be expected, and that Tally had urged her to touch base with me. It was a short conversation.

Wednesday after work I'd changed into jeans and a sweatshirt, and Henry and I were sitting out in the patio garden watching the evening grosbeaks and purple finches filch seeds from the feeders. I was sipping a Sam Adams lager wondering what I'd do about supper when my cell phone began hopping around on the arm of my chair.

It was Horowitz. "You home?" he asked.

"I am."

"I'm parked out front. Got a beer for me?"

"Sure. Come on in."

I went to the front door and let Horowitz in. He trailed me back through the house to the kitchen, where I snagged a bottle of Sam from the refrigerator. I handed it to him, and we continued out to the backyard.

I sat in my chair, and Horowitz sat at the picnic table. He lifted his beer bottle, took a long swig, said, "Ahh," and plunked the half-empty bottle down on the table. "That hits the spot," he said.

"There's more where that one came from."

He nodded. "Good to know. What're those yellow-and-black birds?"

"Evening grosbeaks," I said.

"They look like they should be living in a jungle."

I smiled. "So what's up, Roger? Or did you come to look at my birds?"

"The birds are nice." He took another sip of beer, then turned to look at me. "So, yeah . . . about your client."

"Sharon Nichols," I said.

"She's no longer a suspect in the Ken Nichols murder." He gazed up at the sky. "Thought you should know."

"Good. Thanks. The daughter, then, huh?"

He looked at me and nodded. "Her finger-prints were all over the vic's hotel room, and one of their security cameras caught her leaving that same evening. That took care of opportunity, and we're already pretty solid on motive. Turns out the weapon that killed the brother was not recovered. Ac-

cording to ballistics, it was not the one Ellen Nichols pulled on you. She did test positive for GSR, and she couldn't account for
her time Sunday afternoon before around
five o'clock, when she arrived at the hospital
in Fitchburg. So we got some good stuff,
and we're still working on it. When we
confronted her and her PD with what we
had, they huddled for a while and then
decided they wanted to plead out."

"You going to negotiate a plea with her?"

He shrugged. "Leaning that way. We're
still going back and forth. We'd love to take
her to trial, but we don't have that steak
knife that killed the vet, and we haven't yet
come up with the brother's murder weapon
or a witness to place her in Websterville that
afternoon. We like our case, but it's still got
some circumstantial elements to it that
make me uncomfortable."

We both sipped our beers and watched
the birds. After a minute, I said, "So drugs
had nothing to do with any of it."

"Doesn't look like it," he said.

"Even though Ken was probably traffick-
ing in ketamine," I said, "and Wayne was
selling stuff to the college kids. Right?"

"Like father, like son." Horowitz
shrugged. "The Maryland cops had their
eye on Dr. Nichols. He had big debts,

including to some dubious people in Baltimore, and he was using his ability to write prescriptions in, um, creative ways, but we weren't getting very far with the ketamine piece of it from this end. We had no luck trying to ID the guy in the hoodie you saw at the hotel that night. The other guy, Clements, he's got a nice motive — our vic owed him a lot of money — but he's also got a solid alibi for the night of the murder. Detective Wexler up there in the Granite State, he said they've had their eye on Wayne Nichols for some time, and the drug connection was his original assumption. Their dogs found his stash in his house, but that just confirmed what they already knew — and there was no ketamine." He took a swig of beer. "If you look hard enough, everybody's got a reason or two to end up with a bullet in them. Anyway, that's immaterial now. We've got a good circumstantial case against the girl. There will be a conviction, one way or the other." He cocked his head and looked at me. "Her fingerprints were on that matchbook in the hotel door."

"She left it there after killing her father?"

He nodded.

"Why would she do that?"

"She knew her mother was on her way,"

he said. "She wanted to make sure she could get in."

"So Sharon would find the body and be an instant suspect?" I asked. "Is that what you think?"

"She's a devious one, that girl." Horowitz shrugged. "I'd love to take her to trial."

"Your case is better than circumstantial, I'd say," I said. "She practically admitted to me that she did it."

Horowitz nodded. "For the money she'd inherit from the grandfather with her father and brother out of the way. She told you that, right?"

"Any idea what Wayne wanted to show me, why he asked me to go up there?"

"We figure it this way," he said. "Wayne had a copy of a document about his grandfather's will. It showed that he and his sister would get the old guy's money now that their father was dead. We figure he called you to show it to you as evidence against his sister, and somehow she figured out what he was up to — maybe they talked — so she went up there and . . ."

"Killed him," I said. "Took the document."

Horowitz nodded. "She's a sick puppy."

I nodded. "It's more than just greed."

"It usually is," Horowitz said. "If we do

end up taking it to trial, we'll call you for a witness. We have also charged Ellen Nichols with ADW, among assorted other charges, for what went down with you the other night in the parking garage."

"I don't want to be a witness," I said.

"Yeah," he said, "nobody does."

I had no clients and no court appearances scheduled for Thursday. This was usually the kind of day when Julie and I worked together to catch up on correspondence, schedule conferences, send out bills, review inactive cases, and generally get organized. At noontime on this Thursday in late April, though, I told her to go home. Her daughter had a soccer game. For once, Julie could get to see all of it.

After she left, I fished out the business card Detective Wexler of the New Hampshire State Police had given me. The first number I tried was answered by voice mail. I left my name and a couple of numbers and asked him to call me.

The second number was apparently his cell phone, and he picked up on the second ring. "Wexler," he growled.

"It's Brady Coyne," I said. "You interviewed me at the Wayne Nichols murder last Sunday."

"Yeah, I remember," he said. "What've you got for me?"

"Just a question," I said. "I was wondering what happened to Sparky."

"Huh?"

"Wayne Nichols had a cat named Sparky. Where is she?"

"Christ," he said. "Wait a minute." I heard muffled voices, and then Wexler said, "My partner says they took that animal to the shelter in Keene."

"You got the name of the place?"

He sighed. "Hang on." Again I heard the voices in the background. Then Wexler said, "It's called the Monadnock Animal House."

"Animal House," I said.

"Yeah, John Belushi," grumbled Wexler. "Funny. So is that it?"

"Yes. Thanks. I appreciate it."

"Seemed like a nice cat," he said.

I called the Monadnock Animal House, and the young woman who answered immediately recognized my description of Wayne's cat. "Sparky," she said. "She's a sweetie."

"Will you hold her for me?" I asked. "I want to rescue her."

"Sure," she said. "Wonderful. That's what we're for."

So I shut down the office, went home and

changed out of my office pinstripe, and an hour later Henry and I were heading north and west for Keene, New Hampshire.

It cost me a hundred dollars, plus another thirty-nine ninety-five for the travel crate, to rescue Sparky from the Monadnock Animal House. She rode in the backseat with Henry, who sniffed the crate a few times and then ignored her. After a couple of plaintive meows, she quieted down.

I called Sharon Nichols on my cell phone from the road. It was a little after four in the afternoon, and she was at the leather shop, working, which I took to be a positive sign.

"When do you get off?" I asked her.

"In an hour," she said. "We close at five. Why?"

"If I meet you at your house, will you have a beer for me?"

"Absolutely. It will be wonderful to see you."

"You sound good, Sharon."

"It's not easy," she said, "but Tally's been amazing. I think I'm getting there. Late at night is the worst, but Tally's given me some tricks." She hesitated. "A customer just came in. Gotta go. See you."

I rang the bell to Sharon's condo in Acton

a little after five thirty, and she buzzed me up.

She was waiting with the door open when I got to her apartment. I went in and put Sparky's crate on the floor, and Sharon put both arms around my neck and hugged me tight. "It's wonderful to see you," she said. When she pulled back, I saw that her eyes were glittery. "What's this?" She looked down at the crate.

I opened it up and lifted out Sparky.

She held out her arms and took the cat, which seemed to nestle against Sharon's chest. "For me?" she asked.

I nodded. "If you want her. Her name's Sparky. She was Wayne's."

Sharon stared at me. "Wayne had a cat?"

I smiled. "According to the girl at the shelter, he took very good care of her. This kitty is healthy and happy. She's been well loved."

She rubbed her cheek against the cat's fur. "I will cherish her," she said.

My phone rang at eleven thirty that night. It was Alex's turn to call. "Hi, babe," I said.

"You all tucked in?"

"I am. You?"

"Mm," she said. "Tomorrow at this time you'll be here tucked in with me."

"If we can outwit the trolls," I said.

"I'm not sure I believe in trolls," said Alex. "I'd rather believe in fairies."

"I think we can have it both ways."

"Trolls and fairies?"

"And wicked stepmothers and fairy god-mothers," I said. "It's a more interesting world with all of them, don't you think?"

"A more complicated world, anyway." She chuckled softly. "I'm at a good place with my novel," she said. "I'm not going to think about it all weekend. I'm just going to hang out with you and Henry. Walk in the woods, paddle our kayaks, cook good food, watch some old movies, and snuggle in bed. I can't wait."

"I'm at a good place, too," I said.

ABOUT THE AUTHOR

William G. Tapply was a contributing editor to *Field & Stream* and the author of numerous books on fishing and wildlife, as well as more than twenty books of crime fiction, most recently *Hell Bent.* He lived with his wife in Hancock, New Hampshire.

We hope you have enjoyed this Large Print book. Other Thorndike, Wheeler, Kennebec, and Chivers Press Large Print books are available at your library or directly from the publishers.

For information about current and upcoming titles, please call or write, without obligation, to:

Publisher
Thorndike Press
295 Kennedy Memorial Drive
Waterville, ME 04901
Tel. (800) 223-1244

or visit our Web site at:

http://gale.cengage.com/thorndike

OR

Chivers Large Print
published by AudioGO Ltd
St James House, The Square
Lower Bristol Road
Bath BA2 3SB
England
Tel. +44(0) 800 136919
www.audiogo.co.uk

All our Large Print titles are designed for easy reading, and all our books are made to last.